TIL DEATH DO US PART

A DARK RUSSIAN MAFIA ROMANCE (KORNILOV BRATVA DUET BOOK 2)

NICOLE FOX

Copyright © 2020 by Nicole Fox

All rights reserved.

No part of this book may be reproduced in any form or by any electronic or mechanical means, including information storage and retrieval systems, without written permission from the author, except for the use of brief quotations in a book review.

❀ Created with Vellum

MAILING LIST

Sign up to my mailing list!
New subscribers receive a FREE steamy bad boy romance novel.

Click the link below to join.
http://bit.ly/NicoleFoxNewsletter

ALSO BY NICOLE FOX

De Maggio Mafia Duet

Devil in a Suit (Book 1)

Devil at the Altar (Book 2)

Kornilov Bratva Duet

Married to the Don (Book 1)

Til Death Do Us Part (Book 2)

Volkov Bratva

Broken Vows (Book 1)

Broken Hope (Book 2)

Broken Sins *(standalone)*

Heirs to the Bratva Empire

Can be read in any order

Kostya

Maksim

Andrei

Tsezar Bratva

Nightfall (Book 1)

Daybreak (Book 2)

Russian Crime Brotherhood

Can be read in any order

Owned by the Mob Boss

Unprotected with the Mob Boss

Knocked Up by the Mob Boss

Sold to the Mob Boss

Stolen by the Mob Boss

Trapped with the Mob Boss

Other Standalones

Vin: A Mafia Romance

Box Sets

Bratva Mob Bosses (Russian Crime Brotherhood Books 1-6)

Tsezar Bratva (Tsezar Bratva Duet Books 1-2)

TIL DEATH DO US PART

My fake husband is trying to take my baby away.

The Kornilov Bratva brothers ruined my life.

Fedor attacked me and shattered my innocence.

Then his brother Viktor forced me into a fake marriage I never asked for.

Now, I'm caught in the middle of a war between them.

And if that's not enough…

It turns out I'm pregnant again.

One baby by each brother.

Two sides of a bloody conflict that can only end in death and destruction.

But I know one thing for certain:

I'll pay any price it takes to keep my children safe.

Even if that price is my life.

1
MOLLY

When I can't sleep, I wander.

In the shelters, it wasn't possible. People would think you were trying to steal their things while they slept. Plus, I couldn't leave Theo in the bed alone. So, I'd lie on the lumpy mattress with him tucked into my side and stare at the cracked ceiling.

Now, I wander through the spacious apartment Viktor is paying for while Theo sleeps in his own room. I know the apartment is luxurious and spacious, but I can't keep myself from growing accustomed to it. To all of the wealth and riches and comfort. I want it to stay new and bewildering, but human nature is to adapt. I know that better than anyone. Now, despite my efforts, I'm adapting to being Viktor's bird in a gilded cage.

Viktor has reminded me over and over again that he is doing all of this to protect us. The apartment and the guards are to keep me hidden and safe from his crazy brother. Theo's crazy father.

That is the memory that keeps me up the most. The one that propels me out of bed in the middle of the night and sends me pacing around the house.

I thought I'd overcome what happened to me. I can't remember the rape, after all, so it seems like it should have been easy to push aside and move beyond. But now that Fedor is threatening my life and coming for my son, the trauma of it rushes back fresh and new in waves that threaten to pull me under.

Those are the times I wish Viktor could be in bed with me. The times I wish I had someone to talk to. Someone to confide in.

I wandered instead of sleeping last night, so when Theo woke up at seven this morning, I struggled through breakfast and rocket-ship building until the nanny could take him for a while. I'm supposed to be studying, but I can't seem to focus. My stomach keeps doing nervous flips, and I want to eat but nothing sounds good. Nothing has sounded good for days.

After I force down some toast with butter for lunch, I call Hannah as per our unspoken schedule.

My old friend Hannah has been a comfort to me. I can't call her in the middle of the night when I need someone most, but we chat a few afternoons a week. Before a few months ago, it had been years since we'd spoken. She helped me out after Theo was born, setting me up with connections who could provide diapers and wipes and free vaccinations. She is the reason I made it through the early months, so now that the shit has hit the fan again, she is the only person I can think of who might be able to help.

I fall back on the bed and stare up at the ceiling. Light is streaming through the wall of windows to my right, and I curl up in the sunlight like a cat. The sun has been the only source of external warmth in my bed for over a month. Mostly because the last man I had sex with locked me in my bedroom and refused to let me leave. Viktor apologized and bought the penthouse to make it up to me, but no matter how accustomed I've grown to the luxury, I won't become accustomed to his betrayal.

"Molly?"

I blink and suddenly remember I'm on the phone. "I'm here."

"You got quiet," Hannah says. "My service is shit, so I thought maybe I dropped the call again. Honestly, it could be my phone or my service, maybe both. But I don't have money to fix either."

The phone in my hand is brand-new. Viktor just set it up for me a few weeks ago. He said he wanted me to be able to talk to my friends and get in touch with anyone if I needed to, but I know he is probably using it to track me. I want to throw the phone across the room, but guilt holds me in place.

Viktor cares about me.

Sure, his care feels like a prison sentence. It is suffocating and overwhelming and toxic in more ways than I can count, but isn't that what I always dreamt of? All those nights sleeping in shelters with Theo tucked into my side, I stared at the ceiling and prayed for someone who would care. Someone who would take care of us. Now, I have it. I wonder how fast Hannah would trade places with me if she could.

"I'm sorry," I say. "I know what that's like."

She sighs and then seems to brighten. "Speaking of, how are things going with your sugar daddy?"

Hannah doesn't know the half of it with Viktor, but she knows that my one free night in a hotel turned into a free apartment. She assumes Viktor is taking care of me because I'm his mistress, and crazily enough, that story is more palatable than the truth, so I let her think what she wants.

"I'm in an interior design class now," I say. "Only one and it's online, but it's a start. I wouldn't have even been able to afford the textbooks before."

"That's amazing. Damn. What do I need to do to find me someone like that?"

Get raped by the brother of a crime boss, have his secret baby, and then go into hiding at his brother's apartment to keep him from killing you and stealing your son.

I laugh and change the subject. "How are you?"

"It's the same old story," she says. "Except now, it's the same old story without Matt."

Matt is Hannah's son. He is almost six. She had him when she was even younger than I was when I had Theo.

"Why? What happened to Matt?"

"He is living with his dad for a while." She says it casually, but I can hear the hurt in her voice. "I just … couldn't swing it. I was working too much to pay for this shitty apartment, and then I couldn't afford day care. Everything was kind of falling apart."

"Why didn't you tell me?" I ask. "We've been talking a few times a week for weeks now. You could have said something."

"Would it have made a difference?" The question isn't meant to be biting, but I feel the sting of it regardless. Hannah helped me after Theo was born. She was most of the reason we made it through the first year at all, and in her time of need, I let her deal with everything on her own.

"Maybe not before, but it would have now. I have help, Han." The words are out of my mouth before I can really consider their meaning.

"What does that mean?" she asks. "Is your sugar daddy a pimp or something? Why would he do anything to help me?"

"Ew. No. I'm not a prostitute. Viktor just … values me," I say, wincing at the words. *Loves me* certainly isn't right, but *values me* makes it sound like I'm a prized hog. Both options suck. "If I tell him my friend needs help, he might help."

I don't know if any of this is true. I never would have guessed Viktor would trap me in a bedroom rather than let me leave his apartment, so clearly I don't have a full grasp of what he will and won't do. But I can't sit by and let Hannah suffer. Not when there is something I could do to help.

"I'll talk to him," I say. "Give me some time, and I'll ask him."

Hannah is in the middle of thanking me when her phone really does drop the call. And not a moment too soon, either. The second the phone beeps in my ear, telling me we've been disconnected, my stomach roils.

I sit up and press a palm to my belly, trying to understand the feeling, but a second later I know exactly what is happening.

I jump out of bed, wrench open the bathroom door, and barely make it to the toilet before my lunch comes pouring out into the bowl. I heave until there is nothing left and then fall back against the wall.

Immediately, I feel better. Though, I wish I didn't. If I still felt terrible, there could be a possibility I was sick. That maybe I'd contracted food poisoning or caught the stomach flu. But I feel amazing.

I curse under my breath and close my eyes.

Viktor and I haven't had sex since he locked me in my bedroom. There were a few times where things got close. The day he moved me into the penthouse, he refused to let his men do all the work and pitched in himself. He carried boxes up the stairs and inside, and when he started getting hot, he took off his sweater and finished the job in a tight white undershirt. The way it clung to his muscled chest was obscene, and when the house was empty save for the two of us, I nearly forgave him just so I could run my fingers across his abs. Just so I could feel his warm, hard body pressed against mine.

Somehow, I resisted. I went to bed with a bundle of pent-up energy inside of me, and I spent it all imagining the things he would have done to me. The way he would have made me feel if I'd let him.

But you can't get pregnant from your own hand.

I curse again. If I am pregnant, it means I'm far along. Almost eight weeks, at least.

My periods haven't been regular since I had Theo. I skip months all the time, so that isn't a sure sign of pregnancy. Nausea and vomiting, though? Check.

I palm my chest and wince. Sensitive breasts? Check.

I bang my head back against the wall and squeeze my eyes shut. What am I going to do?

I allow myself sixty seconds of wallowing before I push to my feet, brush my teeth, and grab my purse. The nanny gives me a silent wave from the couch where she is reading a romance novel from the large collection she keeps in her purse. Theo is sleeping, but if he wakes up, she'll be here to take care of him. I walk through the small kitchen and to the front door. The guards downstairs follow me wordlessly out of the apartment, into the lobby, and then down the street. Screaming at them to leave me the fuck alone doesn't work—I know that because I've already tried. Besides, I'm slightly grateful for their presence today. Focused as I am on the possible baby growing in my uterus, I'm not as aware of my surroundings as I could be. If Fedor is ever going to attack me, today would be a good day to do it.

The shop on the corner has everything, including a cat who lies on top of the warm coffee maker and hisses when customers get too close. I'm in and out of the store within a minute, six pregnancy tests in hand.

If the guards know what is hidden away in my plastic bag, they don't say anything.

When I get back into the apartment, the guards take up their posts once again near the front door, and I run up the stairs and back into the bathroom.

Each of the tests is different, so they all have different instructions, but I'm not patient enough to read right now. As long as my pee gets on the stick, I'm doing enough things right to get the answers I'm looking for. So, I tear a pink package open with my teeth, yank my pants down, and pee on the stick for five seconds, though it feels like an eternity.

As I pace the bathroom and wait, I flash back to being eighteen years old in a convenience store bathroom, throwing up in the disgusting toilet while I waited for the pregnancy test to tell me what I already knew.

This time is different, however. Not only am I in an immaculate, spacious bathroom that is nicer than any house I've ever lived in, but I wanted this sex. Regardless of how I feel about Viktor in this very second, the last time I had sex with him was incredible. It was hot and full of passion. Most importantly, I remember every pulsing, aching second of it.

This baby is wanted.

Fear clenches my heart, making it difficult to breathe, but the truth remains. If I really am pregnant, I want this baby.

When I found out I was pregnant with Theo, I didn't want him. I knew I couldn't get rid of him, but I wasn't happy. The warm glow of love didn't wash over me when I realized I had life growing in my belly. I felt used and hollowed out and raw. I'd been raped, and my life was veering off course and there was nothing I could do.

Of course, Theo is my everything now. He is my reason for living and breathing and fighting, but I didn't know that at the time.

Now, knowing how much I love Theo, I know how much I would love this baby, too. *That* is what scares me. Caring for another person that much when life is so insane and dangerous. I spend half of my time studying for my interior design class, the other half caring for Theo, and during all of that, I'm worried sick for Theo's safety. There isn't a second of my day where I get a reprieve from worrying about him. From wondering when Fedor will strike next.

Can I handle feeling that way about *two* human beings?

My phone beeps to tell me the three minutes are up, and I reach for the first test more out of instinct than a conscious decision. Before I can steel myself to see the results, there is a blue plus sign staring up at me from the display screen.

Confirmed. I'm pregnant.

Viktor studies me as we eat a family dinner and play in the living room. Even as he hikes Theo over his shoulder and stomps around the house, laughing and tickling him, I feel Viktor's eyes on me.

I haven't asked him to visit us once since we moved into the apartment. He has, of course. Theo gets upset if he sees Viktor any less than five or six times per week. But I've never asked Viktor to come over, until now.

The second Theo is in bed for the night, Viktor sits on the couch next to me and frowns. "Okay. What's going on?"

I almost don't want to tell him. He deserves to know—believe me, I've more than learned my lesson about keeping a secret child from a crime boss—but I'm afraid of what will happen when he does. Like me, Viktor worries. He is terrified of what Fedor will do, which is why he locked me in the bedroom in the first place. It's why he bought me an apartment in the most secure building in the city and still posts guards at my door twenty-four/seven. And that was to protect his brother's child.

How much more will he worry when he finds out I'm carrying *his* child?

"Molly," he says softly, reaching for my hand. I pull it away before we can make contact, and he sighs. "Clearly, you didn't ask me to come over to chitchat. So, what is it?"

Heat pools in my stomach as I understand his meaning. Part of him hoped I'd asked him to come here because I wanted to see him. Because I wanted to do more than just see him.

I swallow back the lust in my throat, chalking it up to raging pregnancy hormones, and spit it out. "I'm pregnant."

Viktor's mouth falls open, and he sinks back into the couch. Then, he sits up, back straight, and shakes his head ... before falling back into the couch.

"We used a condom."

I nod. "We sure did."

"So, you can't be pregnant."

"Except I am." I shrug. "I took six tests. All positive."

"When?" he breathes. His usual stern mask has slipped. He looks younger when he is confused, softer. It makes me want to reach out and stroke his hair.

"When did I take the tests or when did I get pregnant?" I ask and then decide to answer both. "I took the tests this afternoon, and my best guess is that I got pregnant the day we got fake married and had sex all night."

His jaw tightens, and he shifts his hips. I wonder if he is experiencing the same rush of heat I am at the memory. Suddenly, he pushes himself to standing, plants his feet in front of me, and turns.

"We have to get married."

I don't know what I expected him to say, but it wasn't that. I blink at him in confusion for several seconds before I gather the ability to shake my head.

"No."

Viktor sighs and spins on his heel, dragging a hand through his hair. "If we get married, my men will protect you. They will sacrifice their lives for yours."

"No," I repeat. "This isn't the 1950s. You don't have to marry me just because I'm pregnant."

"This has nothing to do about social obligations, Molly. I'm in a war. *We*," he says, gesturing from himself to me, "are in a war. Fedor wants Theo, and he wants you dead."

"And now that I'm carrying your child, you care more about my life than you did before?"

His lips turn white, and his nostrils flare. "Don't say that like I haven't spent countless hours and a fortune keeping you safe. Don't act like I haven't made it clear I care about you."

Guilt swirls in my stomach, making me nauseous for a different reason. "Then you can continue keeping me safe whether we are married or not."

"Not the same way I can if we are married." He steps forward and grabs my elbow. His touch is gentle, but I feel the strength in it. The passion coursing through him. He is serious about this offer.

There is a part of me that wants to lean into his touch. Viktor has made mistakes, but he has also proven that he cares about me. He has proven that he will be a good father figure to Theo and will take care of us.

It would be so easy to give him what he wants. To surrender myself to him and let him lead me through life by the hand, providing what I need along the way.

His hand slides up my arm, cupping the back of my arm and drawing me closer to him.

I could lay my head on his chest, curl into his warmth, and nod my head. That's all it would take.

"Marry me," he whispers, his breath warm on the top of my head.

Goose bumps trail down my back, and I push him away and shake my head to clear it.

"No."

He growls, frustrated. "Why are you making this so difficult?"

"Why is marriage your solution for everything?"

He narrows his eyes. "Fake marry me, at least. Let me tell my men this is real. They all know the justice of the peace before wasn't real. We aren't living together, so they've worked out that this isn't a serious arrangement. Pretend."

I've been there before. I fake married Viktor—though I didn't know it was fake at the time—and I can't go back to that. Letting people think he's my sugar daddy is one thing, but pretending to be his wife when really we are … I'm not sure what we are. No. I can't do it. I won't.

"I'm done pretending."

His hands fist at his side, and he turns away from me, his body shaking. "You are carrying my child, but you won't let me do anything to protect it. I have a say."

"Not over me and my body, you don't."

We stare at one another, a silent standoff. I refuse to back down. Not on this. I've been pushed around by so many people in my life, but I'm done with that. Not anymore. Not again.

Finally, Viktor turns away. "This isn't over."

"Yes, it is." I grab his keys from the coffee table and hold them out for him. "I think you should go."

He could tell me that I can't kick him out of a house that he pays for.

That I don't have any control over him. I almost expect him to say all of those things, but instead, he snatches the keys from my hand and storms towards the door.

"This isn't over," he repeats again before the door slams closed. He locks it before stomping down the hallway.

2

VIKTOR

The bar is dim. The windows were long ago blotted out with signs and black smears of paint, giving it the appearance of eternal night. Right now, I'm grateful for the gloom. It makes the scene in front of me easier to digest.

I feel a tacky squelch under my boot. Petr grabs my arm and pulls me to a stop.

"Careful." He points to the right of where I was walking, and I see the source of the mess on the floor.

The body is wedged between the barstool and the wood paneling of the bar like it slumped down there and didn't move again. Not surprising, considering the person's head is sitting in a bowl of peanuts on the bar. At least, I think it's the same head. There are several other dead bodies missing heads of their own.

Fedor sounded normal on the phone. Normal for him, anyway.

I was in my office when he called. Going home to the apartment I used to share with Molly and Theo was depressing, and I couldn't go back to Molly's. No matter how badly I wanted to talk with her and figure out what we were going to do about the baby, she didn't want me there. So, I stayed at the office even later than usual. Maybe I should've thanked Fedor, after all. Because of him, there was plenty to keep me busy.

He took half of my men, and the men who stayed behind barely trusted me. I had lost Molly and Theo, and now, because of the brother who should have been my right-hand man, I was looking at losing my control of the Bratva, too. Everything was going to shit.

When Fedor called, I naively thought it could be to make amends. No matter how many times Fedor fucked me over, I wanted to think of him as my little brother. As the boy I'd cared for and protected our entire lives. I didn't want to see him as the monster he'd become.

"Working late?" he asked.

I didn't want to think about how he knew. About whether I was being watched or followed or what it could mean for Molly. If Fedor knew she was pregnant, he'd go after her in a heartbeat. I couldn't let that happen. For sanity's sake, I convinced myself it was just a lucky guess.

"What do you want, Fedor?"

He let out a sharp, bitter laugh. "Well, I was going to see if you wanted to get a drink with me, but I can guess what your answer will be. You don't sound very happy to hear from me."

"Maybe that's because you betrayed me and took my men," I growled.

Fedor sighed. "They came with me willingly, brother."

"You've always had a hard time distinguishing between the two," I said, grinding my teeth at the thought of Fedor touching Molly. Hurting her.

This time, Fedor genuinely laughed. The sound was so sharp it surprised me. "See, brother? You need to come down to the bar. The patrons here would laugh their heads off at that joke."

Something in the tone of his voice alerted me to a scheme. He wasn't calling for a chat. He sounded too proud of himself. As soon as I hung up the phone, I called down to the bar where our men liked to hang out. When no one answered, I called Petr, and we went to investigate.

"What the fuck?" Petr mumbles, pressing his forearm to his nose to keep out the coppery smell of the blood. "What kind of monster could do this?"

"Who do you think?" I know the answer, but it doesn't seem real. I keep expecting it all to be fake. To realize the bodies are props and the blood is corn syrup. Because imagining my baby brother could be capable of bloodshed and carnage like this is beyond me.

There is no doubt Fedor did this, however. I told Molly we were in a war. Maybe she'd finally understand what I mean if she saw this.

I dismiss the idea the moment it pops into my head. I don't want her or anyone else to see this. It's horrific and a sure sign of how far gone my brother is. Besides, in her condition …

I haven't seen her since last night, but I had a doctor sent over early in the morning to confirm everything. I'll probably get an earful about that later for not running it past her first, but that argument would be a welcome reprieve from what I'm seeing now.

"But there are civilians here," Petr says. "By my count, he only killed two of our guys."

By my count, too. My guess is Fedor didn't want to kill too many potential soldiers. That's what my men are right now—potential recruits for Fedor's growing army. As he continues his random trail of terror, he is scaring once loyal men into fighting with him. They are so afraid for their lives that they are pledging loyalty to someone as obviously out of his mind as Fedor.

"The Italians can't agree with this." I pinch the bridge of my nose and close my eyes, trying to think. Trying to be logical. Rage and frustration and a hopeless sadness sink inside of me, and I try to rise above it. I can't let my emotions get in the way of my judgment. That's what Fedor wants. "They've always abided by the unspoken rule of leaving civilians alone. Doing otherwise is dangerous. It risks police interference and jail time."

"I think the game is changing," Petr says, his voice muffled by the sleeve of his shirt. "We've always drawn lines in the sand, but Fedor doesn't have those lines. His army is growing, and he is willing to do things we aren't. If he keeps it up, we won't be able to play anymore."

"This isn't a fucking game."

Petr stiffens at my sudden snap but doesn't retreat. There is nowhere to retreat. We are standing in the only bit of unbloodied floor in the entire bar.

"Are you suggesting we do … this?" I gesture around the bar as though there is any way he could have missed the carnage. "Because if this is what it takes to keep up, I don't want to play."

"Of course not," Petr says. "I'm just passing on what I've heard."

I sigh. If Petr is passing on information, it means there is talk. Fedor's level of crazy is making me look weak. My men are terrified of my baby brother, and I'm not sure how to reassure them.

I clap a hand on Petr's shoulder and squeeze. Then, with our silent apology out of the way, we leave so the bar can be scrubbed and cleaned and the bodies disposed of.

I'm jittery after four cups of coffee and two hours of sleep, but the adrenaline coursing through my veins assures me I won't get tired. Not until after this is done.

Petr put out feelers and heard word back early this morning that Fedor is holing up in an Italian warehouse on the edge of the city. He knows if he shows his face in any of his old haunts or any of the Kornilov turf, he'll have to face me. So, I'm going to go face him.

My men need to know I'm not afraid of a fight. They need to see that I'm willing to go to war for them, that I will do what I can to neutralize any threats against our family and our business. Even if that threat is my own flesh and blood.

"I think you should stay behind," Petr says again, adjusting his bulletproof vest and checking his gun for the third time. "It doesn't make sense for you to lead the charge. If you are killed, how long will the Bratva last? What chance do any of us have?"

Petr is the obvious next choice for leader of the Bratva, though clearly, he doesn't have much faith in his own abilities. Honestly, with Fedor becoming a rival, I have to agree with him. Under normal circumstances, Petr is good with people and knows how to make hard choices, but no one is prepared to counter my brother's level of crazy like I am. I've been talking Fedor back from moral ledges his entire life. This ledge is a little more precarious than the others, but I have hope I can do it again.

"If I'm seen hiding behind my men, how long will it last then?"

Petr doesn't answer, and I know it's because he agrees with me. Everyone is afraid, and I have to be willing to stand up and show them I'm not if I want to save what I've built.

The warehouse sits at the back of a large, empty plot of land. We are not discreet as SUV after SUV rolls down the road towards the warehouse. I have about twenty men in total with weapons, ready to take down anyone who comes into our path. I would never allow my men to take out civilians and innocents, but anyone involved in the attack we saw at the bar last night is not innocent. They deserve to pay for what they did.

The plan is to jump out the moment the cars stop and lay waste to the warehouse. Bust out windows, shoot through walls, and storm inside and take it if the opportunity presents itself. I don't want to lose any men—I don't have many left to lose—but I want to make Fedor understand that I will not roll over and let him treat the city like his own hellish playground. I want him to know I can kill, and I will if pushed.

As soon as the SUV screeches to a stop, Petr and I share a look before throwing open our doors and jumping from the car. I take cover behind the armored car door and am ready to fire when the metal double doors of the warehouse open and a woman comes walking out.

A pregnant woman.

The animal part of my brain sees the long brown hair and the obviously pregnant stomach and thinks of Molly.

She is carrying my child and now Fedor has her. He has captured her and is going to kill her in front of me.

I'm so overcome with terror and rage and blind panic that it takes me several seconds to realize Molly isn't showing yet, and Fedor doesn't know she is pregnant. This woman can't be Molly.

I lift a hand for my men to hold, and on cue, Fedor comes walking out of the warehouse with his gun raised, pointed directly at the pregnant woman's head.

We are far enough away that I can't make out the woman's face, but I can tell by the shaking in her shoulders that she is sobbing. Her arms are raised in surrender, and my plans of revenge fall around me like ash.

To take out Fedor, I'd have to kill a pregnant woman. He knows I never would. He is counting on it.

Petr's words from the bar ring in my head: *His army is growing, and he is willing to do things we aren't. If he keeps it up, we won't be able to play anymore.* I can't play anymore. Part of me wishes I could rationalize this woman's life as a necessary cost of ending my brother. After all, killing her and her unborn child would be far less than the death toll Fedor could rack up if left unchecked. In a utilitarian sense, killing her is the right thing to do.

Still, I can't stop myself from lowering my gun.

I can't.

I won't.

I signal for my men to stand down and then rise to my feet. Petr hisses through the car to ask what the fuck I'm doing, but I can barely hear him over the blood pounding in my ears. I walk out from behind the car door and start moving towards the warehouse. I only vaguely recognize someone is standing next to me, and I turn and realize it is Petr. His eyes are wide, scanning the warehouse windows, looking for snipers or anyone who would shoot at us, but I can't be worried about that right now.

This needs to end. Now.

As we approach, I can see Fedor is smiling. He is grinning, actually. His face is split wide with obvious joy at what is happening, in stark contrast to the sobbing woman in front of him.

Her eyes are red and puffy, snot is dripping from her nose, and her entire body is trembling.

"Did you really think you could just show up and kill me so easily?" Fedor asks, peeking out from behind the pregnant woman but keeping most of his body shielded behind hers. "I thought you'd be smarter than that, brother."

"And I thought you'd be a human being," I snap back. "Who is your human shield?"

Fedor's lips pull back in disgust. "Just some slut."

There is no warmth in his eyes. No caring for the woman or the life she is carrying. There is no sign of humanity in his electric green eyes, and I feel like my brother is dead. Because the man standing in front of me is not the brother I knew.

"This isn't you," I say, deciding to speak my mind. "Come on, Fedor. You are better than this."

Fedor shrugs. "Perhaps. Though, I honestly think this plan is pretty smart. Especially given my time constraints. We hit the bar last night, and I only realized afterwards that you might be a little upset about it. So, I rounded up some passersby and brought them back to the warehouse."

Passersby. "There are more?"

"Inside," he says with an excited nod. "About ten of them. Well, eleven if you count the baby."

He points his gun at the woman's stomach, and she flinches. Fedor grins even wider at her fear.

"Stop." It's a sharp command, and for a second, Fedor listens. His smile fades away, and his expression softens. He looks like a guilty little kid. Like the brother who drew on the walls and stuffed a whole roll of toilet paper in the toilet and cried when he was caught. For the briefest of seconds, I see the boy he once was. "You are not a monster, Fedor. Don't become one."

Then, his green eyes burn brighter, and his smile is back, but this time it has an edge. "I'm not a monster, brother. I'm a leader."

As he speaks, people separate from the shadows behind him, and I recognize the dons of the Mazzeo family, Mario and his son Rio. They flank Fedor on either side, arms crossed over their chests.

They'd make a powerful picture if Mario didn't have a large bruise under his right eye. Clearly, the old man has been beaten recently. I wonder if it was Fedor or one of his men. I wonder how many people he is threatening to maintain his power.

"Mario," I say softly, appealing to the mercy I know he has. "This is madness. Don't support this."

His soft chin lifts, but his son moves to stand partially in front of him. "Don't address my father," Rio snaps.

Fedor's chest inflates now that he has backup. "You are the only one unwilling to do what is necessary to take control, Viktor. Everyone else understands that sometimes people have to die. The sooner you realize that, the better chance you'll have of saving a scrap of what you've built."

"Innocent people never need to die!" I shout, hands fisted at my side. "What you did to those civilians at the bar is unconscionable."

Mario flinches like the imagery of what happened there pains him, but Fedor laughs. "I hoped it would make an impression. My idea! Every person who spoke ill of me in that room had their tongue removed."

My stomach turns. "You fucking psycho."

His nostrils flare, and he readjusts the gun in his hand. I'm afraid I've pushed him too far and he's going to shoot the woman just to make a point, but he doesn't. His entire body stills.

"You've always thought you were better than me. You've always seen yourself as better than me and our father and our family. But deep down, we are the same," he hisses. "And if you are going to win this, you are going to have to let go of this high and mighty bullshit, brother."

There will be no talking him down from this. I see that now. It is hopeless. I have to fight if I want this to be over. But not today.

"What happens now?" I ask. "How do we walk away from this?"

"We don't walk away. *You* walk away."

"So you can shoot me in the back?" I shake my head. "Not a fucking chance."

"You're the one who came here with an army," he says. Then, his mouth curls into a smirk. "You know what? Take the pregnant woman."

He shoves the woman towards me, and she stumbles, catching herself before she falls. Then, she freezes. Like me, she is wary of Fedor's motives.

"Consider it an act of goodwill," he says. "I'll let her go with you, you can feel like a happy little hero, and I won't shoot you in the back."

"Why should I believe you?"

Fedor shrugs. "You said it yourself, brother. I'm not a monster. I guess you're just going to have to hope you're right."

I don't believe that anymore, but Fedor is right. If I stay here, he may grow bored and decide to shoot me for fun.

I hold out a hand for the pregnant woman to take, and she looks at it with wide eyes. I know she wants to reach out, but she is too afraid to move. So, I take a careful step forward and wrap my hand around hers. Her fingers are ice-cold, but she grips my hand like her life depends on it. And right now, it does.

"Don't forget. There are nine more innocents inside," he says, hitching a thumb over his shoulder. "Don't be stupid."

Slowly, we all back away. The tension in the air is thick. It feels like walking backwards through a minefield, holding my breath, waiting for the earth to explode around me.

When we finally reach the car, Fedor lifts his hand in a wave and then ducks back into the warehouse. I don't even begin to relax until the warehouse is out of sight and we are back amongst the tall buildings of the city. But really, I won't be fully relaxed until Fedor has been dealt with. I won't be able to stop looking over my shoulder until my baby brother is dead.

3

MOLLY

My interior design textbooks sit in front of me, open but unused. I can't force my mind to focus on the task at hand. I'm distracted. Beyond distracted.

I haven't seen Viktor since he stormed out of the apartment after I told him about the baby. He sent a doctor over yesterday morning, though.

I want to be angry with him for scheduling a doctor visit without my permission, but I'm just relieved. Hearing the baby's heartbeat and being assured that things are progressing normally has been a huge weight off my shoulders.

Plus, on some level, Viktor's care and concern feels nice.

Though, it's also alarming.

Yet again, I am going to have the child of a Mafia member. No matter how much concern Viktor has for my safety and the safety of his child, he inherently puts us at a higher risk. His activities bring danger to our doorstep every second.

Not to mention, the Mafia members in question are brothers deadlocked into a violent war.

The only way I can see to get out is to not have the baby, but the second the thought crosses my mind, I push it away.

I had Theo when the entire world was against me, and I still love him more than myself. I can't imagine my life without him, and I know I'll feel the same way about this baby when he or she arrives.

Vaguely, I hear the door open, and I assume it's the nanny bringing Theo in from their daily trip to the park. I'm still staring blankly at the book in front of me when I see movement near the door. I paste a smile on my face to keep Theo from knowing anything is wrong, but when I look up and see Theo in the arms of a man I don't recognize, my entire body goes cold.

The smile slips from my mouth and shatters on the floor. I jump to my feet, my body rigid and coiled, ready to strike.

"Who the fuck are you?" There is a knife in the drawer closest to me, but my gun is upstairs. Why didn't I bring my gun down with me?

I assess Theo. He isn't noticeably injured, and either he is relaxed or he is too stunned to be upset. He is stiff and staring at me, his hand resting on the strange man's shoulder.

He isn't hurt and that's a good sign ... I hope.

"Fedor sends his regards," the man says. His voice is deep and low and robotic. It sounds like he has been programmed to speak, but that doesn't stop his words from slicing through me like a blade. *Fedor.* I feel like I've been split open, exposed to my core. "You aren't as safe as you think."

My hands are shaking, and I ball them into fists.

This is my nightmare. This exact moment is what I've feared for weeks.

I don't take my eyes off Theo. If he understands the meaning of the man's words, he doesn't show it. His face is an emotionless mask, which is more concerning. If he was crying, I would understand that. I don't understand this.

The thought crosses my mind that Fedor is hurting Theo even when he isn't *hurting* him. I can't protect him from this emotional trauma. From the fear and the distrust this will sow in him.

"Please." The word scratches out of me. It's all I can manage to say. *Please don't hurt him. Please put him down. Please leave.*

The man's face twitches in annoyance, almost like he wants to roll his eyes, and he bends and sets Theo on the ground.

I want to run to him and scoop him up, but I'm afraid of what will happen if I make any sudden movements. It feels like we are standing in the center of an iced-over pond and the ice could crack beneath me at any second.

The man glares down at Theo, his eyes hungry and violent, and then he turns and leaves. I don't stop him to ask where the nanny went. God only knows what happened to her. At best, she was paid off. At worst…well, it's best not to ask.

The second the door clicks closed behind him, I drop to my knees and hold out my arms. Theo looks at me for a moment, too stunned to move, and then his lower lip starts to wobble. By the time he walks into the circle of my arms, he is crying, though I'm not even sure if he understands why.

I know why I'm crying, though.

∽

"He paid them off."

Viktor is pacing around the living room, running his hands through his hair and tugging on the strands.

"Fucking money," he growls. "That's what it took for my men to turn on me. He offered them some cash, and they folded and walked away."

I called Viktor the moment Theo had calmed down enough. He instructed me to lock the door—I already had—and stay inside until he could get here. He showed up four minutes later. I didn't ask how many traffic laws he broke in order to make that happen.

He fists his hands at his side and then drags them through his hair again.

"We're okay," I remind him. I'm scared. So scared I'm not sure I'll be able to fall asleep tonight, but I'm fine. Theo is sleeping upstairs. He is fine. "We are fine."

"He could have killed you both," Viktor says, spinning on his heel and facing me. His eyes are bloodshot, and I wonder how long it has been since he slept. "Fedor offered my guys some money, and they left you open and unprotected, and there was nothing I could do to stop it."

"Why didn't he?" Viktor looks confused, so I clarify. "Why didn't he kill us? Or take us with him? Isn't that the point—he wants Theo. Why would he let us go?"

"He feels invincible." Viktor starts to pace again and lets out a sharp laugh. "He is trying to prove a point. He wants me to know that he has access to you whenever he wants, that he is in control. Fedor is too theatric to just take what he wants. He has to be a showman about it first. It's why he held a pregnant woman at gunpoint."

I frown, and Viktor shakes his head, not wanting to talk about it. "I took care of her. She is back home and safe ... for now. But Fedor won't hesitate to hurt her or you. Right now, he is still just toying with us."

"Lucky us, I guess."

Viktor crosses the room in two steps and drops down in front of me, grabbing my hands from his lap. "Yes, Molly. Lucky. You and Theo were so, *so* lucky that all Fedor wanted to do is scare you."

I blink at him, surprised by the sudden warmth of his skin on mine and surprised by how badly I need the human touch. I squeeze his hands so he won't pull away.

"But I want you to be more than lucky," he says. His blue eyes are liquid and raw, and even though I know what he is going to say, I lean in closer. "I want you to be queen."

His voice breaks on the word and he holds my hands so tightly they hurt, but I don't pull away.

"The men who left you open for Fedor won't live to see tomorrow, but I need my remaining men to see you as more than just my kept woman. These men respect titles. They need to see you as my partner."

"Viktor..." I sigh, shaking my head.

He pulls his hand away and grips my chin with his thumb and forefinger. He curls his thumb around and brushes it across the point of my chin, drawing a line down my neck. "Even if it is in appearances only, Molly. Even if it's fake. That is still better than nothing."

My mind cries out that I have some dignity. I can't be fake married to Viktor again. It's demeaning.

But then, I see Theo's shaking body in my arms after the man left. Unbidden, the image of what could have happened flashes in my mind.

Theo could have been taken. I could have been killed. I could have never seen him again.

There is more at stake here than my dignity and my freedom. Theo's life is at stake. My unborn child's life is at stake. I have to think about the bigger picture, and when I step back and take it all in, I see the sense in Viktor's proposal. It isn't the only solution, but it is one of the easier solutions.

"Okay." My voice is barely above a whisper, but Viktor tenses as I agree. I hold up a hand before he can say anything. "*But,* once this war is over, Theo and I have to be free to leave."

"We'll discuss that when the time comes," Viktor says.

I narrow my eyes. "We have to be free to leave. I can't enter into this if it's going to end with me locked in a bedroom."

"How do you feel about a bathroom?" he raises a brow, his mouth quirking up in a barely-there smile.

"I can't believe you're making jokes at a time like this." I'm appalled, but also grateful for the lightness. The day has felt heavy. It's nice to see him smile.

He lets my chin go and leans back. "If you really want to leave when this is over ... we'll talk about it."

I want him to agree to my terms, but I know this is the best I can hope for right now. So, grudgingly, I nod and agree.

If Viktor's idea of a fake marriage isn't the best solution, it is certainly the most expedient.

By midafternoon the next day, we are standing in front of a justice of the peace—a different one from the first time we were married, though Viktor assured me he is still only an actor—and reciting our vows.

The crowd for the wedding is intimate, limited to Petr and a few other high-ranking members of the Bratva who will serve as witnesses. Viktor looks dashing in a dark gray suit that squares his shoulders and highlights his trim waist and strong thighs. My dress is simple, but white—the only thing that matters according to Viktor. The straps are thick across my shoulders and the neckline is deep, showing off a good amount of cleavage that Viktor can't seem to stop staring at. From there, the fabric hugs my waist and then falls in a gentle A-line shape to puddle around my feet.

Simple or not, the dress is more than I ever dreamed of. Living on the streets and sleeping in shelters, I fantasized about meeting someone I wanted to marry. A dress never factored into it. I'd get married in jeans and a T-shirt if it was for love.

Viktor's eyes are piercing as he studies my face and recites his vows. It's the second time he has spoken these words to me, vowing his protection and love and generosity. I smile, selling my role as the blushing bride, but inside, I try to bat his pledges away. I try to keep them from sailing into my mind and heart and taking root there.

This marriage is fake. He doesn't mean it.

The ceremony is over almost before I can grasp that it has started, and Viktor grabs my hand and pulls me through the temporary office space and into a large room in the back. Long white fabric panels hang from the walls and the ceiling has been decorated with a tangle of fairy lights and tulle. Soft music is playing through a set of speakers and there is cake and punch.

I open my mouth to try and give voice to my surprise, but none come. Viktor squeezes my hand and presses his warm palm to my lower back. "I didn't ask them to do this. They did it for you."

For the first time, I let myself look at the faces of the men standing around the room. Many of them have women tangled in their arms. They are all smiling and at ease, but more pressingly, they are looking at me. At us.

"They wanted to please their queen," he says, lifting my arm over my head and spinning me gracefully away and then back into his body.

I press my hand to his chest to stabilize myself and marvel at the solidness of Viktor's body. It has only been a few weeks since we've been together, since I've seen all of him bare and exposed, and I'm still consistently surprised by the strength of his body and the feel of it under my fingers.

Viktor cradles my body to his gently, swaying us around the dance floor as music plays. When the song is done, he keeps hold of my hand and leads me around the room, talking to each guest. Almost all of them congratulate us and then take my hand and press it to their foreheads.

"Their loyalty," Viktor whispers in my ear. His breath is warm on my neck, and I shiver, wishing he would never stop whispering to me.

The night is a whirlwind, and we leave to cheers and whistles and excited applause. Viktor helps me into the passenger seat of his black car, ensuring my dress doesn't get stuck in the door, and then drives us quietly and expertly through the city, navigating traffic fearlessly.

I'm surprised when he pulls up in front of my apartment rather than his own. We haven't discussed it, but I assumed we would be consolidating our living arrangements post-marriage. Yet, Viktor helps me out of the car and allows me to unlock my own front door and step inside.

Theo is with a new nanny and several guards who have proven themselves incredibly loyal, so the apartment is quiet. I feel Viktor behind me as I walk into the kitchen, but when I turn around, his hands are in his pockets. Almost like he is trying to restrain himself.

"Should we have a drink?" I offer, unsure how else to end this night. Then I remember the baby and laugh, breaking the tension. "Not for me, though."

Viktor smiles and moves to get glasses from the cabinet. "Virgin?"

"Considering our last fake wedding night, you know the answer to that," I joke.

Viktor smiles, but I notice a tension in his jaw.

I defer the drink mixing to him. Viktor made sure the liquor cabinet was well stocked before we moved in, so I assume he will make a better drink than I ever would. I watch as he slips out of his suit jacket and begins measuring and shaking and pouring. His button-down shirt is pulled tight across his muscled back and his biceps. I like watching Viktor move. He has an inborn grace, a rhythm entirely his own that lures me in like a siren's call. No matter how complicated being with him is, I can't seem to pull away. I can't seem to want to distance myself from him the way I know I should.

When he hands me a deep red drink, I take a long swallow without asking what it is.

"Juice, sparkling water, and a lime," he says with a shrug. "Virgins aren't my specialty."

I snort, almost sending the mocktail out my nose, and clamp a hand over my mouth. When I manage to swallow, I laugh. "That feels like an understatement."

He seems to relax as he makes his own drink, his shoulders easing, a small smile on his mouth. It's nice to see him like this. I tilt my head to the side and watch him until I feel butterflies fluttering in my stomach. It's too early for it to be the baby and the drink is sans alcohol, so there can only be one cause.

Viktor puts the lid on the shaker, grips it with both hands, and mixes it vigorously. His muscles flex and strain under the thin fabric of his shirt, and he nips at his lower lip. I spin away from the sight and walk out onto the balcony for some fresh air.

Fake wedding. Fake wedding, I remind myself.

I didn't even want to do this. I had to be convinced to marry him, so I can't possibly be enjoying this. It wouldn't make any sense.

The evening is cool, and I feel goose bumps spread across my back and shoulders. As soon as they appear, a warm hand smooths across my skin, and I gasp.

"Sorry. I didn't mean to scare you," Viktor says softly, his words whispered on the back of my neck.

"You didn't," I assure him. I turn around, pressing my back to the railing, and face him. "I don't have a reason to be scared anymore, right? I'm safe now?"

Viktor tips his glass back, swallowing half of the drink in one go, and then presses his lips together. "You're safe. One hundred times safer than you were before, at least."

"Good."

He nods and then swallows back the rest of his drink. Mine is still mostly full, but my stomach is too busy doing flips to enjoy it. I don't know if it's pregnancy nausea or nerves or both.

"There are guards at your door who know failing to protect you will be the end of their lives," he says. "You will always be protected. Even when you're alone in the apartment, you won't really be alone."

I set my glass down on the glass table and fold my hands in front of me. "What about tonight?"

"The guards followed us from the venue. They are on duty right now."

I shake my head and step forward, grabbing Viktor's glass. It is empty, so he doesn't resist as I pull it from his hands and place it next to mine. When I turn back to him, I can't look up at his face yet, so I stare at my hands as they work their way up the hard planes of his chest.

"I mean, will I feel alone tonight?"

He pauses for a second and then lays his large hands over mine. "Only if you want to, Molly."

Finally, I let myself look into his face. His eyes are a wide-open sky blue, and I see hope in them. Desire. And, even though our wedding was a farce, I see a promise there, too.

Viktor will take care of me. He'll protect me and Theo and our unborn child. He is going to do everything he can to keep us all alive, and for right now, that is the only vow that matters to me.

I shake my head. "I don't want to be alone. I want you to stay."

He lets out a breath and then we are kissing. His hands pull me against him, one around the back of my neck, the other curled around my waist. My body molds to his in the same way my mouth does—soft and warm and eager.

A breeze cuts through the balcony, and I shiver. Viktor shifts his arms to my waist, picks me up, and carries me inside without ever breaking the kiss.

I reach for the couch as we pass it, assuming we are going to stop there, but Viktor growls and shakes his head. "On the bed. I want you on the bed tonight."

Tonight. Our wedding night.

Again, I remind myself this is fake, but it doesn't feel fake. When he lays me down in the bedroom, he steps back and lets his eyes devour the sight of me. He bites his lower lip. "That dress is sinful."

"It's white," I smile, hoping it's dim enough he can't see how easily I'm blushing.

Viktor crawls over and lifts me up against his chest. He pulls the zipper slowly down my back and then works his hands over my shoulders, pushing the straps down my arms.

"It's a lie," he whispers in my ear. He grips the neckline and begins peeling it down my body, revealing more and more of my skin with each inch. "You aren't innocent. Or *pure*. You're wretched, Molly. Just like me."

Distantly, I think I should be offended, but Viktor speaks each word like a caress. As he shimmies the dress over my hips and trails his fingers along my thighs, I want to be whatever he says. Whatever Viktor is, I want to be the same. If that's wretched, so be it. I can be wretched.

The second the dress is off my legs, Viktor throws it over his shoulder, and I lunge forward and begin undoing buttons as fast as my fingers will go. Viktor leans forward and licks the side of my neck from my collarbone to my ear. He sucks my earlobe into his mouth, and my body is on fire. There is heat pooling between my legs, heavy and pressing, and it needs attending to urgently.

Viktor must sense the need because his hand cups the delicate lace at my center, and he rolls his palm over my heat. My lips part in a moan, and I buck my hips against him.

"Wretched," he purrs into my neck. "Wicked."

I tear his shirt from his shoulders and begin working at his pants all while Viktor is undoing me with his lips, kissing and sucking and nipping at my skin until I'm wild with lust.

His finger smooths a path across my panties before dipping inside. I still as he finds my opening and presses inside. Then, he curls his finger, needlessly beckoning me closer as if I'm not already under his spell, and I melt. I fall forward, my cheek against his chest, and spread my knees wider on the bed to stabilize myself.

Viktor is on his knees, too, and from my lazy position lying against his warmth, I slip my hand inside his unbuttoned suit pants and stroke the hard length of him. He growls, the sound rumbling through his chest and into my body. The animal in him calls to me, daring me to push him further, to make him as wild as he is making me.

I hook my fingers in the waist of his pants and push them down around his thighs, freeing him. He springs out of them, excited and ready, and I stroke my hand down at the same time he curls a second finger into me. I gasp and brush my thumb over his tip, eliciting a shudder.

Viktor works a third finger into me, and I'm falling apart. I moan and bite his collarbone, trying to reclaim my grip on reality, and he lets out a soft curse.

I've never felt so connected to my own body yet so tuned in to every brush of skin on skin. The thumb Viktor circles over my center is the only thing holding me to the planet, and it isn't enough. I need more. I need all of him.

I grab his wrist and pull him out of me, feeling the loss immediately. Then, I push him back, and Viktor sees where we are heading. He stretches his legs out in front of him, grips my lower back, and guides me onto his lap.

He presses himself against my opening, and then we sink together. I'm not sure whether I'm going under or Viktor is coming up. It doesn't matter. The laws of physics don't seem to have any hold on us as we rock together.

I hug Viktor's head to my chest, clawing at his silky hair, and roll my hips again and again.

Viktor's large hands spread out on my back as I lean away from him to get better leverage. He tips forward and sucks my breast into his mouth, his lips soft even while his teeth nip and tug and punish. I cry out from the cacophony of sensations. From the pain and pleasure and warmth even as goose bumps shoot down my arms. It's more than I've ever felt, and Viktor was right, I'm safe.

I can feel it with him. A perfect bubble around us, protecting us from the rest of the world in a way I've never experienced before.

My legs start to shake with the beginnings of my climax, and Viktor tips me back, back, back until I'm lying down and he is over me. His elbow presses into the mattress on one side while his other hand explores the topography of my body, brushing my nipple and strokes my waist and grips my hip.

I bring my knees up and wrap my legs around him as he dives into me again and again, and when my orgasm comes, I bury my face in his shoulder, clinging to him with all of the strength I have left.

He falls not long after, his lips pressed to my neck, whispering words I can't hear but can feel. They are his vows. His wicked, wretched vows, whispered in the throes of passion, and they mean more to me than anything he said in front of the witnesses.

When he is done thrusting, and his weight presses down on me, I curl my finger around his square jaw and draw his lips up to mine. Against his mouth, I whisper my own wretched vows.

I give him the only thing I have left to give: my trust.

4
VIKTOR

I left Molly's late in the morning before Theo was set to arrive home with the nanny.

We slept next to each other all night and woke up together like any normal married couple— except, we weren't married. Molly tucked her body against mine like a small spoon, nudging her hips back until I slid into her and took her gently like it was normal. Like we spend every morning this way.

Except, we don't.

There are lots of reasons to maintain two apartments. My men won't ask questions if we don't give them reason to. Which is why we have to do the swearing-in ceremony.

When I told Molly about it the night before, she was hesitant.

"I thought we already said our vows," she said.

"*We* did, but the ceremony is a chance for the Bratva to pledge their loyalty to you, as well."

She frowned, a wrinkle forming between her brows. "Wasn't the reception enough? They all seemed respectful."

I shook my head and pushed a strand of hair behind her ear, ignoring the nervous flutter of her lashes at my touch. "This is how things are done. I want my men to view you as their queen. I want them to know that your life is as important as mine or Theo's. You will be as good as blood now."

"Won't they be upset with you when they find out this is fake?"

The question plays in my mind again now as I towel off my damp hair and slip into a fresh suit.

The short answer is: yes. They will be angry.

The more complicated answer is that I hope they will never find out the marriage is fake.

My secret hope is that Molly will realize this marriage is more than just protection. I hope she'll come to enjoy my company and decide to stay. If she does, we'll file the paperwork and have a private ceremony all to ourselves. Outwardly, nothing will change, and my men will never know I violated a sacred Bratva ritual.

I know there is a possibility Molly will leave once this war is over. I know there is a possibility I'll have to confess everything to my men and risk losing even more of their trust. But I can't think about that now. Right now, the only thing that matters to me is keeping Molly and Theo safe. Even my allegiance to the Bratva has to come second —another thing I hope my men never find out.

Petr knocks on the bathroom door, pulling me from my thoughts. "I have to leave to set up. Are you picking up Molly or should I have the guards bring her?"

I know the men I have posted at Molly's apartment are trustworthy, but I still can't bring myself to let them drive her around the city. Especially before the ceremony has been performed.

"I'll pick her up."

"Okay." Petr's voice tapers off, but I don't hear his footsteps walking away. After half a minute, I walk over and pull the bathroom door open to find him still standing there.

"What is it?"

He looks ashamed to have been caught, but then his shoulders slump forward. "I was debating whether I should say something sentimental."

I raise a brow. "Like?"

"Like how you are not only my leader but my family," he says, looking down at the floor. "And as my family, I'm happy that you are happy. I know this marriage to Molly is partly out of a desire to protect her from Fedor, but I know you care for her, and I'm happy for you."

I clear my throat. "You're right. That was sentimental."

Petr runs a hand over the back of his neck and takes a step back from the door. "Yeah. I think I've decided against saying it."

"Probably a good idea," I say, trying not to smile.

Petr lifts a hand and disappears down the hallway. When I close the bathroom door, my smile fades.

I'm lying to everyone. Fooling even my top advisor in order to protect Molly.

I hope, in the end, it is all worth it.

～

Theo is sitting on the living room floor with a mountain of blocks in front of him. He is arranging them into a single tower, his tongue sticking out the side of his mouth from concentration, so he doesn't notice my entrance.

The nanny is sitting at the kitchen table with a book and a cup of coffee, and after a quick glance to see who I am, she goes back to her book. I don't blame her. I love Theo, but I learned how exhausting he can be when Molly ran away for a week.

He stands up to place another block on top, holding it carefully in his small hands. As he places it, however, the whole tower wobbles and topples over. The second it does, I grab him from behind and swing him off his feet. He shrieks and then giggles when I tickle his side.

"I didn't know you were coming." He grabs my face and then wraps his skinny arms around my neck.

If someone had told me six months ago I'd be the pseudo-father to a four-year-old boy, I would have told them they were crazy. Yet, here I am.

"I'm here to get your mommy. We are going out."

"Me too?" he asks, his eyebrows lifting to his hairline with expectation.

He looks so much like Fedor. So much I feel my heart squeeze. They have the same pointed chin and narrow nose. People who don't know any better will say he looks just like me—we are related, after all—but knowing Fedor as intimately as I do, the truth is obvious. Theo is Fedor's.

I sit down on the couch and plop him on my knee. "Not today, I'm afraid. We are going somewhere that is just for grown-ups."

He frowns, but I flick my thumb over his lower lip and release it quickly, making a loud popping noise that, despite his disappointment, makes him smile.

"Next time," I promise.

He climbs off my lap and goes back to working on his tower, enlisting my help to gather up all of the blocks that skittered under the couch after the first collapse. The tower is half as tall as it was before when I hear the muffled shouting upstairs.

I turn around and the nanny is glancing towards the stairs as well. When she sees me looking at her, she nods for me to go and walks over to keep Theo busy. I thank her with a half-smile and hurry up the stairs.

Voices are coming from Molly's room, and as I approach the door, I can hear sobbing mixed in.

"I can do something else with it, Mrs. Kornilov. If you don't like it—"

"Don't call me that," Molly interrupts the hairdresser. "Molly, please. Call me Molly."

I walk into the room without knocking.

Molly and the hairdresser both start, eyes wide. Molly's dark hair is half up, twisted into a crown of braids on the top of her head with the bottom half curled and flowing down her back. She looks incredible, even more enchanting than normal.

The hairdresser backs away from Molly and goes to the vanity table, needlessly rearranging her supplies. Molly sags onto the bed, her shoulders hunched forward. She looks nothing like the happy, sated woman I left in bed this morning.

"What's going on?" I ask, turning my ire on the hairdresser. "Why did I hear my wife screaming?"

Don't call me that. Call me Molly.

She is regretting her decision already. Less than twenty-four hours later, and she wants to back out. When Molly agreed to the fake arrangement, I knew I needed to act quickly before she could change her mind, but maybe this was too fast. Maybe it was too much, too soon.

Though, the alternative was to wait and allow more of my men the opportunity to defect to Fedor's side of this war, and the Bratva can't afford anymore losses. Neither can Molly. Fedor got close enough the night he sent one of his men into the apartment holding Theo. I couldn't let him get any closer. This was necessary, regardless of how Molly felt about it.

"It's nothing. It's not her fault," Molly says, shaking her head. She sits up, a breath hitching in her chest like she is going to say something, before she sinks back down and shakes her head again. "It's nothing."

"Yeah, it seems like nothing," I say, voice thick with sarcasm. I move to sit on the bed next to her and lay my hand on her knee. "What is it?"

All of a sudden, Molly stands up, slipping out from under my touch, and begins to pace across the room. I can clearly see she is upset, but I also can't take my eyes off the figure she cuts in her dress.

She is in a black dress that I hand-selected for her. The wedding was about love, but the ceremony tonight is about loyalty. It is about the men seeing Molly as their leader, not as an innocent, pure bride. They need to respect her authority.

The top is rigid and structured in a bustier style with a tight skirt that hugs her body close through mid-thigh. Then, over top, is a layer of lace that drapes to her knees. It is sexy and powerful—a dress befitting a Bratva queen. A dress befitting my wife.

"I can't do this," she says, waving her arms over the dress and her hair. "*This*. All of it. I just … this isn't who I am. I don't wear fancy things or have my hair done like this. I feel—"

"Different?" I ask, standing up and walking over to her.

Molly pulls her hands away when I reach for them, but I grab them anyway and lay them against my chest, pinning them there with my own hands. "You *are* different now. You should feel different."

"Not really," she whispers, glancing nervously towards where the hairdresser is pretending not to listen to us.

I know what she means. She isn't really different. We aren't really married.

I shake my head. "No, really. You are."

"But I'm not." Molly raises her voice and pulls away from me, tucking her hands behind her back. "I've been dirt poor my entire life, and now, overnight, I'm some rich Bratva wife who has a hair stylist. This. Isn't. Me. I feel ridiculous."

I don't know how to fix this right now. Not when we need to be at the ceremony in twenty minutes.

"If it is about your hair, I'm paying this woman twice her normal fee. She can change it."

The hairdresser turns around, her cheeks flushed with embarrassment, and nods. "I can. I'll do whatever you like."

"It isn't the hair," Molly says more gently, addressing the stylist. "It's fine. I'll be fine. Let's just finish up and get this over with."

Molly turns away from me and goes to sit at the chair in front of the vanity again. I can see tension in the hunch of her shoulders, but I can't do anything about it now. Based on what I overheard before walking in, my presence is only making things worse.

So, I turn and leave, pulling the door shut firmly behind me.

I'm not sure what happened between last night and now. I'm not sure how Molly went from clutching me and surrendering to me to this, and even worse, I can't fix it.

As her husband, I should know how to calm her. I should know what to say. Yet, I don't.

I run a frustrated hand through my hair before I remember it has been gelled into a respectable style. I try to flatten it back down as best I can and then go back downstairs to sit with Theo until Molly is ready. Once we get through the ceremony, we can talk about everything. I can comfort her.

At least, that's what I tell myself.

~

Molly claims she isn't ready to be a Bratva wife, to be the queen, but she could have fooled me.

The ceremony is a success.

She smiles and looks at ease, even as her finger is pricked and her blood is spilled over the Bratva symbol. When she is asked to repeat her oath of loyalty, she stumbles over a few of the words, but she remains confident and strong. I can tell my men respect her when they make their own oaths. I can feel it in the tone of their collective voice. They will protect her.

When we walk back to the car afterwards, I open Molly's door for her and then walk around the front, hoping the strangeness from before has passed. Hoping I can chalk it up to pre-ceremony nerves.

Those hopes are dashed the second I close the car door.

"How much did I fuck up?" Molly asks, dropping her head in her hands.

I'm so surprised by the sudden change in her that I don't say anything for a second.

Molly tips her head back against the seat, her eyes closed. "Everyone knew something was wrong. I used the wrong silverware and misspoke during the ceremony. And God, my hands wouldn't stop shaking. I might as well have hung a sign around my neck: FAKER."

"No one noticed anything. I thought you did great."

She looks up at me, her face twisted in disbelief. "Don't lie to me. You more than anyone know how important it is that we each play our parts, and I'm fucking it up."

"No, you aren't," I say, this time more forcefully. "My men loved you. If they don't now, they will. You did great. You're safe now. We are safe."

She takes a deep shuddering breath, and I can see her lips trembling. Her hands shake in her lap. "You don't know what it is like to be me, Viktor. You have always been wealthy. You've been a part of this world forever, and you are always, *always*, in control. Of yourself. Of those around you. You don't know what it feels like to be tossed around by life."

I want to let Molly think whatever she wants. I want to throw the car into drive and speed away from this night, from this conversation. Soon enough, Molly will find her footing. Everything will work out, I'm sure.

Still, for some reason, I stay put. For some reason, I tuck the car key in my pocket and sit back in my seat, settling in to tell a story I never planned to tell.

"Did I ever tell you how my parents died?"

Molly goes still the way all people do when I bring up the subject of my parents. No one wants to touch it. It's uncomfortable and messy and, more importantly, I don't like to tell it. The story makes me look weak. It isn't something I broadcast.

She shakes her head, and I take a deep breath.

"It was a fire while we were sleeping. The only reason I woke up is because Fedor came into my room to tell me. I'm still not sure why he didn't go to our parents' room. Maybe the way was blocked with smoke or ... I'm not sure. I never asked, and I guess I'll never know now." I shake my head and try to get back on track. "He woke me up, and I knew I had to save him. The house was already starting to come down and there was smoke everywhere. The only thing I could do was get him out through the window. I didn't have any other choice."

Molly reaches out and lays her hand over mine the way I tried to do with her. Except, for me, it works. Her touch is gentle and it soothes me in ways I didn't know I needed. I continue.

"We stood in the yard while our neighbors called for help. Fedor fought against me, desperate to get inside and save our parents, but I couldn't let him go back in. It was too dangerous. He asked me to go in. He begged me to save them, but I couldn't. I just stood there in the grass, watching our house and our parents burn up."

"You were young," she says. "What else were you supposed to do?"

All of the possibilities flash through my mind. I've had many years to imagine the many different ways I could have rescued my parents and pulled them from the flames. I've also had years to imagine how my actions could have changed things for Fedor. Would he have gone through the same struggles he did if our parents had been around? I'm not sure, and it doesn't do any good to ask. Things are the way they are.

I pat her hand and then remove it from mine, turning the car on and shifting it into park. "I know you are overwhelmed right now, but don't be fooled into thinking my life has always been easy. I may look like I'm always in control, but that is the point—that's how I *look*. Like you, like everyone, I'm doing the best I can with what I have. From here on out, I expect you to try and do the same."

5

MOLLY

I push the fruit around my plate and try to bite back a yawn. The wives of the Bratva have been in my dining room for going on two hours, and I'm exhausted.

Not just from today, but from the unending string of events that seem to come from being Viktor's wife.

Before, people saw me as a girlfriend, at best. An on-call prostitute, at worse. They didn't want to get to know me or understand me because they didn't have to. They didn't owe me any loyalty, and I showed no interest in them.

As soon as Viktor and I became "legally" wedded, however, their priorities shifted. Now, being close to me could benefit them. Perhaps their husbands will rise through the ranks of the family. Perhaps I can whisper in my husband's ear and tell him who is most devoted.

Viktor claims the women simply want to be my friends, but we both know he is lying. He just doesn't want another meltdown like I had in the car the evening of the loyalty ceremony. Viktor claims I didn't make a fool of myself that night, but I saw the way the women watched me eat—like vultures circling over a starving animal. They were waiting to pick me apart. But as I continue on day after day, they put away their claws and replace them with smiles.

"Molly, aren't you hungry? You've barely eaten, dear. You need to keep up your strength." Nadia has dyed blonde hair and each of her boobs is as big as my head. I know that her husband is a lieutenant, but I can't remember which one.

Another woman—Tasha or Mila, I can't remember—wags her brows in my direction. "Especially as a newlywed. I'm sure Viktor keeps you busy."

"Bratva men are insatiable," Nadia says, adjusting her V-neck shirt to show even more of her cleavage. "Five years in and Michail still can't keep his hands off me."

I assure them I ate a large breakfast, but the truth is that pregnancy nausea has made it impossible to eat anything other than plain crackers or, bizarrely, onion rings from the diner George is working at now. He owned a liquor store, but after becoming my personal guard for a short time and getting tangled up in the Bratva mess, the location became too messy. So, he bought out part of his brother's diner, and now sends Viktor home with giant bags of onion rings for me and the growing baby.

I could use some of those onion rings right now.

The women talk about the other Bratva wives who aren't present at our little powwow, but I don't recognize any of their names and don't care enough to ask for further clarification. So, I just nod and smile with the rest of the group and hope they don't notice I'm drinking sparkling juice instead of champagne.

It has been a week since the wedding, and I've only seen Viktor a total of ten hours maybe. He has been sleeping at his place, partly because I haven't invited him to stay over at my apartment again, and partly because his place is closer to a lot of the motels the Bratva is running. Viktor is still working to undo the damage Fedor caused when he set fire to several of the motels and destroyed the product they had hidden away there.

A lot of the renovation is done, from what Viktor has said, but they are still trying to recover the money they lost in weapons and drugs. Ironically, Viktor is pushing for better promotion of the motels to bring actual customers in. Prior to the fire, they didn't care about people visiting the motels at all since that wasn't how they made their money, but now Viktor is accepting extra cash flow wherever they can get it. I joked a few nights ago that he was becoming a legitimate businessman, and he laughed at the idea. It was nice to see him smile.

Now, he is busy, and I have to keep the Bratva wives happy. Even though I'm surrounded by people, I feel entirely alone.

When the women finally finish the champagne and decide to leave, I'm happy to be alone. At least when I'm alone I don't have to pretend.

The moment the women are gone, I change out of one of eight identical skintight dresses Viktor had delivered and into my favorite pair of gray sweats. I wrap myself in a fluffy white sweater, grab my design textbook, and head down to the living room. The class I'm in is online and mostly self-led—all of my assignments have to be turned in by the time the final is administered—so I have time to get everything accomplished, but with my new responsibilities to the Bratva, I'm going to have to set aside time to study if I want to stay on top of it.

Though, what is the point of it all now?

I've done my best not to think much about my future. If I think about things one day at a time, it keeps me from feeling an overwhelming sense of existential dread. However, the sudden realization that this might never end washes over me.

Getting out of this kind of lifestyle is hard. I know better than anyone that even the smallest amount of contact with the people in it can yank you in. So, what if I can't leave? What if, even after the threat of Fedor has subsided, I can't get away? The Bratva wives will find it strange if I want to get my degree or do an internship. I certainly wouldn't need the money.

I try to push the thoughts from my head, instead focusing on the hope that it will all work out, but they crowd into my brain until I can't think about anything else.

Just as I slam my textbook closed, there is a knock at the door.

Since the wedding, I don't have to answer my own door, but I still get up out of habit. I'm halfway across the living room when the guard comes inside to tell me there is a woman at the door for me. I assume it is one of the Bratva wives who forgot something, so I don't ask who it is and tell him to let her in. A minute later, the guard ushers in a woman I barely recognize. A woman I haven't seen face-to-face in years.

"Hannah?" I ask, mouth hanging open.

Hannah rushes across the room and wraps me in a hug, and it is all I can do to force my arms to encircle her.

I told Hannah I'd ask Viktor about sending her some cash, but things have been so crazy that I forgot. About the money and Hannah, if I'm being honest.

"What are you doing here?" I ask, holding her back by the shoulders. "How are you here? What—?"

"All good questions," Hannah says, tucking a greasy strand of hair behind her ear and turning in a circle to take in the apartment. Her sneakers are filthy, her jeans have worn holes in the knees, and she is wearing two oversized jackets instead of a coat. When she finishes her circle, her eyes are wide. "But my question is: what do I need to do to get a place like this?"

I ignore the question and grab Hannah's arm, dragging her towards the couch. "Sit down and tell me how you are here."

She runs her hand over the couch cushion, admiring the fabric, and then sighs. "I lost my apartment."

I slide my touch from her elbow to her hand and squeeze. "Shit."

"Yeah, shit," she agrees. "I couldn't have my son with me since I didn't have a place to stay, and I couldn't get a job to get a new place. I was in a shit-filled rut, and I thought a small trip would help me get out of it."

"A trip?" I ask, trying to follow her thinking. "Like, a vacation? How is that going to help? What are you going to do?"

Hannah looks up at me, her eyebrows raised and expectant. "I kind of hoped *you* would be able to help." As if to drive the point home, she looks around the apartment again. When she turns and sees my balcony and the view of the city, she sighs. "Wow."

Guilt coils in my stomach. "I'm sorry. I told you I'd talk to Viktor, but I just got ... distracted."

"It's okay," Hannah says, folding her hands in her lap. "I hate asking for handouts anyway. You know I wouldn't if I wasn't in trouble."

"I know. You helped me when I had no one else, so I owe you."

She gives me a nervous smile, her eyes going glassy, and then she blinks away the emotion and leans back in the cushions. "How is your sugar daddy, anyway?"

I quickly battle with myself, trying to decide how much I can/should tell Hannah about my situation here, before I decide I'm keeping track of too many lies as is. I might as well be consistent.

"He is my husband now."

Hannah's mouth falls open, and I'm tempted to reach out and close it for her. "Shut up."

I nod. "A week ago. It was a small ceremony."

The baby is my secret. Mine and Viktor's. It's too soon to be telling people, anyway. Plus, I'd like to wait until Fedor has been neutralized before I tell anyone else. He will be sure to strike where Viktor is weakest, and if he knows I'm pregnant, he'll come after me.

I quickly talk Hannah through the justice of the peace, leaving out any mention of the loyalty ceremony with the Bratva, and then turn the questioning back to her.

"You still haven't explained how you are here," I say. "How did you know I was living here?"

"Do you promise not to be mad?"

No. I nod. "I promise."

Hannah sighs, her shoulder sagging forward. "I guessed your Find My Phone password."

I blink, stunned at the admission, and Hannah holds up her hands as if to physically stop my train of thought.

"I guessed the secret question to your account and got access. God, I know that's terrible. I could have just texted and asked to come, but I was desperate and, if I'm being honest, afraid you'd say no."

I would have. It feels terrible admitting it to myself, but I would have turned Hannah away. I would have told her things were too crazy, and I couldn't handle guests right now. It would have been true, but only partially. The other reason would have been that she might end up involved with dangerous people who could kill her to get to me.

I wonder if I shouldn't still refuse her. If I shouldn't call the guards to escort her out. Even if she never spoke to me again, at least she'd be safe.

Hannah slaps a hand over her forehead and shakes her head. "I'm an idiot. I betrayed your trust and now I'm sitting here asking you to let me crash with you for a while. What was I thinking?"

"You weren't." I pull her hand from her face and look into her eyes. As soon as I do, I recognize the same desperation that used to be in my own eyes. "When you are living day to day, you don't think long-term. You do what you have to do to survive. I understand."

Once again, her eyes go glassy.

"Stay," I insist before I can second-guess myself. "I have a guest room, and you are welcome to it. Stay."

"Oh my God, Molly. You are an angel. An absolute angel." Hannah throws her skinny arms around my neck, and I pat her sleeve, cringing away from the sour smell coming from under her arms.

"Two things," I say. "First, don't hack into my accounts again, okay? Not cool."

She nods in agreement.

"Second." I peel her arms from around my neck and push her up from the couch and towards the stairs. "Go take a shower. You stink."

She sniffs herself and then wrinkles her nose, laughing in embarrassment. "It has been a few days. No showers on the bus."

I give her some clothes and a fresh towel and leave her to shower, hoping I can figure out what I'll say to Viktor when he arrives later this afternoon.

～

"Who the fuck is that?" Viktor asks. His voice is quieter than normal, but he is practically hissing in anger.

Hannah was playing with Theo in the living room, getting to know him when Viktor arrived. I'd planned to tell Viktor I'd invited

Hannah to stay with me later when we were alone, but Theo said it before I could.

"Mommy's friend is living with us now."

The second the words were out of his adorable little mouth, I could see Viktor's forehead wrinkled in confusion and then his eyes turned to me, narrowed and serious. I dragged him to my room before he could make a scene like the one he is making now.

"You let someone come and live in my apartment without asking me first? Who is she? How do you know her? What were you thinking, Molly?"

"*My* apartment," I correct him. "You pay for it, but you told me it was mine to do with as I wish. And right now, I wish to help out a very dear friend of mine."

"I've never even heard of her. How dear could she be?" Viktor snaps.

I place my hands on my hips. "You don't know everything about me, Viktor."

That wounds him more than I thought it would and some of the anger leaves his face, replaced by wistfulness. A second later, he blinks and it is gone. "Who is she?"

"Her name is Hannah, and she needed help. She came to me with no place to stay and no money. She just needs somewhere to crash while she gets back on her feet."

"How did she find you?" Viktor asks.

"I told her where I was living," I lie, thinking quickly. If I tell Viktor how easily Hannah gained access to my location, he'd lock me in a cage and throw away the key. He'd never let me out of his sight again. If I want any semblance of freedom, I have to lie to him. Besides, I'll change my passwords later. It won't happen again, so there is no need to worry him.

He folds his arms over his chest. "What else did you tell her?"

"I told her you're my husband."

His eyes flick down the length of me and then away. He nods. "Have you told her about the Bratva or … Fedor?"

It's hard for him to even say his brother's name.

I shake my head.

"Good. Keep it that way."

I cross my arms to mimic his posture. "Is that an order?"

Fire flares behind his eyes. "It is. And it's for your own safety *and* hers. The less she knows, the safer she is."

I know Viktor is right. It's why I didn't tell Hannah about everything immediately. I don't want her getting tangled up in this. Still, Viktor's command chafes like a collar around my neck. I don't like being told what to do.

"Plus, the less she knows, the less she can pass on to our enemies," he adds.

"She wouldn't do that," I insist.

Viktor shrugs. "You never know."

"I do," I say. "I trust Hannah. She has always been there to help me when I need it. I know her better than you."

I regret the words the moment I say them. Mostly because they aren't true. Not anymore, anyway. I have only spoken to Hannah a handful of times over the last few years. I don't know much about her life at all anymore.

Viktor turns away, waving over his shoulder. "I won't spoil your fun, then. Good night, Molly."

I hear him say a short, but sweet goodbye to Theo before the door closes and he is gone.

6

VIKTOR

I call Petr again and let it ring five times before the automated voice clicks on to tell me the recipient of my call can't make it to the phone and his voice mail is full.

I know. I'm the one who filled it.

We are supposed to meet this morning to talk about consolidating the business. The renovation to the motels is costing more than we expected, and I'm not confident we'll make back the money we are spending fast enough for it to matter. Besides, we are operating with fewer men now that Fedor took half of them, so fewer moving parts mean fewer things to guard. It might make more sense to sell off a few nonessential motels that we aren't currently using for stash houses, consolidate our men, and use the money from the sale to cover losses. I planned to talk it over with Petr. Except, he hasn't shown up.

Petr has never been late to a meeting before. He has shown up half drunk and in pajama bottoms before, but he has never been late.

All I can think is that he is dead. Somehow, Fedor got to him and he has been killed.

I call anyone who might have an idea where Petr is and ask everyone at the office, but no one has seen him all morning.

Shit, shit, shit.

I call him again and again for almost an hour, growing more frantic with every unanswered call.

Then, just when I've decided to get up and go search the city for him myself, he answers.

"Hello," he says, out of breath.

I let out a relieved breath, and then my relief instantly shifts to fury. "Where have you fucking been all fucking morning?" I growl.

I can practically see Petr wince through the phone. "I was tied up. I'm sorry, I'm sorry."

"Unless you were actually tied up, you should have been able to answer your phone. We had a meeting this morning. Or, we were supposed to. Where were you?" I press.

There is a moment of hesitation, a beat of silence too long to miss. Then, he answers. "My mom is sick, and I don't have cell signal in her apartment. It's a dead spot for some reason. I'm sorry."

"Aunt Vera?" I ask. "Why didn't you just say so?"

Petr and I have a working relationship, but he is still my family. I'm his boss, but I like to think I'm not a monster.

"I don't know," Petr sighs. "I didn't want you to think my attentions were divided. I thought I could handle it all without telling anyone. I'm sorry."

I'm still frustrated, but it feels wrong to yell at him about this.

"Just get your ass to the meeting," I command. "That will show me your attentions aren't divided."

Petr agrees with my plan to drop a few of our fronts to consolidate, and even though it was my plan, I'm disappointed.

I built those businesses myself. I put them in place and kept them running. They made us money and operated as stash houses for our less legal dealings. Even though I didn't go around bragging about them, I was proud of what I'd built. And now, because of my own brother, I have to give some of them up to protect what I have left.

It is necessary, but the meeting leaves me feeling restless. I have too much energy to just go home. I need to go out.

Before Molly, that would mean stopping off at the club, tossing back a few drinks, and then dragging one of the willing club girls back to my bed. I'd fuck her until exhaustion and then kick her out to find her own way home.

Now, I just want Molly.

I've been trying to keep my distance from her. Not only to give her time to adjust to this new element in our relationship, but also because I need to keep my sights focused on Fedor as much as possible. I need to stay cold so I can react and make decisions as necessary, and being with Molly gets me anything but cold.

I'm calling her before I even realize what I'm doing. She sounds hesitant when she answers.

"Hello?"

"Do you want to go out with me?" Again, I'm operating on autopilot. The question blurts out of me before I can find a more eloquent way to phrase it. "Like, to lunch?"

The silence stretches out so long I'm sure she has hung up, but finally, Molly clears her throat. "Hannah would have to watch Theo."

That isn't a refusal. She's willing.

"I'll call the nanny to come back over, too." I hope she can't see my offer for what it is—distrust of her friend. "Just in case," I add.

To my surprise and delight, Molly doesn't argue or refuse. She tells me to pick her up in twenty minutes.

She meets me outside wearing a devastating pair of jeans and a low-cut gray sweater, and I whisk her towards my favorite lunch spot—a quiet Italian joint with flickering candles on the tables and soft music in the background. When I'm halfway there, however, I remember the night after the ceremony. The way Molly felt uncomfortable in the fancy environment of etiquette and gowns. The Italian place isn't fancy, but it isn't what she is used to.

On nothing more than a feeling, I turn away from where I was headed and casually scour the roads as we drive, searching for a suitable alternative. When I see a greasy spoon I've been to a few different times, I pull over and help her out of the car.

The booths are lined in red vinyl, neon lights wrap around the ceiling, and pictures of Elvis and Marilyn Monroe cover the walls. It is Americana in all of its glory. The menu is, too—nothing but hamburgers, French fries, and milkshakes. Given Molly's recent penchant for onion rings, I know she'll approve. The smile on her face as we are seated confirms it.

"I can't believe a lunch with Viktor Kornilov involves paper cups of ketchup," she says, dunking a French fry in the sauce.

"What did you imagine?"

"Silver serving trays and five-hundred-dollar bottles of wine."

"Only five hundred?" I ask, brows pinched together in mock surprise. "You insult me."

She laughs, and the sound of it rings in my chest, opening my lungs for what feels like my first breath of fresh air in weeks. *This* is what I want my marriage to Molly to look like. My entire life has been heavy.

Death and drugs and crime. It is the life I've known and, there is no sense denying it, loved. But it feels good to balance that with Molly's lightness. Her laugh and her ease. I worry every day that my darkness will drag her down with me, but I pray that isn't true. I hope, once everything with Fedor is settled, she'll pull me a little closer to the light.

"This is amazing, though. Really." There is a soft emphasis in her voice, and she purses her pink lips together until I can't think about anything other than leaning across the table and kissing her. It has been several days. Too many days. I miss her.

I ask her how classes are going, and she tells me she is as determined as ever to get the necessary certifications to become an interior designer. She wants to own her own company and have employees, and hearing her talk about her future makes me wonder if I'm part of her plans.

If we make our marriage official, she certainly won't need a job, but I would never tell her she couldn't have one. My brother derailed her life, and maybe this is just another instance of me wanting to clean up his messes, but I would like to help her put it back on track. I want Molly to accomplish all of her goals. I don't want Fedor's action to steal anything from her.

"You did amazing with Theo's nursery at my place," I say. She designed the room when she and Theo were living with me. "I'm sure you could have your own design business right now if you wanted."

"Thanks, but that was just a small project," she says. "With help from your designer. I don't know enough to do it all on my own yet. But I will."

She lifts her chin and pushes her shoulders back, and the confidence is sexy on her. It also doesn't make my attraction to her any easier to ignore. I want to throw her over my shoulder, carry her to the car, and have my way with her in the back seat.

"Dessert?"

Our waitress is holding out a dessert menu, but Molly waves it away before I can answer and orders us a milkshake to share. It feels a little *Happy Days* to me, but I'll do it. Especially if it keeps the smile on her face a little longer.

The waitress goes back to the kitchen to put in our order, and Molly opens her mouth to continue talking but is cut off by the sound of her own name.

"Molly?"

We both turn and see a thin blonde woman with fake lashes and bright red lipstick. Her arm is wrapped around the arm of a man with shoulders as wide as mine but a gut twice as big. It hangs over the edge of his pants a bit, and he has to keep adjusting his shirt to make sure it is covered.

Molly blinks in surprise. "Angela?"

The blonde woman smiles and rushes forward, arms open for a hug. "Holy shit. I haven't seen you since ... high school. Really? Has it been that long? Damn. How are you?"

Molly looks at me over the woman's shoulder, stunned. When they pull away from the hug, she manages to arrange her mouth into a smile. "I'm good. How are you?"

"You had a kid, right?" Angela looks around like she expects Theo to come crawling out from under the table. "Right after high school?"

Molly nods. "Yeah, Theo. He's four."

Angela whistles. "I can't imagine having a four-year-old. Man, that's crazy. Who was the dad? There were rumors, but—"

"How are you?" Molly asks, cutting her off.

"Amazing," the woman says, excited enough to talk about herself that she doesn't mind the sudden change in conversation. She holds out an arm for her male friend to take, but when he doesn't, she clears her throat to catch his attention. He jumps forward to take his place. "Brad and I got married a few years ago, so we've been living the high school sweetheart dream. "

The woman turns towards me and seems to *see* me for the first time. She blinks and her cheeks flush. "Who is this? I'm sorry, did I interrupt a business meeting or something?"

"No," Molly says nervously. "This is ... um ... my—"

"Her husband," I finish, standing up to take the woman's hand. "Viktor."

Angela flutters her absurdly long lashes at me as I stand and move around the booth to slide into the same seat as Molly. I wrap my arm around her shoulders and gesture. "Join us. Please."

Molly explains how they all know each other as the two take their spots across from us. "Brad played football for our high school, and Angela was a cheerleader—"

"Head cheerleader," Angela corrects, pushing her blonde hair back over her shoulder. "I always lobbied for you to make the team, Molly. I just couldn't get the other girls on board."

The way her mouth turns up in a smile at the memory tells me Angela probably wasn't on Molly's side.

Molly waves it away. "It was a long time ago."

"You didn't make the team?" I ask, feigning confusion and tucking her into my side. "But you are unnaturally flexible. Really," I say, turning towards our stunned lunch guests. "I've seen Molly get in positions that you wouldn't believe."

Angela's face goes red, and Molly hides a laugh with a cough into her elbow.

"It was about more than flexibility," Angela says. "You have to know what to do with that flexibility, unfortunately."

"Oh, she knows what to do with it," I purr, wagging my brows at Molly.

Molly grips my thigh under the table. It's a warning, but it only serves to speed up my heart and spur me on.

Angela lets out a humorless laugh and cuddles up to her husband, who is too busy looking out the window at the parking lot to even pretend he is paying any attention. "Are you two newlyweds? It sure seems that way. Brad and I were the same way after we got married. He couldn't keep his hands off me. Honestly, he still has a hard time."

"We got married in Paris last year, but it wasn't legal, so we just had the small ceremony last week," I say before Molly can answer.

Angela's eyes bulge out. "Paris? That's …"

"Beautiful," Molly interrupts. "He proposed to me at the top of a mountain in Switzerland, we were married in Paris two months later, and now it is finally official. It has been a whirlwind."

"Jet setters," Angela says, bitterness obvious in her tone.

The waitress brings out our shake with two straws, and I'm now grateful for the iconic symbol of cutesy romance. Molly and I both drink from the shake while staring into each other's eyes and trying not to laugh.

Angela talks about her job as a legal assistant and Brad's position at the construction company, but Molly and I one-up each of her stories with tales of our fictitious travels and wealth. By the time we finish our shake, Angela is begging her husband to slide out of the booth so they can escape.

"It is late. We should really order and get going," she says, pinching her husband's arm. "It was great to see you, though, Molly."

Molly squeezes my bicep and waves to her high school "friend," and the second Angela and Brad are out of earshot, she collapses into a fit of laughter, her head on my shoulder.

She stays close to me all the way out to the car, and when I climb into the driver's seat, she sighs.

"That was amazing. Do you know how long I've wanted to stick it to Angela? God. She is unbearable."

"She seemed it," I agree.

Molly reaches across the console and grabs my hand, squeezing my fingers. "Thanks for that, Viktor. Even if it was all bullshit, it felt good."

It did. It felt so good.

I wish I could whisk Molly and Theo off to Switzerland and Paris. I wish I had the time to woo them both the way they deserve, but keeping them safe is my main priority right now. It has to be. As much as I want to daydream about a future where Molly and I are carefree jet setters, I have to be practical.

Right now, I have to be a mob boss above everything.

7
MOLLY

"We should go to lunch sometime," Hannah says. "I'm not used to being cooped up in an apartment all day. Maybe tomorrow?"

She volunteered to watch Theo while Viktor and I went to lunch today, but I still feel guilty about using her for babysitting her first whole day in town. "Sorry you felt cooped. You can go explore and do whatever you want, you know?"

"It's not your fault," she says, reaching out to ruffle Theo's light hair. "I enjoyed my time with the little dude."

I know she misses her own son. I can see it in the way she looks at Theo.

"I just think it would be fun for the two of us to get out and do something together. On my way here, I saw a deli that looked really good. Maybe we could try that?"

I've been avoiding leaving the house with Hannah simply because I don't want to have to try and explain why I have guards trailing me everywhere we go. I could just tell her Viktor is extra cautious, but even that would barely explain it.

"Sure, but I can't tomorrow. Viktor and I have plans."

"Oh right," she says, suppressing a smile. "I forgot you have the old ball and chain you have to run things past now."

"He's hardly a ball and chain." Really, Viktor has been keeping his distance. Lunch today is the first time I've seen him for longer than half an hour in days. I would never admit it out loud, but I've missed him.

Theo is coloring a picture of a dinosaur, decimating the wax point of his crayons, and Hannah slides back to lean against the couch, giving him some space. "What is Viktor like? I only saw him for like a minute two days ago. Since I wasn't invited to the wedding, the least you could do is give me the inside scoop."

"No one was invited to the wedding," I remind her. "It was kind of rushed."

"I wouldn't have been able to go, anyway," she says with a dismissive wave. "But I don't even know what he does for a living."

I've avoided the topic because, yet again, I have to lie. Everything in my life feels like a lie these days. I wanted to have just one person I wasn't keeping things from. Apparently, that won't be possible.

"He is a business owner," I say. "He has a few motels around town. Nothing fancy, but they bring in good money."

A partial lie, but if Hannah knew the truth, she'd recognize it as a lie by omission. Viktor's main source of income is far from legal.

"I'd say so," Hannah says, gesturing vaguely to the apartment. "He has enough money to set you up in a place like this, and he must have his own place, right? He hasn't stayed here the last few nights."

There is a question behind the words: why aren't you and your husband living together?

"He has been busy with work lately, and we just haven't consolidated our stuff. Then, I asked him to keep his distance for a few days to give us girl time."

"You don't have to do that on my account." Hannah checks to make sure Theo isn't listening and then holds a hand to her mouth, whispering to me. "I would not want to be a cock block to the newlyweds. Trust me, I'm a hard sleeper."

I laugh and it feels genuine. Just like it did today at lunch. In the scheme of things—especially recently—today has been a good day. Maybe I should invite Viktor over for the night.

Just the thought has heat pooling low in my belly.

"That is very good to know. I'll be sure to let Viktor know he can come over whenever he wants."

Hannah nods, pleased. "Okay, so he is a rich businessman, but what is he *like*? Funny? Generous? Sarcastic?"

"Serious."

Hannah winces. "Ouch."

I shake my head. "No, it's a good thing. Viktor takes everything he does seriously. If he makes a promise, he'll keep it. Maybe 'focused' is a better word? He puts all of himself into the task at hand."

Hannah raises a racy eyebrow. "I'm sure that is a very good thing when you are the task at hand."

I suppress a smile, warning her with a wide-eyed glare. "You are bad."

"I'm horny," she whispers. "I haven't been with anyone in months. It's hard to find the motivation to get out and date when you can't even find a job, you know?"

The stark realities of Hannah's life—the realities I knew all too well only a few months before—sober me.

"I'm sorry." She groans. "I really killed the mood. We were having fun."

I nudge her with my socked foot. "We are still having fun."

"I'm having fun," Theo says, holding up a picture of a purple and yellow dinosaur for us to admire.

"Look at your little Picasso," Hannah says, oohing and aahing at the photo, making Theo feel special. "Can you make me a dragon? I want it to breathe green fire."

Theo sets to work, excited to draw his first commissioned picture, and Hannah smiles at me, a tinge of sadness around her eyes. "I hope you know I'm happy for you. Even if I sound bitterly jealous, I'm happy you've found this."

I nod, unable to say anything. My pregnancy hormones have made me especially weepy lately, and having one of my only real friends congratulate me on my fake happy ending is enough to push me right over the edge.

"You have a great kid, and Viktor seems like an awesome father figure for Theo. I think this is a good thing you have going here."

I wonder what Hannah would say if she knew who Theo was to Viktor. If she knew he was actually Theo's uncle and the brother of my rapist.

I want to tell her, desperately. I want someone to understand the complexities of our relationship and tell me if I'm crazy for wanting to be with him anyway.

"I sure hope so," I say, taking a deep breath. "Because I'm pregnant again."

Hannah's eyes go wide, and her mouth falls open in a smile. "Are you serious?"

I nod and hold a finger to my lips, gesturing to Theo. We still haven't told him the news. It seems like too much to pile on him right now, especially after nearly being kidnapped by Fedor twice. I want him to have some normalcy. "We weren't even trying. It just … happened."

"Trust me, I've been there. I'll never be rich like the one percent, but I sure as hell will fall into the two percent of people that condoms fail. Just my luck, right?"

I chuckle and give her a high five. "Amen."

She sobers and shrugs. "But, at least Viktor stepped up and put a ring on it. Matthew's dad is a piece of shit, but if he'd stuck around, I'd probably still have an apartment and custody of my kid."

"I'm lucky," I admit, hoping it doesn't sound like I'm bragging.

"You are," she says, her eyes narrowing. "But make sure you are safe, too."

I frown, unsure what she means. "It's a little late for the safe sex talk, Han. But I'll keep it in mind in nine months."

"I mean," she says, lowering her head and looking up at me beneath her brows. "I know your story about Viktor's day job is bullshit. I saw the guards standing in the hallway. They are covered in tattoos and scars. Clearly, Viktor is involved in something criminal."

I open my mouth to argue, but Hannah holds up her hands to stop me. "Far be it from me to judge you. Believe me, if I could lasso myself to a wealthy criminal and live in a place like this, I would. But please be careful."

"Viktor isn't like that," I say when she is finished. I can tell by the knowing slant of her mouth that Hannah doesn't believe me, so I continue. "He isn't always aboveboard, but he is a good man. He defends the innocent and protects people."

"That may be, but I've known men like him. He will do whatever it takes to save his own skin. I just want to make sure you and Theo won't be caught in the crosshairs."

The image of Theo wrapped in the stranger's arms fills my mind, and I blink it away, fighting back frustrated tears. "Viktor would never choose to put us in harm's way. He loves us both, and he'd rather die than let something happen to either of us."

She pats my hand and gives me a condescending smile. "Whatever you need to tell yourself to get to sleep."

Fire fills my chest, and I stand up, yanking my hand away from her. "Don't come into my house and tell me who my husband is."

"Molly, I'm sorry—" she starts, but this time, I wave her words away, silencing her with a flick of my wrist.

"You don't know me or my husband. You don't know what he does for a living, so don't come in here and tell me to be careful. *You* be careful, Hannah. I'm happy to help you the same way you helped me years ago, but I will turn you away if you speak ill of my family."

Without another word, I grab Theo's hand and lead him upstairs to my room, leaving Hannah alone on the couch.

～

My vision is blurry when I wake up. I try to lift my arm to wipe the sleep from my eyes, but it feels heavy and dead. I look over and realize Theo is lying on it, fast asleep.

He curled up next to me to watch a movie after we came upstairs, and we must have both fallen asleep. The television is still on, an old cartoon from when I was a kid, playing for all of the nostalgic adults up late after their kids have gone to sleep. I gently pull my arm out from under Theo's head, shaking the pinpricks out, and turn the TV off.

I try to listen for signs of Hannah moving around the house, but it is silent. She is probably in bed. Or gone.

From the way she made it sound, she doesn't have anywhere else to go, but given what she seems to know about Viktor's business and the way I spoke to her, she might be in fear for her life.

I sigh and press the heels of my hands into my eyes, trying to rub the exhaustion from them.

I shouldn't have gotten angry with Hannah. Her words came from concern, I know that, but she doesn't have the first idea of what I'm going through. She imagines me as some wide-eyed woman in love. Or, if not love, then lust. I could see in the way she spoke to me that she thought I walked into this relationship blind, wooed by the wealth and finery to the point I would risk the life of my own son.

She doesn't know the first thing about my relationship with Viktor.

She also doesn't know anything about Viktor.

I've had more than a few complaints about his conduct over the last few weeks, but at the end of the day, everything he has done is to protect me and Theo. I can't fault him for that.

My phone vibrates next to me in the bed, and I see Viktor's name on the screen. It is late—far later than he has ever called me before—and my heart leaps into my throat as I answer, afraid of what news I'll find out.

"Hello?" My voice is raspy, and I clear my throat.

"Sorry, did I wake you?"

"I was already awake. What's going on?"

"Nothing." He sounds out of breath and exhausted.

"Did you call to talk to Theo?" Viktor rarely calls to speak with me. If he has something to say to me, he'll come by the house. But he has called to talk to Theo a few times. Their connection is growing stronger every day, and while it is precious to see how much Theo likes Viktor, their bond concerns me as well. What if we leave and Viktor can't be there anymore? How will Theo handle that?

"No, no," he says quickly, almost emphatically.

"Are you okay?" If he doesn't want to tell me what he has been doing, then fine. I trust him to tell me things when and if they concern me. But I still want to check on him. If he has been in a fight or some kind of conflict, I want to ensure he hasn't been hurt.

He sighs. "I'm fine. Just tired."

"Go to sleep," I say. I'm tempted to tell him to come here. I'll clean him up and put him in bed next to myself and Theo. A happy family.

But the image feels like a pipe dream.

"I will soon. I wanted to talk to you first."

There is a long silence, neither of us saying anything. I keep waiting for him to deliver some piece of news or ask me a question. Finally, I realize he just wants to talk. To hear my voice. The realization makes my stomach flip.

"Theo is asleep next to me, so I'm probably talking quietly," I say, unable to think of anything else. "Can you hear me?"

"I can hear you," he breathes. "How are things going with Hannah?"

If I tell Viktor what Hannah said about him, what she may or may not know about his business, he might request that she leave. Honestly, that might be the safest thing for Hannah to do, anyway, but I'm not ready to get rid of my friend. The other Bratva wives don't understand me at all. They know who I appear to be now, but they don't know anything about my life growing up or what I've been through. It feels good to have someone around who I can relate to. I want Hannah to stay.

"Fine. She wants to go to lunch soon."

Viktor hums, concern clear in his tone.

"We'll take the guards with us," I say, assuaging his worries before he can give them voice. "I'll be careful."

"Just tell me where you decide to go. I want to know where you are."

I agree, and we slip into silence again. I don't have anything else to say, but I don't want to end the conversation until I know Viktor doesn't need anything from me. Finally, Viktor speaks.

"I guess I also called to gauge your interest in coming to a dinner I'm hosting in a few days," he says. "For the Irish."

"Like, a party?"

He hums an assent. "Fedor has allied with the Italians and taken some of my men, so I need to do what I can to strengthen the alliances we already have. I've rented out a restaurant and have everything set up. You would just need to go and stand by my side … my beautiful wife."

There is real tenderness in his voice, and it makes me feel lightheaded. I think that might have been the point.

"You called to gauge my interest or to tell me I need to be there? Because it sounds like this isn't something I can skip."

He hesitates and then sighs. "I need you there."

"So, you're telling me where I need to be."

"I'm asking you to … to want to be there with me," he says, sounding more exhausted than I've ever heard. "I know you don't like these kinds of events. After the loyalty ceremony, I wanted to give you space from those people and that environment, but this is important. The Irish can offer support that will change the outcome of this fight. Plus, it will be delicious food, gowns and suits, and live music. I'll try my best to make it bearable for you."

The fact that he cared about my discomfort and sought to separate me from it is heartwarming, but that isn't the only thing filling my chest. To my surprise, excitement is bubbling up. I want to go.

After our lunch at the diner, I realized I like pretending to be Viktor's wife. Out in public, in front of other people, even though it is a lie, it is an easy lie. I can let myself lean into him and gaze at the handsome lines of his face and body. At home, I have to distance myself. I have to think constantly about what my next move will be after this war is over and how attached Theo is growing to Viktor. When we are out together, however, I can just be with him. I like that feeling.

"I'll need a new dress," I say, biting my lip to keep from openly grinning.

"Done," Viktor says quickly.

"But I'll do my own hair."

He chuckles. "Again, done. Whatever you need, Molly. Tell me, and I'll make it happen."

When we hang up, the smile is still teasing the edges of my mouth, and when I turn off the bedside lamp, I finally let it spread across my face. For now, Theo and I are warm and safe, and I have a date planned with my husband. It almost feels perfect.

8

VIKTOR

George's diner is a nice place. Clean. Quaint. A far cry from the rundown liquor store he owned before.

Technically, it is his brother's diner, but now George owns fifty percent. Apparently, his brother was in financial trouble and George wanted to get out from under the liquor store where he nearly died—where I almost killed him, to be specific—so a partnership worked out for them both.

It worked out for me, too. Molly has been craving onion rings since becoming pregnant, and George sends them home with me free of charge.

I sip my black coffee, surprised by the smoothness. Most diner coffee is burnt tar water, but this cup is rich and nuanced. George walks over without a word and tops off my mug. When I look up, he tips his head towards the back door and gives me two fingers.

Meet me out back in two minutes.

I take a burning mouthful of coffee, count to thirty, and then drop a ten on the counter and leave.

The alley is dark and damp and it reeks of grease and rotting lettuce. George is leaning against the brick wall with a cigarette dangling from his lip, trying to light it. He looks up as I round the corner and walk towards him.

"How did you know I needed to speak with you?" I ask.

He circles his hand around his face. "I could see it in your expression. You were trying too hard not to look at me."

There is a reason I hired George as Molly's personal guard for a while. He is observant. He pays attention. He can read people.

I don't like exactly how well he can read me, but as long as he stays on my side of this war, he doesn't have anything to worry about.

"So, what's going on?" he asks, shoving his lighter in the front pocket of his jeans. They hang off him a little looser than they used to. He's lost weight since I first met him, and his arms are a bit thicker around the biceps. Having his life put in danger probably gave him good reason to want to get back into military shape.

"I need your help. Well, actually, I want your help."

"You have guys. What could you need with me?"

"That's the problem. I don't know who my guys are right now. How much do you know about Fedor's operation?"

"As little as possible," George says, holding up a hand to stop me. "And I'd like it to stay that way. I knew too much before, and I don't want to get into trouble again. I'd be happy to flip burgers and refill coffee until I die, thank you very much."

I respect that. Sometimes, I have the same dream. Getting away with Molly and Theo, starting over somewhere else. I've considered it, but like it or not, this life has its hold on me, and I won't be getting out anytime soon. I'm not even sure I actually want out.

"Then I won't tell you more than you need to know," I assure him.

"Basically, I'd like to hire you to be my eyes. One of my guys is sneaking around on me, and I don't trust him. Normally, I'd confront him, but something like that could split loyalties in the Bratva in two, and I can't afford that right now. I need this to be discreet."

George flicks ashes on the ground. "What do you think he's doing? Could this get me killed?"

"Not unless you're stupid, which I'm pretty sure you're not."

He raises an amused eyebrow at me. "Your confidence in me is inspiring."

"I don't know if he is skimming money or meeting with my brother, but I want to figure it out, and I'd like to pay you to help me," I say. "My rate is far higher than what you make here at the diner. It shouldn't take more than a few days."

George clears his throat and stands tall, his cigarette dangling from his hand at his side. "I don't owe you anything anymore, Viktor. I paid my debt. We are square."

"If anything, I owe you," I tell him. "You saved my wife and son."

Once again, he raises an eyebrow. This time, in surprise. I hadn't told him Molly and I got married.

"We don't owe each other anything," he says. "This is a business deal. I'm doing this because I trust you. I trust you not to risk my life and to pay me fairly."

"Done."

George drops his cigarette and crushes it under the toe of his boot before extending his hand. We shake on it.

"What's the name?"

"Expect all of the details soon, but his name is Petr."

His brows pinch together. "Your consigliere?"

I nod solemnly. "The very same."

"Shit," he breaths.

Shit, indeed.

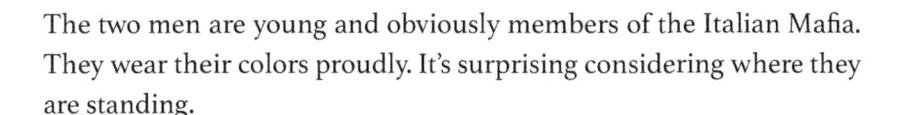

~

The two men are young and obviously members of the Italian Mafia. They wear their colors proudly. It's surprising considering where they are standing.

On my corner.

I was driving to the club to put together the information for George and get him the full details on Petr when I saw the men two blocks up. I parked the car and watched them for a few minutes to be sure I understood what I was seeing. A young girl, barely sixteen if that, walked over to them while I waited, and they shook hands. Innocuous enough if you aren't paying close enough attention, but I wasn't fooled. Even after only a few minutes, I knew there was no mistake.

The Italians are dealing on my turf.

The corner was contested territory a few years before, but I long ago settled that dispute. Prior to Fedor partnering with the Mazzeos, the Italians knew better than to send their men to my territory. Yet, here they are.

I know Fedor is behind it. Just like when he had a man waltz into Molly's apartment with Theo in his arms, he is doing this to show me that he can. To show me he will take what he wants without consequence.

Well, fuck that.

The intersection is one block removed from the busier road, but there are still a fair number of people on the sidewalks and in the road. I shift the car into park and blend in with them.

I cross the street, watching as the men laugh and joke with each other. They make suggestive comments to women as they pass and pantomime things they want to do to them.

They are children. Idiots. They'd have to be to side with Fedor in this fight.

Well, I'm going to show them what a mistake that was.

As I approach them, one of the men with a thick head of dark hair looks at me and then away. Just as he is turning back towards me, eyes wide with recognition, my fist connects with his face.

He flies sideways, hitting a metal sign before sinking to the ground. His friend stands in stunned silence when I hit him with a one-two, knocking his head back and forth like a bobblehead.

They aren't well-trained. The second man throws up an arm to protect his face, and I kick him in the stomach. He doubles over and falls.

"Who the fuck sent you here?" I roar at them.

Distantly, I recognize people on the street are startled and fleeing. I can't stay here long. The police will be along soon, and even though I have some of them in my back pocket, I know the Italians do too. There's no saying who will show up, and I can't afford to be arrested right now. Not when my Bratva is being divided and my top advisor might be betraying me.

Both men get back to their feet and jockey back and forth, ready to fight.

"Get out of here before you get hurt."

"You leave before you get hurt, old man," the dark-haired kid says. He pulls out a switchblade, flicking it open, and lunges towards me.

He moves slowly enough that I dodge what could have been a deadly blow and instead feel a burning sensation across my arm. I don't need to look to know he got me. There is blood on his knife.

I drive my elbow up and over, hitting his arm and sending the blade skittering across the ground and into the gutter. He curses, and I drive my fist into his nose. Blood spurts down his face and over his lip.

"Leave. Now," I command. "And tell Fedor if he has a message for me, to deliver it himself."

The second man seems torn between running away and defending his friend, but he settles on grabbing the dark-haired man's arm and pulling him towards a car halfway down the block.

Adrenaline is humming beneath my skin, keeping me from feeling the ache in my fist and the cut to my arm. I know I'll feel it later.

Luckily, neither of them landed any punches, so I shouldn't have any obvious injuries to my face. If I'm careful, no one will know about this.

I turn to go back to my car, the crowd parting, and that is when I see her.

Molly.

She is standing across the street near my car, her hand wrapped around Theo's, with her friend standing behind her. But all I can really focus on is the shocked expression on her face. And the anger.

A million questions run through my mind in a matter of seconds. What? How? Why?

Then, I see the guards tailing them. And the greasy bag of food in Molly's other hand.

She told me Hannah wanted to go out for lunch soon. Apparently, they did. Unfortunately, they chose this exact time and place.

I rush down the block towards them, and Theo pulls away from me, partially hiding behind his mom's leg.

"It's okay, bud," I say softly, holding out my hand. My knuckles are bloody, and I pull my hand back, tucking it behind my back. I can't even look at Molly. "What are you doing here?"

She holds up the diner bag silently.

I take a deep breath. One problem at a time.

I kneel down and hold out my other hand to Theo. "I know that was scary, bud, but those were bad guys. I was just … taking care of them."

Theo is peeking out at me from behind Molly's legs, and I don't blame him for being scared. He has never seen that side of me before. I've kept it purposefully hidden from him and Molly, for that matter. If they don't need to see my violent side, then I don't want them to. It isn't my best quality.

"It's okay," Molly says, ruffling Theo's hair.

I'm surprised she is encouraging Theo to forgive me, but then I realize it is for Theo's sake, not mine. Molly doesn't want Theo to be afraid of me, even though she knows he probably should be.

Eventually, Theo lays his hand in mine and lets me hold it.

Molly, I know, won't be as easily swayed.

Hannah is standing behind her, eyes wary. Molly just looks livid. If smoke could come out of her ears, it would.

"Molly, what—"

"Your arm," she says, nodding to the cut. "You should go to a hospital."

I shake my head. "It's fine."

I want Hannah to disappear. I want to be able to talk to Molly, to explain what she saw. I lost my temper. The thought of Fedor pushing boundaries upset me, but remembering how he invaded Molly's space and put Theo in danger, that set me off. I lost control and did something stupid, and Molly witnessed it.

"You should clean it," she says. "It could be infected. I doubt that man cleans his knife very often."

"I have a first aid kit in my car."

Molly asks Hannah to watch Theo and then motions for me to follow her towards the car. I'm not concerned about the cut, but I do want to talk to her alone.

We climb into the front seat and Molly pulls out a small first aid kit from the glove compartment. She moves quickly and efficiently, her hands steady.

Hannah and Theo are looking in the window of a toy store on the street. I see the guards in the rear-view mirror, so I allow myself to ease back and focus on Molly for a second.

"Molly—"

"Not now." She shakes her head and then grabs the hem of my shirt and pulls it up. "Take your arm out."

I do as she says, surprised by that fact. In different circumstances, I'd grab her face and force her to look me in the eyes. I'd pull her brown eyes to mine and make her listen to me.

With Molly, however, I don't want to push her away.

My fondness for her is a weakness. One I don't want to be rid of anytime soon.

She dabs a disinfectant to the cut and it stings, but I don't wince or pull away. I've handled far worse pain than this.

"I came here to—"

"Not. Now," she repeats. Her pink lips are pressed into a thin line, and she tucks a strand of dark hair behind her ear before unwrapping a large bandage and placing it over the cut. Blood starts to leak through the bandage immediately, and her brow furrows. "You need stitches."

"I'm fine."

Molly rolls her eyes and gestures to the wound. "You might bleed out on the way home, but sure, you're fine." Then she looks down at the console. "There is blood all over your car."

"I don't care."

She ignores me and pulls a wrap out of the kit and begins winding it around my arm. The pressure seems to help and after a few layers, there is no more blood seeping through. As soon as she finishes, I reach for her hand, but she pulls away.

"I'm not ready to talk to you," she admits, taking a deep breath. "I don't know what to say."

"You were supposed to tell me when you left the house."

She looks up at me, her eyes fiery and sharp as a blade. "I'm going to go."

"Let me drive you. The guards can take Theo back. We need to—"

"I'm going to take my car." She pulls away and is out of the door before I can stop her.

9

MOLLY

Hannah is pale and silent the entire way home.

When we get back to the apartment, I go lay Theo down for his nap and then find Hannah in the kitchen. She is eating some of her leftover French fries that have to be cold by now. She looks up as I enter and gives me a small smile.

"How freaked out are you?" I ask, not wanting to avoid the elephant in the room.

"I'm worried about you," she says, even as her voice breaks. "That was ... quite a scene."

I don't know what to tell her.

I could tell her the truth, that Viktor's life looks like that a lot. It was the first time I'd really seen it firsthand, but I've bandaged him up enough times to know he puts himself in harm's way every day. However, I don't think that information would comfort Hannah at all.

I could lie, but she would see right through it. After seeing Viktor fight that way, taking down those two men like it was nothing, no one could deny he is very practiced in hand-to-hand combat.

I could also be honest with Hannah and myself. Because until this point, I've been lying to myself, too.

The truth is, I saw Viktor take out those two men, and while I was horrified that Theo and Hannah saw him that way, and that he had put himself in danger, I also found it incredibly attractive.

Viktor's body was strong and capable, and he overpowered two men by himself. It was barbaric and harsh and violent, and underneath my horror, was lust. A primal attraction to the strongest man in the vicinity.

That reality scares me more than anything else.

I am still trying to decide what to tell Hannah when the door to the apartment bursts open and Viktor comes charging into the kitchen. The second he sees me, he tips his head towards the hallway. "We need to talk."

He is fuming. In the car, he was quiet and respectful. He allowed me to bandage him without complaint and talk back to him, but it is clear he is done with that now. *Now*, we are going to fight.

Hannah's eyes go wide, and she disappears into the living room without a word. I follow Viktor into the hallway and towards the study on the opposite end of the apartment.

The second I close the door I spin around and start talking before he can.

"You attacked two men on a street corner in the middle of the day. What in the hell were you thinking?" I say, fighting the tremor in my voice. "You could have been killed. You were alone. Where was Petr or any other enforcer to help you? And you did it in front of Theo."

I try to organize my anger into coherence.

"I've been terrified for weeks that something would happen to you or someone would break into this house and hurt me or my son or my unborn baby, but turns out, I should have been worried about you walking around and putting yourself in life and death situations. I mean, for God's sake, Viktor, what would happen to all of us if you died on a street corner fighting off dealers? Where would we be then?"

Viktor steps forward into my space, his body close enough that I have to stop to draw in a sharp breath.

"You were supposed to tell me before you left the house," he says, reminding me of my promise. "I had no reason to believe you or Theo or your friend would be anywhere close to that scene today."

"Hannah. Her name is Hannah, and so much for keeping your business secret from her. She got an eyeful today."

"Fuck Hannah," Viktor says harshly, his neck turning red. "I'm worried about you. Why didn't you tell me where you were? What would have happened if you'd run into those two men on your own? They recognized me, so I have every reason to believe they would have recognized you, too. You could have been hurt or kidnapped or worse."

"We had guards," I say, rolling my eyes as if that very scenario hadn't already played in my mind. "Besides, that area was supposed to be Kornilov territory, right? Even if I had told you we were going there, you wouldn't have done anything differently. Or have territories changed since the last time we spoke about it?"

"No," he says, nostrils flaring.

"Okay, then." I cross my arms and hold my ground. "So, if I'm not safe in territories that are supposedly 'safe,' then where am I safe?"

The question comes out hot and angry, but there is a current of fear beneath it.

Where are we safe?

Viktor steps forward until his chest is pressed against mine. I want to pull away from him for the simple reason that his nearness makes my head fuzzy, but I don't. I stand firm.

He lays a hand over my bicep and drags it down until his fingers tangle with mine. "You're safe here. With me."

The words crack the ice around my heart, and I can feel myself melting into him. Despite everything I've seen today and all of the chaos happening inside my brain, Viktor's touch has a way of slicing through all of it and getting straight to the heart of me.

I tip my head up to look at him, and his blue eyes are studying my features, outlining my every edge like he is trying to memorize me. Then, his lips are on mine.

I don't know if I lean into it or if it's Viktor who closes the entire distance on his own, but once his lips are on mine, I don't care. I arch my back against him, tangle my hands in the soft hair at the base of his neck, and inhale him like my life depends on it.

Viktor's hands are gentle on my waist for a second, and then his touch burns. It scorches. He grips my waist and molds me against his body. I wrap my legs around him instinctively, and he sits me on the edge of a small desk he bought for me to study on. I prefer the kitchen table for homework, so this is the first time I've used it. And I'm guessing, after we are done, I won't be able to sit at this table and focus on anything academic ever again.

His body is warm on the inside of my thighs, but there is too much material between us. Too many layers separating our bodies. I slide my hands down the hard plane of his stomach and unbutton his pants, and Viktor stops kissing me to glance down and watch me peel his pants down to the tops of his strong thighs.

I cup the bulge in his boxers and rub the heel of my palm down his ready length. Viktor tips his head back and groans. When he looks down at me again, his eyes are dark and wild, and I can barely draw in a breath before his mouth is on mine again. His tongue swirls into my mouth, drawing mine out for a dance, and his hips roll against my hand.

"Hannah is waiting for me," I say, hating the part of me that is being practical. I don't want to think about anyone or anything beyond this room. Not right now. Not while his body is pressed against mine.

"Fuck Hannah," Viktor repeats, though this time his voice is a gravelly whisper.

I slide my hand inside his boxers, and he tenses as my fingers wrap around him. "I'd prefer if you fucked me, instead."

Viktor's mouth tips up in a wicked smile. "Gladly."

His mouth curls around my jawline and down my throat as I stroke him. He licks my collarbone and rolls his palm over my breasts while I smooth my thumb over his tip.

"Quieter," he says in my ear, his teeth nipping at the lobe. I realize all at once I was moaning, and I bite my bottom lip. Viktor pulls back to look at me, and groans.

"Quiet," I tease while teasing my hand down the length of him at the same time.

"It's hard when you look that good biting your lip," he admits, the words almost lost in the huskiness of his voice.

His fingers dig into my hip, and then he pulls me down off the desk and puts my feet on the floor. I reluctantly relinquish my hold on him and am immediately rewarded by Viktor dropping to his knees and unzipping my jeans.

He pushes them down and then walks his fingers up the outsides of my thighs when he returns to my panties. My knees feel weak. I have to grip the edge of the table to keep from falling over. The feeling is only compounded when he lets my panties drop to the floor and presses my knees apart.

His lips are soft on my calves, the backs of my knees, and the untouched skin of my thighs. My entire body is shaking by the time I feel his breath on my center, and I can't stand the wait anymore. I curl my fingers in his hair just as he buries his face in me.

A stifled scream forces its way out, and I lean back against the table to keep from falling. Viktor sucks and probes and nips as though he knows better than I do what I need, what feels good. No, not good. Incredible.

My vision is stars and fireworks, and my stomach is a puddle of heat.

Viktor grips my thighs and presses his tongue into me, and I think I've never been tasted so expertly before. Then, he circles his thumb over my center, and I'm gone.

I clap my own hand over my mouth to keep from shouting as shakes and tremors roll down my arms and legs, radiating outward from my epicenter.

I'm still shaking when Viktor stands up and peels my hand from my mouth. His lips are gentle against mine—much gentler than they just were down south—and I wrap my arms around his neck and my legs around his waist as he lifts me back onto the desk.

My body is aching for his even as my mind is a mass of confusion. Especially after my first orgasm, I wonder how we've found ourselves here. How this has happened again. I'm angry with him, but the need inside of me feels like a sinkhole, yawning open and taking all of my rational thoughts with me. I'm so ready for him that it only takes one thrust for him to be deep inside of me.

We both moan with the connection, and I find myself staring into his blue eyes. They are lidded, pupils blown wide, but I feel safer with this wild version of Viktor than anywhere else in the world.

How is that possible? His life is violence and crime and constantly checking over your shoulder. The lifestyle of Viktor's family is why I'm in this mess to begin with. And yet, I want to roll into a ball and curl myself against his muscular chest. I want Viktor to smooth his large hands down my spine to help me fall asleep, and I want him to press himself inside of me to wake me up.

Knowing what I know about him, I still want him with me. Now and later. Always.

The thought splits something open inside my chest, and I gasp. Viktor takes the sound as a sign of my pleasure and thrusts into me with more urgency. Our bodies slap together, rattling the table, until I'm clawing at him with my hands and pulling him closer with my legs. I roll my body against him with every connection, losing control with every passing second, and Viktor buries his face in my neck. His warm breath washes over my skin, coming faster and faster until he moans with release.

I fall with him.

We cling to one another as the waves of pleasure ebb and then flow away. As our hearts slow and return to normal. As the fog in my mind dissipates, leaving me with a clear picture once again.

"I can't do this," I whisper, pushing gently on his chest and untangling my legs from him.

Viktor frowns. "It's already done. Twice for you."

I slide off the table, and my jelly legs prove his point. I pull on my panties and my jeans and then gesture between our bodies quickly. "We've always been able to do that, but I mean ... the other parts of it. You say I'm safe with you, but I don't feel safe."

It's a lie, but it feels like a necessary one.

Viktor's eyes widen in shock from the blow, but he rearranges his face into a neutral mask as quickly as possible.

"Too much has happened, and I have to focus on Theo and the baby. I can't spend all of my energy worrying about you and what's going to happen next."

"Then don't," he snaps. "Don't worry about me and what happens next. Let me take care of you now."

"I can't depend on you." My voice is higher than I expected, and I clear my throat and lower my voice. "Your life is dangerous, and if I depend on you, I'll be lost when you are gone. So, I can't."

Viktor's hands clench, his knuckles going white. He winces and glances down at the bandage I put on his arm in the car, and then pulls on his clothes angrily. I'm not sure where we go from here. I'm not sure what decision we've just come to. Just as I'm about to ask, Viktor runs a hand through his hair to smooth it down and turns to me.

"Stay with me until this is over," he says softly. "Until Fedor isn't a threat anymore. Then, do whatever you want." He pauses for a long time, like he wants to speak but can't find the words. When he does, his voice is so quiet I can barely hear it. "Leave if you want. Take Theo and the baby and go. I won't stop you."

I blink at him, unable to believe the words coming out of his mouth.

Leave?

I must have spoken out loud because Viktor nods. "If that's what you want."

"What about what you want?" I ask. For weeks, I've just wanted permission to leave. I wanted Viktor to tell me I was free to go. Now that he has, the victory tastes bitter in my mouth. If I go, who will be here with Viktor?

He shrugs. "All I want is to take care of my family."

I want to ask whether he is talking about me or the Bratva, but I'm not sure I want to know.

Viktor glances up at me one more time. Just a quick flick of his eyes over my face. And then he turns and leaves.

～

Hannah has been quiet all afternoon and evening. While we were playing with Theo, she'd talk to him, but she barely looked at me. I wanted to ask her what she was thinking, but again, I was afraid of the truth. The same way I am with Viktor. It feels easier to not know how she feels.

By the time we are halfway through a mostly silent dinner, however, Hannah is fidgeting with her glass of wine. Finally, she folds her hands in her lap and looks up at me.

"What happened today?"

I blink, trying to decide if it's possible I could play dumb. Pretend I have no idea what she is talking about. "What?"

"The fight," she says, one brow arching upward.

I shrug and wave a dismissive hand in her direction. "That was—"

"If you say 'nothing,' so help me." Hannah's eyes narrow for a moment and then soften. "Come on, Molly. We both know that was something. And the way he came in here and demanded to speak with you. What is going on?"

I lay my fork down next to my plate, no longer hungry. "I don't want to talk about it."

"Neither do I," Hannah says. "It's why I waited all day to bring it up. But I'm too worried about you to keep quiet. Something is going on, and I'm scared for you."

My vision goes blurry, and my chin wobbles.

It has been so long since I've had someone who genuinely wanted to talk to me about my life that I can't handle it. Her basic kindness overwhelms me, and before I know it, I'm sobbing into my napkin and Hannah is kneeling next to me, her hand rubbing circles on my back.

"It's okay," she whispers. "Just tell me what is going on? Who is Viktor?"

Through hiccups and sniffles, I tell Hannah everything. I tell her Theo's father is Viktor's brother, Fedor. I tell her Viktor was sent to kill me, but took mercy on me and Theo and tried to hide us from his brother. Then, when his brother found out about Theo and wanted to take him away from me, Viktor put us in this apartment to protect us.

"And you fell in love?" Hannah asks, blinking as she processes the story.

The opportunity to tell her the entire truth presents itself—about the first pretend marriage and the current one, as well—but I'm embarrassed. Embarrassed that I could allow myself to be controlled by a man, but also the idea of Hannah thinking my entire relationship is fake is embarrassing, too.

Because it isn't fake.

Not all of it.

Not what just happened in the office this afternoon or the concern Viktor has for me and for Theo. Or the concern I have for him.

Despite the marriage being fake, our feelings aren't. So, I just nod.

"Yes, I fell in love."

"Oh man," Hannah says, shaking her head. "That's the scariest part of everything you just told me. A woman in love makes the stupidest decisions."

Despite the raw ache in my chest, left there by Viktor's announcement that I can leave once Fedor is dealt with and by

Hannah's kindness, I laugh. I wipe my nose with my sleeve and shake my head.

"I've definitely made some stupid decisions."

Hannah wraps her arm around my shoulders and presses her cheek against mine. "That's okay. I'll be here for you. You aren't in this alone anymore."

I'm so relieved I feel like I could cry more.

10

VIKTOR

It has been two days since Molly and I were together in her office, and nothing has gone right since.

She told me she didn't want to do this anymore. *This. Us.*

I knew that she had doubts about our arrangement, but I always assumed she'd come around eventually. The way she looks at me makes it obvious there is a connection there. Something more than just the physical. I assumed once Fedor was taken care of, we would have time and space for that connection to grow.

Now, I'm not sure.

She expressed her desire to leave, so I compromised. My big stupid mouth said she could leave when this was over if she wanted.

I can't hold her against her will. I mean, I can ... but I shouldn't. I won't.

So much of Molly's life has been without her consent, and I don't want to be responsible for any other bad memories for her. Telling her she can leave was the right thing to do, but now there is a time bomb ticking over my head.

Between it and the actual bombs Fedor has been setting off, it's a wonder I haven't lost my mind.

Three Kornilov Bratva hangouts have been targeted in just two days. The warehouse where Fedor was staying before is empty now, and I have no idea where he is or where he is launching these attacks from. The only thing I know for sure is that he is ruthless. Men, women, and children have been caught in the crosshairs, and he doesn't seem to mind.

He is a far cry from the boy I remember screaming at me the night our parents died.

Fedor fought my tight hold around his middle, digging his fingernails into my arms to try and free himself to get inside and save them. He was so angry at me for holding him back, for sacrificing our parents to save him. I'm not sure when that little boy lost his humanity and became the Fedor I know today, but I wish more than anything I could go back and fix it.

My men have avoided their regular haunts and are keeping a low profile while I try to figure things out, but morale is low. This dinner with the Irish couldn't have come at a better time. We need allies. Now.

I park along the curb in front of Molly's apartment and just before I turn off the car, my phone rings.

It's George.

"What do you need?" I ask shortly, not wanting to chitchat. "I have plans tonight."

"And I have information." His voice is gruff. "I've been monitoring Petr the last few days, and I've seen him driving into an Italian stronghold every day."

"To see who?"

"I don't know." He sighs. "The damn streets are so narrow that I have to keep my distance to avoid him seeing me, and I lose him every time."

I curse. "That isn't good, but I need more than a suspicion. If I cast doubt on Petr, the entire Bratva could fall apart. If even my right-hand man is betraying me, what would keep everyone else from deserting me? I have to be absolutely certain Petr has turned his back on me before I do anything rash."

"I'll keep tailing him," George says.

We hang up, and I take a deep breath, trying to release the tension building in my neck and shoulders. I look over and see one of my men parked across the road to keep eyes on the street outside Molly's apartment. He rolls down his window an inch and sticks a finger out in a small wave. I tip my head in his direction, straighten my suit jacket, and head inside.

Molly told me she'd need a new dress, so I had one sent over for her this morning. She isn't far enough along in her pregnancy to be showing yet, so the measurements I had taken after she first came to live with me still work. Eventually, I'll need to buy her maternity clothes.

For our baby.

How can I let her walk away with my baby?

The question has been floating around in my brain for two days, and I'm no closer to having an answer. Perhaps we can arrange some kind of custody deal, but I'm not sure Molly would agree. Being close to me at all puts her and the kids in danger. She might want to cut ties with me completely, and I have to figure out whether I'm okay with that. Whether I can live knowing my child is out there in the world without me.

I knock on Molly's front door three times in the specific pattern I devised with the guards and then unlock the front door with my key.

One of the guards peeks his head around the corner to be sure it is me and then disappears, worries assuaged.

The living room is empty—Theo is with the nanny, and I'm not sure where Molly's house guest is—so I mount the stairs to her room. I'm just about to knock when I hear voices.

"You don't have to go." I recognize the voice as Hannah's. "Tell him you're sick. Or that you are nauseous. You're pregnant. He can't argue with a pregnant woman."

"I'm always nauseous," Molly says. "Even before the pregnancy. This life gives me anxiety."

I fight back the flare of anger and concern that rises up in me.

"That is why you need to get out of here," Hannah says. "Let's do it. Right now. We'll leave, pick up Theo, and run. Who is better at living under the radar than a formerly homeless woman and a current one? We are society's undesirables. Let's embrace our invisibility and run."

There is silence for a long time, and I start to worry Molly is considering the offer. But she wouldn't ... would she?

Running now would be so foolish. Fedor would find her in a second, and with no one to protect her or Theo or the baby, she'd be killed. Or worse.

"I can't," Molly says at last. "I have to think about Theo. Plus, I'm pregnant."

"We were both pregnant the first time we slept under a bridge," Hannah says. "We can do it again."

Molly doesn't say anything, but her answer must be clear enough because Hannah sighs. "Okay, but just know I'll support you no matter what you decide."

She sounds so sincere, but she is also trying to convince my (fake) wife to run away with her and take Theo and my baby with them, so I don't think it is a good idea to let them spend anymore alone time together. I push open the door without knocking and stand in the doorway, arms crossed.

Hannah jumps back, yanking her arm from Molly's shoulder, and Molly yelps, her eyes going wide.

"You should be dressed by now," I say.

Hannah steps forward again and lifts her chin. "She isn't feeling well."

I glare at her and then tip my head towards the door. "I'd like to speak to my wife alone."

Hannah's eyes narrow and she lays a hand on Molly's shoulder. "Only if Molly wants me to go."

We both look at Molly, and she seems to shrink under our gaze. Then, she pats Hannah's hand and assures her it is okay.

"Of course it's okay. I'm your husband," I say. "I'm not going to hurt you."

Hannah doesn't look convinced of that fact as she slinks from the room, sliding past me. I slam the door shut behind her.

"What the fuck was that about?"

Molly is sitting on the edge of the bed in maroon sweatpants and a zip-up hoodie. I can see that her dark hair is curled in soft waves, and her brown eyes are rimmed in smoky eyeshadow and mascaraed. She is partially ready, at least, but the dress is nowhere to be seen.

"She was helping me get ready."

I roll my eyes, not wanting to argue with her right now. "She was doing a bad job. Where's your dress?"

Molly points to the closet, and I open the doors and pull the slinky silver dress out from where it had been stuffed in the back.

"Do you not like it?"

"It's beautiful," Molly says softly. "It's just ... it's not me. None of this is me."

She gestures to her makeup and her hair. "I'm not a woman who goes to fancy dinners and mingles with the most powerful men in the city. I feel like everything in my life is a game of pretend, and I am so tired of playing."

My anger dissipates when I look into her eyes and see the sadness there. The resignation.

Molly looks exhausted, and I wish I could lay her back on the bed, tuck her into my chest, and sleep next to her.

But I can't.

We have to go.

I hang the dress from the top of the closet door and move to sit next to Molly on the bed. She instinctively turns towards me as I sit, and I reach out and lay a hand on her knee.

"Molly, you don't have to pretend to be the most beautiful woman in any room."

She gives me a small, sad smile, but I can tell she doesn't believe me. So, I grab her hand and bring it to my chest, letting her feel my heart beating beneath my ribs. Letting her know I mean every word.

"You are my queen, Molly. I know you find it difficult in these situations, but it is only because you have spent so long fighting. You know what it means to struggle, which makes you stronger than any of the silver-spoon women you are going to talk with tonight." I bring her hand to my lips and press a kiss to the center of her palm. "Plus, I'll be with you every step of the way. Right by your side."

Molly's lashes flutter closed, and she nods. "I know. I know you'll make sure nothing happens to me, but I'm just ... scared. I'm so scared. For myself, but mostly for Theo and our baby. It makes it hard to leave the house."

I drop her hand and slide mine to the front of her hoodie. To the place where our child is growing inside of her. "I'll protect all of you."

It is too soon to feel any kicks or movement, but a warmth seems to radiate from her center, and I find myself drawn to it, desperate to know the child growing there.

I can't let her walk away with my baby.

The answer to the question I've been asking myself rises in my mind, and I yank my hand away quickly.

Emotional attachments are dangerous. They clutter my mind and muddy my thinking.

If I want to keep my family safe, I have to stay cold. Unaffected.

When Fedor is gone and no longer a threat, I can think about this. But right now, it doesn't matter. Nothing matters until I know they will all be safe.

I stand up and straighten my jacket. "I'll let you get dressed."

Molly looks confused, but I see her stand up and move towards the dress just before I shut the door and walk back downstairs. Hannah is smart enough to know she shouldn't be lingering in the living room. Wherever she is, I hope she stays there. I don't trust her.

∽

Molly's silver dress is simple, but sexy.

The neckline plunges across her chest and snaps around the back of her neck, leaving her back exposed down to her waist. I lay my hand on her lower back as we walk to the car, and it's physically difficult to release her. I'll have to fight the urge to touch her all night.

"Are you nervous?" Molly asks.

The question pulls me from my thoughts—mostly thoughts of touching all of her exposed skin—and I realize my fingers are digging into my knees hard enough my knuckles are white.

I loosen my grip. "No."

"Are you sure?" she asks. "You've looked a little nauseous ever since I walked downstairs. Are you sure you aren't the one who is pregnant?"

We are separated from the driver with a soundproof sheet of glass, but I still turn to Molly with a warning in my eyes. No one else should know about her condition ... not yet.

"He can't hear us," she says a little louder, a smile tugging the corners of her mouth up. She leans forward and cups a hand around her mouth, directing her words towards the divider. "Take the next right."

The car continues moving straight and steady. No deviation whatsoever.

"Go back to the apartment. I forgot my panties!"

This time, I reach across the seat and lay a hand over her mouth, though I can barely keep the smile from my own face. "What is wrong with you? Weren't you nervous just a few minutes ago? You better not have taken any drugs. You're pregnant."

Her eyes go wide. "Are you not supposed to take drugs while you're pregnant?"

For a brief moment, I think she is being serious. Then, I see the spark of amusement in her eyes and shake my head. "You are bad."

"And you're smiling," she says softly. Her hand lifts like she wants to reach out and touch my face, and I resist the urge to curl against her palm like a cat. Then, she drops it in her lap, her smile dimming slightly, becoming more restrained. "If we both went into tonight nervous, I'd never make it through. You're supposed to be the one holding me together. So, whatever has you worried, I want to help take care of it."

"Sorry." I run my hands through my hair and lean back in my seat. "I've been distracted lately."

It is more than I usually admit to anyone, but I don't feel vulnerable. Not with Molly. I feel safe.

The realization hits me all at once, and the thought once again arises unbidden in my mind: *I can't let her go. I can't let them go.*

Molly reaches across the seat and lays a hand on my wrist. Her fingers are long and thin, and her skin is warm against mine. "Well, no matter what else is going on, all we need to focus on tonight is being a convincing married couple."

I turn my hand over and thread my fingers through hers. "I think I can manage that."

Her eyebrow arches up in a challenge. "Are you sure? Because, as a wife, I can be quite demanding."

She shifts slightly in the seat, her legs uncrossing, knees falling apart slightly. Without permission, my eyes trace the curve of her breasts in the dress and dip lower, falling into the shadow beneath the slit of her dress. I swallow back the desire clogging my throat.

"What kinds of demands?"

Molly drops her hand to the exposed skin of her thigh and slides it slowly up, her fingers whispering over her skin in a way that makes me want to grab her firmly, the way she needs to be grabbed. "Well, for one thing, you'll have to stay close to me."

I nod before she is even finished speaking. "Done."

Her mouth puckers to one side, hiding a smile. "And keep me satisfied."

My gaze flicks back up to her face and then down again. "In what ways?"

She shrugs, her hand moving higher, pushing the fabric of her dress aside to expose her upper thigh. So much of her leg is showing that I have to wonder whether the joke about forgetting her panties was real or not.

"Food if I'm famished," she says, her words breathy. "A drink if I'm parched."

Suddenly, I am parched and my voice is dry when I speak. "Okay. I can do that. What else?"

Molly curves her fingers around her thigh, inching closer to her center, and I can't peel my eyes from her body. I want to watch her touch herself. Even if the driver is only a thin piece of glass away from us. I lick my lips.

With her free hand, Molly reaches out for me. She slides her hand down my arm until her fingers brush across my palm and then grip my own. She draws my hand across the space between us and towards where her other hand is dangerously close to her sweet heat. The only thing better than watching Molly pleasure herself would be pleasuring her myself. My mind is empty of everything but her as she lays my hand on her thigh. I want her. Now.

"More than anything, I want you to ..." She leans forward, her lips parted in delicious seduction. My fingers grip her soft skin through the material of her dress, and I want to tear the fabric off her. She is too beautiful to be covered. Her breath is warm against my mouth when she speaks. "Open my door for me."

I blink, confused.

Molly tips her head behind me, and I look over my shoulder.

"We're here," she says.

I groan and fall back against my seat, and Molly laughs behind me. "Come on, husband. It's time to make an alliance."

That was my priority ten minutes ago. Now, the hardness between my legs has other ideas.

I rearrange myself before getting out of the car and doing as my wife asked. I open her door and escort her inside.

11

MOLLY

The restaurant is at the top of a skyscraper downtown. Three of the four walls in the dining room are floor-to-ceiling windows, and the room is bathed in the faint glow of the city. Candles flicker on the round tables, a four-piece band plays softly in the corner, and everyone is dressed in their best.

And looking directly at me.

At us, really.

Viktor has his arm wrapped tightly around me, his fingers splayed across my hip, and I know I should feel nervous. Hell, an hour ago I was contemplating faking being sick and hiding under the covers. But now, standing next to Viktor with his arm around me, I can't find the fear.

Somehow, while distracting Viktor in the car, I managed to distract myself, too.

The way his eyes traced my shape, the way he devoured me with his gaze, made me feel powerful. If I can bring a man as fierce as Viktor to his figurative knees, then what do I have to fear from anyone in this room?

He told me back at the apartment that he would take care of me—that he would take care of all of us—and I wanted to believe him. At least for tonight, I want to trust that I will be in good hands. I want to trust that he won't let me make a fool of myself. So, to the best of my ability, I shed my nerves and fear and trepidation over meeting new people and making new alliances and focused on the one thing Victor and I have always had in abundance: chemistry.

Viktor wears a kind smile as we move through the room and greet his guests, but it is surface level. It doesn't reach his eyes the way his smiles in the car did. This is business Viktor. Mafia boss Viktor.

And I'm his queen.

I hold my head high and shake the hands of women who, only a few months ago, would have found me undeserving of the energy it would take them to spit at my feet. Now, they bow their heads in small signs of respect and don't make eye contact with Viktor as we pass. But I can feel their attention snag on the two of us. On Viktor's hand claiming my waist and my body molded against his as though we are carved from the same clay. They may doubt whether we are equally matched in our marriage, but they won't doubt whether there is passion.

In the center of the room, with a wide berth around them, stands a couple who I assume are the Irish boss and his wife. Viktor hastily described them in the elevator on our way up.

Seamus and Niamh are older than I expected them to be. He has a shock of gray hair and hers is pure white, but trimmed neatly around her ears. They smile as we approach, and Seamus extends his hand to Viktor while his wife smiles warmly at me.

I'm not sure what I expected of them, actually. Viktor told me this dinner was to create an alliance. I think I expected things to be more tense. To feel more like a hostage exchange. Instead, there are suits and kind smiles and pleasantries.

"Viktor," Seamus says, turning to me and winking. "Your new wife is lovely. I expected nothing less."

I meet his expectations even if he didn't meet mine. That seems like a good thing.

It seems everyone was waiting for us to arrive because as soon as we greet Seamus and his wife, the rest of the guests begin moving towards their tables. Viktor presses his hand to my exposed lower back and leads me to a table just big enough for the four of us in the center of the room.

"You don't even have to speak to impress these people," Viktor whispers in my ear. "Your natural charm shines through."

I'm not so sure Seamus wasn't just commenting on my physical appearance, but I take the compliment, either way. Viktor's confidence gives me some of my own.

I sit between Viktor and Niamh, and the two men begin talking immediately, speaking in quiet tones. I know they are talking business, but they look relaxed. I suppose they would. Criminal affairs are their work. Why should they be bothered about discussing such things openly?

"Hardly any small talk before they get down to business," Niamh says next to me. She rolls her eyes playfully when I look at her. "Seamus has always been ninety percent business."

"What of the other ten percent?" I ask.

Niamh's eyes spark with mischief. "The other ten percent is why I married him, and I'm afraid it's indecent dinner conversation."

I cover my mouth with my hand and laugh, surprised by her forthrightness.

"I'm sure you understand," she says, tucking a strand of white hair behind her ear. "Why did you marry your Viktor?"

My Viktor. I do think of him that way. But only sometimes, when I lower my guard. When my thoughts are running away with themselves.

"I was drawn to him the first moment I ever saw him," I say. "He seemed bigger than life. Tougher than everyone around him and firm in what he wanted. He overwhelmed me, and I couldn't deny our chemistry."

My answer is meant to make Viktor look strong, dominant. But I realize, halfway through, that the answer is true, too. For all of our struggles, I admire Viktor's strength and our connection.

"He is protective, too," I continue, brow knitted in thought. "Of me and our son. He loves the people in his life fiercely and is loyal to those who are loyal to him. He is a good man."

I blink as if coming out of a trance and smile at Niamh. She is no longer looking at me, however. She is looking over my shoulder. I follow her gaze and see Viktor smiling at me. He was apparently eavesdropping on our conversation.

"What about you, Viktor?" Niamh asks. "Why did you marry Molly?"

"My wife, the romantic," Seamus says, reaching over to squeeze her hand.

Viktor smiles, lifts his chin in thought, and then smiles down at me. "Molly is strong and resilient. She overcomes whatever obstacle is placed in front of her and never views herself as a victim. She is one of the strongest people I've ever met, but also one of the gentlest. Her heart is kind and big, and in the end, I just knew I had to find my way into that heart. I knew I had to make her my wife."

Viktor's eyes are honest as he studies my face. Then, he blinks and turns back to the table. Seamus and Niamh are both looking at him with a newfound appreciation.

I find I'm seeing him in a new light, as well.

"Molly is a great designer." Viktor says the words casually while he stabs a piece of tortellini on his plate.

Viktor rented out the restaurant and then catered in some of the best Italian food in the city. I wouldn't have thought something like that was possible, but apparently, money can do anything. The waitstaff at the restaurant doesn't seem to mind, anyway.

"I don't have any formal education," I say, ignoring the rush of heat in my face.

"Talent needs no formal training." Viktor smiles at me and then takes a bite, his knee nudging mine under the table.

Niamh is sitting taller, her eyes on me. "Do you think you could help me? I want an entire redesign of our library. It's so dark. It's like a cave."

"If I remember right, that's what you said you wanted, dear," Seamus says, a knowing smile on his face. "I remember you saying it would be nice to escape from the world."

"I did say that, but that was before I realized reading by artificial light would strain my eyes and make me sleepy." She rolls her eyes at me in a commiserating way, but her lips smirk up in a small smile.

Niamh and Seamus clearly have a loving relationship. They tease one another and push each other, but there is genuine fondness between them.

I shouldn't be surprised. Of course, crime bosses can have loving relationships with devoted partners. They aren't all like Fedor.

Before Fedor discovered Viktor's lie—that he hadn't killed me like he said and was instead letting me live in his house—Viktor was gentle and kind and loving. Maybe things could be that way again.

Though, I don't see how that would really matter. Viktor told me I could leave. He told me I could take Theo and the baby and get away from this life, and after all the violence I've seen, I'd be stupid to stay. It's a dangerous life. I have to go.

"Do you think you could help?" Niamh presses, laying a hand on my elbow. "I just want to get it right."

"But don't let that scare you," Seamus says. "She has redone it three times in the last two years. So, if you take the job and she does hate it, she won't tell you. She'll just redo it again."

Niamh glares at him and then pats my hand. "I doubt I'll hate it."

"You might," I laugh. "I've only done a nursery before. And it was for my son."

Niamh claps her hands in front of her and grins at me. "It's decided. I'm hiring you. I'll have a contract drawn up. Then, when you become famous, I'll be able to claim I was your first official job. I love being on the cutting edge."

"This was your plan all along," Seamus says to Viktor, raising his glass for a toast. "You know I can't deny my Niamh anything. If she likes your Molly, I have no choice but to work with you."

"Everyone knows it's the wives who really make the alliances," Niamh whispers to me. "The men only think they are in charge."

I laugh into my hand, and Seamus nudges his wife's shoulder. "We can hear you, darling. Speak more quietly so we can maintain our illusion of power."

The night is going so much better than I ever would have imagined. I'm comfortable and genuinely having a good time. The other women in the Kornilov Bratva seemed catty and only wanted to gossip. Half an hour with Niamh, and I already feel like she could be my friend. Perhaps there is truth to her statement. Because I will do everything in my power to ensure Viktor never betrays Seamus' trust. I would hate not being able to talk with Niamh.

Everyone is still chuckling when suddenly, Viktor leaps out of his seat.

His thighs hit the underside of the table, knocking everything sideways. Niamh's wineglass tips and spills red across the white tablecloth, and Seamus grabs her arm to steady her.

I yelp, but Viktor doesn't stop. He knocks his chair back and starts moving around the table towards Seamus' side.

For a second, I wonder if he wasn't offended by the idea that he isn't the one in control. I've never seen him lose his temper so recklessly before, though. Especially when we are here for the purpose of making nice with the Irish. But the way he is charging around the table towards Seamus makes my heart rate spike. What is going to happen? We are surrounded by the Irish. Viktor and I came alone as a sign of good faith. Surely, he wouldn't risk our lives because of a joking comment.

Seamus lifts his hands in defense and leans back in his chair just as Viktor grabs the serving tray from the waiter standing near our table, sends the dishes crashing to the floor, and then swings the tray, hitting the waiter square in the face.

"Viktor!" I stand up, hand inadvertently falling to my stomach. My instincts tell me to run, to get out of here and find out what is happening later.

But my heart is worried about Viktor. What is he doing?

The entire room goes quiet for a moment, though it feels like hours. Everyone is waiting with bated breath. The Irish have stood up all around the room, the men ready to act, the women ready to hide. Everyone is on high alert.

Niamh is the first to move. She looks from me to Viktor and then lays a hand on Seamus' shoulder.

"Viktor, what—" Seamus starts to say.

Before he can finish, the waiter reaches for his hip, and Viktor drives the heel of his foot into the man's chest. He flies back, hitting the table next to ours. The occupants scatter as their drinks spill onto their plates and dribble onto the floor.

Just as the waiter hits the ground, Viktor presses a foot to the man's chest, pinning him down, and then kneels and grabs for the waist of his pants. The waiter is frantic, his eyes huge and panicked, and he doesn't look older than twenty. He barely has any facial hair, and his arms are long and scrawny. This isn't a fair fight.

"Viktor," I say, taking a step forward.

Niamh grabs my elbow, and I still. I'm not sure what is going on, but I trust her already. I stay where I am, watching as Viktor pulls a gun from the man's hip.

He holds it in the air and then gestures for some of the Irish to come forward. "Would someone help me restrain this piece of shit?"

Seamus nods at his men, and they obey his order, coming forward to help Viktor by holding the young waiter down.

When Viktor stands up, he rolls his shoulder awkwardly, and I remember the bandage on his arm from his fight the other day. Clearly, it is smarting, but Viktor is trying to play it off.

"Sorry to interrupt the festivities," Viktor says, his tone light but strained. "But I thought allowing an assassination attempt on Seamus' life might dampen the mood even more."

Niamh gasps and grabs her husband's arm. "What is he talking about, Seamus?"

"What are you talking about?" Seamus asks Viktor, repeating his wife's question.

"I noticed the waiter studying you closely," Viktor said. "He kept circling around our table unnecessarily, and on his last pass through, I noticed the bulge at his hip. His hand hung near it nervously, like he wasn't sure when to grab for it. I recognized the signs and made a call to attack him before he could attack you."

Seamus looks from Viktor to the waiter lying pinned on the floor, and shakes his head. "Well, then thanks are in order."

Viktor shakes his head. "Not necessary."

"It is necessary." Seamus steps forward and extends a hand to Viktor. The two men shake. "You saved my life, and I'm grateful to you. The real question, however, is why was it necessary? How the fuck did this man get in here?"

Seamus' lip curls in disgust as he takes in the waiter lying on the floor. "How did you get in here?"

"Please," the waiter says. "I didn't do anything. The gun was just for—"

Seamus tips his head and one of the men holding the waiter drives an elbow into his mouth. Blood spurts from his mouth and dribbles out the sides.

How *did* the man get in here? There were guards waiting at the elevators to check everyone before they entered the party. How did they overlook the waitstaff?

Suddenly, the image of the strange man walking into my kitchen with my son in his arms returns to me, and I shiver. Once again, I'm reminded of how I'm never safe. Not really. Danger can slip in through the smallest of cracks.

"This man intended to kill me, so I find it is only right if we return the favor." Seamus tells his men to lift the waiter to his feet and then asks Viktor for the gun. Viktor flips the gun around and gives it to Seamus handle first. Yet another show of trust between the two men.

The conversation in the room rises to a moderate din, and everyone seems to be in agreement. This man needs to die.

Seamus lifts the gun to the boy's forehead, and he is so pale he looks half dead already.

"Wait." I speak before I can think better of it.

I meet Viktor's eyes, and he seems to be begging me to stay out of it. This situation could have gone sideways in a thousand different ways. Seamus' men could have thought Viktor meant to attack their leader and killed him before he could have stopped the waiter. Seamus could have thought Viktor set up the assassination attempt as a way to build trust between them.

This, right now—the murder of a young waiter in the middle of the party—is the best possible outcome for me and my family.

And yet…

"The man hasn't given you any information," I say quickly, the words coming out breathless. "You should keep him for more information. Find out who wanted to do this to you."

Viktor blinks at me and then turns to Seamus to gauge his reaction.

Seamus' hand flexes on the handle of the gun, clearly itching to pull the trigger. Then, Niamh pats my shoulder gently before walking over to her husband. She speaks into his ear, but it is loud enough that everyone in the immediate area can still hear her.

"Besides, honey. The blood will make a mess and ruin the rest of the evening."

The soothing sound of his wife's voice makes Seamus loosen his hold on the gun and eventually lower it to his side. Then, he wraps his arm around her shoulders and turns to me. "Like Niamh said before, the men only think they are in charge."

I'm worried Seamus is angry with me, but then he smiles, giving me a wink, and turns to Viktor. "You are observant and your wife is wise. It would be foolish of me not to align myself with you. Clearly, you are an asset to our operation."

It's remarkable how quickly the party returns to normal.

The Irish enforcers drag the waiter from the room—I do my best not to think about where they are taking him—and then everyone returns to their seats. The rest of the staff is checked for weapons once again, and then the overturned drinks and food are replaced. The mood is light and festive, almost as if the unpleasantness never happened.

"Is your arm okay?" I ask Viktor a while later. "You shouldn't be doing anything too physical with that cut."

Viktor lays his hand over where mine is on his arm and squeezes my fingers. "I'm always fine when you are by my side."

"You aren't angry?" I ask. "I probably shouldn't have said anything."

Viktor lowers his head, his eyebrows drawn together and serious. "Yes, you should have. You should always speak up when you feel the need. I don't want you to be silenced."

His words feel like a balm on my nerves, and my mouth twists into a nervous smile. "Thank you."

Viktor grabs my hand and brings it to his lips, his breath warm across my knuckles. "Thank *you*, Molly. I couldn't have done this without you." He kisses my knuckles again and looks up at me with his devilishly handsome blue eyes, making my stomach turn. "My Bratva queen."

Once again, logic wars with my heart. I should want to run as far from Viktor and this lifestyle as possible. Especially after what I just witnessed. Yet, I find myself warming to the idea.

A Bratva queen.

His queen.

12

VIKTOR

When I knock on Aunt Vera's door, conflicted feelings swirl inside of me.

I don't want Aunt Vera to be sick. And yet, I also hope she is. Because if she is, it means Petr was telling me the truth. It means that he was visiting his mother when he disappeared off the radar and his mother's house really is a cellular dead spot. It means there is a reasonable explanation for why George saw him in Italian territory last night.

If Aunt Vera is sick, it means that my cousin and second-in-command isn't a lying piece of scum who I'll have to kill.

As soon as she opens the door, however, my heart sinks.

"Vikki," she says, calling me by the name she and my mother used to taunt me with as a child. "What a surprise."

Aunt Vera has always been a stout woman. There is something square and solid about her. Broad shoulders, a thick middle, and legs like tree trunks. When she pulls me into a hug, her grip is firm and strong. So, her ailment certainly isn't physical.

"Good to see you, Auntie." I hug her back and then hold her at arm's length. "But you still can't call me Vikki."

She barks out a sharp laugh. "I'll call you whatever I like. Now, come inside. I've been cooking."

I slip my shoes off at the front door. Aunt Vera is always cooking. She likes to have a well-stocked kitchen and something hot to offer anyone who might stop by. For years, her house was full of hungry boys. After her older sons got themselves into trouble and died in prison fights, there is just Petr.

I hate the thought of taking him away from her, too. But I'll do whatever is necessary to protect my Bratva and my family. Anything.

"Are you feeding an army?" I tease as I walk into their kitchen. There is a tower of baklava on the table along with a stack of buckwheat pancakes and an entire loaf of sourdough bread. "Where is Petr? Baklava is his favorite."

The question is casual, but important.

"Busy with all the work you give him," she says, narrowing her eyes at me. I know she is only teasing. Aunt Vera has told me many times how happy she is that I keep Petr busy. No woman in our family wants her son to be involved in our dangerous lifestyle, but being consigliere to the boss is better than being a soldier. Petr is safer at my side than anywhere else in my operation.

I only hope I haven't risked my own safety by trusting him.

"He hasn't been by to see you recently?"

Aunt Vera shakes her head and then squints to think. "Not for a couple weeks. That toad. You should tell him to visit his mama. Make it an order."

"I'll do that." I try to sound light, but my entire body is tense. How much betrayal can one man handle?

I clear my throat and take a bite of baklava. The honey and walnut balance each other well, and I take momentary solace in the flaky pastry. I might not be getting another one in a long time, if ever. I doubt Aunt Vera would forgive me for killing her last living son, no matter how justified my reasons.

"How have you been?" I ask.

She waves away the question. "Same. I'm a boring old woman now."

"You're healthy?" I prod.

Aunt Vera glances up at me, eyes narrowed. "Do I not look healthy? Are you implying I'm old?"

"You just called yourself old."

"I'm allowed to do that, but not you," she says with a stern finger point. "Your job is to tell me I don't look a day over thirty."

"You don't," I lie with a forced smile. "But you didn't answer my question."

Aunt Vera cuts off a slice of sourdough and slides it across the counter to me on a napkin. "I'm healthy as a horse, you worrywart. I feel great."

I want to believe she is lying, trying to protect me from the truth of some terminal illness, but I know she isn't. If anything, Aunt Vera would come to me first if she was sick. She would want to protect Petr from the news and from having to take care of her.

If Aunt Vera was sick, she'd tell me.

Which means Petr is lying.

"I hear you got yourself married," she says, lifting her chin and turning away from me. "Though, I missed the invitation."

"It was a quick wedding," I say. "I'm sorry."

She turns back to me, her eyes assessing. "A quick wedding? Is it because she is carrying your baby?"

Damn, I almost forgot how astute Aunt Vera can be.

When I don't answer, she shrugs. "Fine, but when you announce the news, I better be one of the first to know. I'll babysit whenever you need me to."

"I know," I say warmly, wishing that were possible. By the time the baby is born, Molly might be gone. And if she isn't, Petr likely will be. The news of why I had to kill Petr will get back to Aunt Vera, and she'll never forgive me. She'll never meet my child or babysit for me.

After my parents died, Aunt Vera was a substitute mother. She has been there for me my entire life, and now, I'm looking into a future alone.

Before I leave, she sends me home with a plastic container of food for Molly and Theo and a kiss on the cheek. I can still feel the residue from her lipstick on my cheek as I call Petr from the car.

He answers on the third ring with a loud *whoop*. "You won over the Irish. Goddamn, Vik. We might actually win this thing."

"We will win," I say firmly.

"Of course, of course." Petr chuckles to himself, excited by the news of the recent alliance. Or, at least, pretending to be excited. "So, what's going on?"

"Nothing. I just wanted to call and check on your mom. Is she still sick?"

There is a pause. "Yeah. Still sick. Thanks for asking."

I close my eyes and shake my head. "Let me know if I can do anything. I can stop by and help with whatever she needs."

"No, that's okay," Petr says quickly. "I can take care of it. Thanks, but I got it."

Petr congratulates me again on the alliance before we hang up, and even now, knowing he is lying to me, it sounded genuine. Petr had me perfectly fooled.

I switch to my texts and message George.

Find out who Petr is meeting with. ASAP.

~

Seamus is sitting with his back against a brick wall, facing the dining room of the restaurant. It's not surprising after the assassination attempt last night. I'd be nervous, too.

I take the seat across from him and grip his hand in a firm shake. "Good to see you again so soon."

"Sorry for the late notice," he says. "I just thought it would be best to talk in person."

"Of course, what have you found?"

Molly was nervous about her interruption at the dinner last night. Admittedly, I was nervous, too. My alliance with Seamus was tenuous, and if it looked like I couldn't control my wife, what would he think?

Luckily, Seamus is familiar with strong, outspoken women. His wife is the same way.

Plus, Molly was right. Keeping the waiter alive and questioning him served a far better purpose than quick vengeance.

Seamus sighs and rolls his eyes. "Just as you suspected. It was Fedor's doing."

"He knows I am trying to take him down. I should have guessed he'd try to interfere."

"It isn't your fault," Seamus says. "My men somehow let the man he hired through the doors. I need to increase security."

How did Fedor know where we were meeting? Obviously Fedor found out, but how?

"Do you have any idea how our meeting location got out?" Seamus asks, giving voice to my own thoughts.

I shake my head. "No idea, but I plan to find out."

Petr is my first thought. He knew where the dinner was being held, and if he is betraying me, he could have told Fedor.

Still, I don't want to put any suspicion on Petr until I'm sure. I don't want to jeopardize a relationship between Petr and Seamus if I don't have to. Plus, part of me is still desperately hoping Petr is loyal and this has all been a huge misunderstanding.

A waitress brings us each an espresso and asks whether we want anything to eat, but Seamus dismisses her with a polite refusal.

"Sorry, but I can't stay long. Niamh is expecting me home soon."

"I need to be getting home soon, too," I say. Even though my "home" is empty. Molly is at her house.

"Niamh can't stop talking about Molly. I'm afraid our wives are becoming best friends."

"Is that bad?" I ask.

Seamus raises a brow. "They are going to share all of our secrets with one another. Soon enough, they'll be working together to control us."

"There are worse things that could happen."

Seamus laughs. "Too right. We should get them together again soon. If we don't, Niamh is going to drive me crazy with asking. She has already drawn up ideas for how Molly can redecorate the library."

"We'll have dinner soon," I assure him.

We finish our espressos shortly and part with a shake and a promise.

"To our alliance," Seamus says.

I grin. "And our friendship."

∽

I'm halfway home when the idea of going back to my empty apartment feels too depressing to cope with. Before I know it, I've turned around and am driving to Molly's.

I knock three times and then let myself in with a key.

"Hello," I call from the entryway, not wanting to startle her. However, my words are lost to the sound of music. Loud music.

I follow the sound to the living room where Molly and Hannah are standing in the middle of the room ... with microphones ... singing.

After the crazy few days I've had, it takes me a second to understand the happy scene in front of me. Two friends singing karaoke doesn't jive with assassins and traitorous friends and brothers. They can't coexist in the same story.

They are singing a duet, and Molly throws her head back during her part, eyes closed, belting it out to the ceiling. Half of the notes are off-key and shrieked, but she is passionate and loud and ... happy.

Then, Molly turns towards me, and her eyes go wide, and her cheeks flush with embarrassment. She lowers her microphone and covers her face with her hand.

She is adorable.

Hannah carries on singing, pointing at Theo and encouraging him to dance, until she notices Molly has stopped and then notices me. As soon as she does, Hannah spins around and turns off the karaoke machine.

"Sorry to interrupt," I say.

"Well, you did interrupt," Molly says, walking across the room, her cheeks still flushed with embarrassment, though her mouth is pulled into a smile. She grabs my hand and pulls me across the room. "So, it's your turn."

I let out a sharp laugh. "Yeah, no. That won't happen."

Theo wraps his arms around my legs and tries to drag me forward. "Come on, *siiiiing*."

"*Nooooo*," I say back to him in the same tone of voice. "It won't happen, but I will gladly watch."

Molly narrows her eyes at me playfully and then shrugs. "Fine, but no making fun of us."

"Never," I say, making a cross over my heart.

Hannah's joy seems to have dimmed since I arrived, and she glances over at me with narrowed eyes before she turns the music back on and continues singing.

I sit on the couch, and Theo practically hurls himself at me. He crawls into my lap and claps as his mom and Hannah sing another song. He even gets me to clap along, however reluctantly.

By the third song, I'm holding onto Theo's hands and waving them in the air to the beat, and he is giggling and joining in with the words he remembers.

The moment feels impossible. More like a dream than reality.

But I smile and enjoy myself so much that I can almost completely ignore the sour looks Hannah throws my way, clearly still upset by the fight she witnessed a few days earlier.

I can focus on Molly and Theo and this moment for our family—a happy break in the chaos.

13

MOLLY

Niamh's library is as big as my living room and dining room put together.

"What do you think?" Niamh asks, carrying in two mugs of tea. "Is it worth your time?"

"Absolutely," I say, unable to hide my enthusiasm. "This room is huge. It has so much potential."

I'm slightly embarrassed by my outburst. Despite living in Viktor's apartment and now in my own luxury space, I'm still not used to exactly how much more the other half have.

Niamh and Seamus have an actual house with three floors and huge windows and chandeliers so big I flinch a bit every time I walk underneath one, afraid it will come crashing down over my head.

She sets our drinks down on a large black rectangle that is serving as a coffee table and gestures for me to sit on the leather sofa next to her. "Good. I'm so excited to bring some life back into this room."

"It's a little dark in here," I admit.

It's an understatement. Heavy dark curtains hang over the windows, the walls are painted a dark gray, and the wood floors have been stained a brown so dark it is nearly black. Any light that manages to come through the open windows is immediately absorbed, leaving the entire room in gloom.

"A little?" Niamh laughs. "I feel like I'm being buried alive. I can't wait for you to use your magic touch on the space. I loved the pictures of Theo's nursery that Viktor sent. It looks lovely."

"A lot of that was Viktor's designer's decision. Honestly, I'll probably reach out to her for guidance through this process. I want to make sure you are happy and that I do a good job."

"You'll do great," Niamh assures me, laying her hand over mine. "Viktor has faith in you, so I do, too."

I smile in thanks and then shrug. "Viktor has more faith in me than I do."

"Because he loves you."

I know it is true, but it feels strange to hear it stated so boldly. Sometimes I forget so many people think we are truly married.

"Part of it is that you are still in the honeymoon period, too," Niamh says. "Seamus is sweet on me, but never quite as sweet as right after we got married. Is Viktor the same way?"

A week ago, I would have had to lie. But not now.

Viktor has stayed with me the last two nights. Ever since he walked in on Hannah and me singing karaoke. He didn't tell me he would be coming over, but I was happy to see him. So, I invited him to stay and then never asked him to leave. We've slept in the same bed and eaten breakfast together and done normal married couple things.

It has been nice.

"He's the same way," I nod.

"Is your boss a boss in the bedroom, too?" Niamh asks, eyebrows wagging.

My entire body goes warm, and Niamh must be able to see my blush because she giggles. "I'll take that as a yes."

The physical part of my relationship with Viktor has never been difficult. It is the emotional part that we have trouble with.

I woke up in the middle of the night last night to Viktor tossing and turning. He was whispering in his sleep. Just the word "no" over and over again. When I shook him awake, he sat straight up, his eyes wide, and then sighed in relief when he realized where he was.

"Bad dream?" I asked, pressing a kiss to his shoulder.

"A memory," he admitted. "The fire."

The fire that killed his parents.

He told me about it only once and had never spoken of it again.

He saved his brother and couldn't save his parents, no matter how badly Fedor wanted him to. Viktor wouldn't admit it, but he felt guilty. I tried to soothe him with my touch, but I could see his eyes were distracted, and eventually, he kissed my cheek and rolled away from me.

I couldn't blame him. I still haven't decided whether I will leave him or not … when this is all over. It makes sense why he doesn't want to be vulnerable with me.

Still, I wish he would be.

"I'm thinking about linen curtains here," Niamh says, pulling me from my thoughts.

She is standing next to the windows. I didn't even realize she'd moved. Hopefully I haven't been so deep in thought I ignored her.

"What do you think?" she asks.

I set my cup down and smile at her. "I think you and I are going to get along just fine. I love linen."

○

Theo and the nanny are coloring in the living room, and I kneel down on the floor next to my son and kiss him behind his ear.

"Where did Hannah go?"

"I don't know," Theo says distantly.

I muss his hair and turn to the nanny. She shrugs. "She just left a little bit ago. She didn't say where she was going. Sorry."

"Don't apologize. You aren't Hannah's babysitter," I joke. Besides, Hannah is free to come and go as she pleases.

She was feeling trapped early on in her stay with me, and after our disastrous lunch out when we ran into Viktor beating up two drug dealers, Hannah stopped going out with me. I don't blame her.

I'm tempted to call her and see, but I don't want it to look like I'm keeping tabs on her. Plus, she might be out looking for a job, in which case, I don't want to distract her. She has been taking calls in her room often. Each time, her eyes get big and she tells me it could be a possible job. Apparently, none of the jobs have panned out yet because Hannah hasn't said anything.

Or, just as likely, she needed some fresh air.

Either way, she'll be home later.

"Tell Viktor to come look at my picture," Theo says.

"Viktor is here?" I ask, spinning around as if he might have crept into the room without me noticing.

Theo nods, but doesn't give me any more information. I leave him to his colors and get up to search for Viktor. I find him quickly enough in the hallway bathroom. When I open the door, I hit his side.

"Sorry."

He steps back to let me in, and I freeze when I realize he is shirtless.

I've seen him naked, but it is still shocking to see the full expanse of his muscled chest without the proper preparation. Especially since he is twisted to one side, his muscles stretched and taut as he messes with his arm.

His arm.

"How is your cut?" I ask, my voice thick with desire. I clear my throat.

"Fine," he says, but I can see it is bleeding again.

I step into the room with him and slide between his body and the sink. "You need stitches."

He snorts in disagreement and continues trying to disinfect the wound himself. His arms are thick with muscle and it's hard for him to reach the spot on the back of his arm. I push his hands away and take over.

"What happened?"

"Nothing." Another lie. I can tell by the way he won't meet my eyes. And by the grazes on his knuckles.

"You can tell me the truth."

"I just did." His voice is flat and emotionless, and the distance has me confused and frustrated.

I never know what to expect from Viktor. Is he going to be warm and gentle? Or perhaps, serious and passionate? Or, worst of all, cold and distant? There is no consistency, and I'm getting emotional whiplash.

"If I'm your Bratva queen, you can't hide these things from me." I press a cotton ball soaked with disinfectant to the wound, and he winces.

"But you aren't," he says sharply. "Not really. We aren't married."

The words feel like a slap to the face, and I bite down on my reaction, trying to remain just as cold as he is. It is clear something happened to upset Viktor, and now he is taking it out on me, trying to pick a fight.

"Whether it's real or not, it feels real," I snap. "The pregnancy was an accident and the wedding was fake, but we are still a team. We still have a life together, and I deserve to know what is going on with you."

Viktor has stilled beneath my touch, and I realize all at once what I've just admitted to.

"It's real for you?" Viktor whispers.

I don't answer and instead slap a bandage over his wound and rush out of the bathroom and back into the living room where Theo is coloring.

A minute later, Viktor follows me.

"Molly," he says sternly, but with a hint of gentleness.

"Theo wanted to show you his picture." Theo jumps up and holds up his drawing to Viktor, and I'm not at all ashamed of using my son as a shield.

I'm not ready for this conversation. I'm not ready to admit my feelings to Viktor because I still don't understand them. I don't understand what they mean for me or my children or our future. Everything is up in the air, and I don't want to make any commitments that I can't keep.

Viktor admires Theo's drawing and pats his head, commissioning Theo to draw him a purple dinosaur blowing green fire. Theo, a born businessman, requests payment in the form of one piece of chocolate from the candy drawer in the kitchen.

"Don't undersell yourself," Viktor says. "You can have two pieces of chocolate."

With the promise of candy, Theo sets to work drawing the best dinosaur he can, and Viktor grabs my hand and pulls me far enough away that Theo can't hear us.

"Did you mean that?" he asks.

My shoulders droop forward, and I place my face in my hands. "I'm tired, Viktor. It has been a long day. Can we just—?"

"No, we can't." Viktor slides his hand from my elbow to my shoulder and squeezes. "Talk to me."

"Talk to me," I repeat back to him, my words shrill and slightly frantic. "Tell me the truth."

"I am telling you the truth," Viktor says, lowering his face to look into my eyes. "Nothing out of the ordinary happened today. These cuts and bruises and scrapes are my normal life, and I promise you, I'd tell you if something beyond the normal happened."

"You promise?"

He nods. "I swear it. We are a team."

My words sound different coming out of his mouth. And they land like physical blows.

"I shouldn't have said that."

His brows pull together and there is hurt in his blue eyes. "Why not? Did you mean it?"

I want to lie to him and tell him it was a mistake. I misspoke and I take it all back. But I can't.

"Yes, I meant it," I admit, twisting out of his touch. I can't think straight with him that close to me. It is why I slipped up in the bathroom in the first place. Having his naked chest two inches from my face makes me a bumbling idiot. "But the way I feel doesn't change the facts."

"It sure as hell does for me," Viktor says, putting himself in my line of sight again. "How does that not change things? If you care about me the way I care for you, then—"

"Then we'll be safe?" I ask, hating how harsh the question sounds. "Then you suddenly won't have any more enemies and my kids will be protected?"

Viktor stares at me, the lines in his face becoming more pronounced as frustration mounts inside of him. The same frustration that is building inside of me.

"See?" I throw up my hands in defeat. "It doesn't matter. This life is too dangerous for my kids, and I won't risk their safety for my feelings. I just ... I won't do it, Viktor."

He clenches his jaw, making it even more square than normal, and I resist the urge to reach out and massage his cheek. I want to be the person who eases Viktor's burdens. Like Seamus and Niamh, I want to be the person who stands by his side and makes this life easier to bear. I want to take his weight and carry it like my own, and I want to give him some of mine.

But I can't put any of that weight on Theo or my unborn baby. I simply won't do it.

So, I keep my hand fisted tightly at my side.

Finally, Viktor shakes his head. "This life is dangerous, but you know I'm working hard to make it less so. I'm doing what I can to get rid of Fedor, and I'm making alliances I never would have made even two months ago ... because of you."

"Don't do it on my account," I say, interrupting him.

"I have to," Viktor grinds out. "You are the reason I'm still fighting at all, Molly. You and Theo and our baby ... without you, I don't have a reason to fight. Don't you understand that?"

My heart cracks. From top to bottom, a line forms in the organ in my chest, and I feel it change irreparably.

My eyes fill with tears, and I blink them away.

"If you were really my wife," Viktor sighs and looks up towards the ceiling, like he is imagining it. "If you and I were really married, nothing would be different for me. I would still go above and beyond to keep you all safe. The only difference is that I wouldn't have to wonder when you're going to leave. But no matter what, I'll protect you and our kids until my dying breath."

Viktor's blue eyes pierce through me, leaving me breathless, and then he turns and walks back into the bathroom without another word. I stand in the same spot for a long time, wishing I could go after him and confess my feelings. But I don't. I stay motionless even as he collects his commissioned drawing from Theo and leaves without telling me where he is going.

14

VIKTOR

It feels good to have work to keep me busy. It's just a delivery of cash. Money made from various deals over the last few weeks that needs to be funneled through the motels I operate around the city. A lot of people pay cash for a night in the hotel, so it is easy enough to do.

Still, I'm grateful for the distraction.

After my conversation with Molly, I feel flustered and vulnerable. I need to get out and do something. Anything.

Usually, I'd call Petr in to handle something like this. Or, at least, oversee that it's done. But I'm not sure I can trust him anymore. George still hasn't gotten back to me about what Petr is doing in Italian territory, and I don't want to rock the boat until I have all of the facts. My boat has been rocked too many times as it is.

Just as I'm climbing back into my car, debating whether I should go back to Molly's place or mine, Molly calls.

"Hi." Her voice sounds small on the other end of the line, and I'm not sure why she is calling me. To apologize. For what? I can't even blame her for being afraid to be with me, even though it has me near the end of my rope.

"What's going on?"

"I just got off the phone with Niamh," she says, the words coming out in a rush. "She called, and I tried to tell her I needed to talk with you first, but she told me I could make decisions for the both of us, and the next thing I knew, I was agreeing to have her and Seamus over to our penthouse for dinner."

I nodded along, trying to take in what she's saying. "Okay, but we don't have a penthouse. Not together, at least."

"Hence the call." She sighs. "I wanted to give you space after ... well, *after*."

After she told me it was never going to happen. After I cut my chest open and handed her my heart, and she stood there silent and motionless.

I push the thoughts out of my head, trying to focus on the present.

"But," Molly continues. "I realized that we don't have a place together, so we'll need to pick one and ... make it home."

"Okay." I still feel slightly lost, but I'm catching up. "We'll just do it at your place."

"That's what I thought, too. Since Theo and I already have our stuff here. Plus, your place is still a total bachelor pad. Niamh would never believe I live there."

I can hear the teasing in her voice and it feels good to have a moment of normalcy. "So, it's settled."

"Yeah, but we still need to make it look like *our* house," she says. "Pictures of us. Mementos from our life together."

Seamus praised my attention to detail at the restaurant when I saved his life, but I know he has a keen eye himself. Molly and I haven't given him any reason to doubt our relationship as anything other than legitimate, but I don't want to give him any reason to be suspicious.

"That's smart. I'll arrange a photo shoot. I'll just make a few calls."

She lets out a small sigh of relief. "Okay. Great. We can just have them printed at the shop a few blocks over, and I have picture frames in the closet."

"And I'll go home, pack up some of my stuff, and bring it over …" I hesitate, still not sure whether I'm going to her place or not. I could easily make the decision, but I don't want to force myself on her. Not right now. If I want any chance of Molly changing her mind, I know I need to let her control the progression of our relationship. I forced her into the marriage, but I can't force her into loving me.

"Tonight," she says.

I've stayed at her house for the last two nights, but it still feels like a big deal for Molly to want me to come back. Especially after our conversation this afternoon. I laid my hopes out bare in front of her. Is this her way of accepting them?

I try not to put too much stock into her invitation, but I can't help it.

"Great. Then, I'll see you in a little bit."

"See you soon," she says softly.

～

At my house, I pack a suitcase with enough clothes to get me through a week, though that feels a bit too optimistic. Molly and I can't spend two days together without getting into an existential fight about our relationship. I might be gone as soon as dinner with Seamus and Niamh is over.

Then, I grab everything I need from the bathroom—I already have a toothbrush at Molly's—and a few pictures from my office of me standing in front of the Kremlin and the Grand Canyon. I leave all of the pictures of Fedor behind. I don't want to look at them anymore, and I know Molly doesn't either.

Just as I'm finishing up, my phone rings again. I answer without looking, assuming it is probably Molly calling to check on my progress.

"Viktor. It's George." George doesn't need to announce himself—his voice is deep enough that it's obvious—but he is too formal for anything less. "I've got news."

"Let's hear it," I say, though I hardly mean it. Whatever he has found out, I don't want to know. Something finally went right. Molly wants me to come over, and I'm excited about it. I don't feel like being brought down with bad news. Yet, I know this information can't be delayed.

"I followed Petr again today, but I didn't lose him this time. I know where he is going." He pauses for dramatic effect. "He has been going to the apartment of a well-known Mafiosi lieutenant."

My hand tightens on the phone and it takes every ounce of self-control I have not to throw it against the nearest wall.

"You're sure?"

"Yes," George says clearly. "He pulled a hat on before exiting his car, but I still recognized him. He was there for almost an hour before leaving. I saw his face as he left."

Shit, shit, shit.

"Thanks, George." My hands are shaking, but my voice is even. I'm grateful for that. I don't want anyone to know exactly how deep this cut goes. "I'll drop your payment at the diner."

As soon as I hang up with George, I call Seamus.

"Eager to see me again?" he asks by way of a greeting. "Niamh just told me we'll be seeing you tomorrow for dinner."

"Something like that," I admit, trying to keep my tone light. "I think I might know who told Fedor where to send the assassin."

"Who?" Seamus asks, all sign of warmth gone from his voice.

"Petr. My consigliere."

"Shit," Seamus says, echoing my sentiments from earlier. "I'm sorry, Viktor. What can I do?"

"Kidnap him and take him somewhere isolated. Somewhere I can question him later," I say. "I would do it, but I don't know who I can trust."

It's a lot to ask for from a new alliance, but considering Petr assisted in nearly ending Seamus' life, I know he won't mind helping out. I'm doing this for his benefit as well as my own.

"Done," he says. "It's the least I can do considering you saved my life. I'll take care of it and see you tomorrow."

I give him a half-hearted greeting and hang up. The moment I end the call, I drop down onto the couch and rest my face in my hands.

For my brother and now my cousin.

Can I truly trust no one?

∼

By the time I get all my suitcases in the car and get to Molly's, it's late. She doesn't respond to my text from the car, so I assume she is asleep as I unlock the door and step inside. The guards are still on duty, and after a quick check to be sure I'm not an enemy, they go back to their allocated corner of the apartment.

I drop my suitcases in the entryway and turn towards the kitchen, headed straight to the liquor cabinet for a drink. Soft footsteps sound behind me, and I smile at Molly's attempt at a sneaky approach.

"I'd make you a drink, but your condition doesn't allow it," I say before she can reach me, my back still towards her.

I feel a hand stroke down my shoulder blade, pressing into my tense muscles, and I relax slightly.

"I hope that isn't true because I've already had several drinks tonight."

The voice does not belong to Molly, and my entire body tenses. I spin around, sloshing some gin across the counter, and face Hannah.

Her eyes are bloodshot, and she is swaying on her feet even though she isn't moving.

"How many drinks?" I ask, my voice harsh and cold.

She lifts an eyebrow and shrugs. The simple movement sends her stumbling forward. She catches herself with a palm to my chest, and I react as though she burned me. I peel her hand off me and throw it back at her side.

"Never mind," I say. "It doesn't matter. You need to get to bed."

"Whose bed?" Hannah asks, her mouth tipping into a sloppy smile.

I sigh. I do not have the patience to deal with this. I've barely tolerated Hannah's presence here, mostly because she spends all of her time glaring at me like I'm scum and trying to turn Molly against me, and now she is coming onto me? No. Absolutely not.

"Yours," I say sternly, sliding down the counter and putting more distance between us. "Or, at least, it is yours so long as you don't touch me again. Where's Molly?"

"Sleeping," Hannah purrs, resting her hip against the counter and crossing her arms.

I realize for the first time that she is just wearing an oversized T-shirt. I assumed she had shorts on underneath, but no. I am seeing far too much of her thighs, and while it isn't tempting, it is maddening.

"What the fuck is your problem?" I growl.

"Yes, get angry," she says, her eyes widening with a perverse kind of pleasure. "I liked seeing you get angry the other day. You have a powerful punch. I wonder what else you can do with those hands."

"I could snap your neck like a twig," I say, my voice a low rumble. "Try to seduce me away from my wife again, and I won't hesitate."

Forgetting my drink on the counter, I walk around the island, grab my bags, and jog up the stairs to Molly's room.

I plan to tell Molly immediately. This is exactly the kind of thing that could be twisted and distorted to make me look like a cheating piece of shit, and I don't want anything to come between us. Anything else, that is. There are already a million obstacles between us and a happy ending, but I won't let a lying bitch like Hannah be one of them.

When I walk into Molly's room, however, she is sitting in bed with the laptop I bought her open, smiling at the screen.

"You're home," she says.

Home. That single word is more powerfully seductive than anything Hannah just tried in the kitchen. The simple idea that Molly is happy to see me and wants me here, that I could ever belong here with her and Theo, is enough to get my engine revved.

"Hi," I say, dropping my bags and crawling across the bed. I lean over the computer screen, stroke Molly's cheek with my palm, and tilt her face up for a kiss. Her lips are soft and pliant, and she releases a small moan as I slip my tongue into her mouth and nip at her lower lip. When we pull apart, her brown eyes are glazed over.

"Wow," she breathes.

I roll over and lie next to her, my hand slipping under the covers to rest on her exposed thigh.

"What was that for?" she asks.

I shrug and circle my finger over her smooth skin. "Just hello."

"In that case, goodbye." She waves at me, her hand curled under her chin. I frown, confused, and then she grins and leans in for another kiss.

This feels perfect. Magical. Dreamlike.

Yet, there is a current of guilt sitting in my stomach as Molly strokes her hands down my chest. I need to tell her what her friend tried to do. She deserves to know.

We are both breathless when she pulls away. "We should say goodbye a lot more often if hellos are going to be that good."

I grab her hand from my chest and kiss her knuckles. "What are you still doing up? I assumed you'd be asleep."

She rests back on her pillow and points at her computer. "Just reminiscing."

I twist over to see her screen, and my stomach drops.

It's a picture of Molly and Hannah when they were younger. Just teenagers. Molly's eyes are bright, her smile carefree and wide. She looks happy, her arm slung over a younger Hannah's shoulders.

"It's the only picture I have of the two of us together," Molly says. "I had to search through, like, twenty old classmates' Facebooks to find it, but there it is. Both of us before life kicked the crap out of us."

She laughs, but then frowns. "Sorry, that sounds dark. It's just …"

"Life kicked the crap out of you," I finish for her. "You don't have to apologize to me."

She gives me a sad smile and sighs. "Hannah gets me, you know? I know the two of you are tense around each other, but she knew me before the shit hit the fan, and I like that we have so much in common. She understands my feelings on a lot of things. In a way no one else can."

The knife in my stomach twists. "Not even me?"

"Not even you," she says gently. Molly curls her fingers around my hand on her thigh. "You've been through a lot, too, but Hannah and I both had kids so young and spent time on the streets. We lived the same way for so long that we can understand each other."

I nod and swallow.

So much has been taken from Molly in her lifetime. Do I really want to take this away, too? She has a friend. Someone she likes and relates to and trusts. Can I really strip that away?

"Viktor?" Molly's voice is gentle. "Are you mad?"

Hannah was drunk. That much was obvious.

Even though her actions were reprehensible, there is every chance she'll wake up and deeply regret them. Or, better yet, that she won't remember the encounter at all. Should I really threaten their friendship over something that might not matter after a good night's sleep and a few painkillers?

"Nothing." I shake my head and kiss her. "It's nothing."

I kick off my shoes, slide out of my jeans, and crawl under the blankets with Molly. She closes her laptop and curls into me, too. As though it is normal. Natural. As though we've done this every night before this and we'll do it every night after.

It feels good enough that I allow myself to forget what happened in the kitchen.

If it happens again, I'll tell Molly. Without hesitation.

But for now, I'll find solace in Molly.

A voice in the back of my head reminds me that I need to stay cold, detached. When I relax and let my guard down, bad things happen. But with Molly's small body curled against mine, her breath warm on my chest, it's impossible to feel anything other than delicious warmth.

15

MOLLY

"Wait, so you are holding a photo shoot today so you have family pictures in your house to impress the boss of an Irish Mafiosa?"

"Exactly," I say, sighing and shaking my head. "It sounds crazy when you say it like that."

"It is crazy," Hannah says, taking a long sip of coffee. "I just don't understand why it is important that you look like a picture-perfect family. Aren't these people your friends?"

"I hope so," I admit. "I really like Niamh, but it is also important for an alliance. We have to make sure they trust us."

Hannah nods. "So, you're going to lie to them?"

I stab my eggs and shove them in my mouth. "I guess so."

"Sounds healthy."

I don't respond. Partly because I've shoved another bite of eggs into my mouth and partly because Hannah's tone is annoying. I'm not sure whether she means to or not, but every comment is a subtle dig at my marriage. At my relationship. I've allowed her to live here with me and it feels like she is judging me and Viktor at every turn.

"I don't understand why you can't just tell them the truth. You are married, but you both like your space." Hannah shrugs. "It definitely isn't normal, and most people would think it hinted at issues in your relationship, but that is between you and your husband."

"Exactly," I snap. "Me and my husband."

Hannah must take my not very subtle hint because her eyes widen in a moment of surprise and then she devotes herself wholly to finishing her breakfast and coffee.

I've confided in Hannah about a lot of things, but Viktor and I are moving towards being in a good place, and I don't want to feel bad about how we got here. I have enough stress in my life without worrying what Hannah thinks of it all, too. I know she isn't entirely happy that Viktor has been staying over, but again, it isn't her business. If she doesn't want to live with him, then she can find her own place.

"Hey," Hannah says, snapping her fingers like she has just had a great idea. "If you two need to take some couple's photos, I can keep an eye on Theo for a while."

"They are family photos," I say sharply. I immediately regret my harsh tone. I can tell she is trying to make amends for overstepping. "But thanks."

"Oh I know. I just know how kids can be taking photos. It might be easier if I just brought him by the shoot a little later so you could get pictures with him after you've done couple photos."

"It will be fine, I'm sure. There will be people there to entertain him if he gets rowdy." I finish off the last bit of coffee in my mug and stand up to head inside. Viktor and Theo are inside playing together. I invited them to breakfast with us, but Viktor seemed reluctant, so I didn't push it.

Hannah follows after me, nearly breathless. "I guess I just wanted some company. The house is so empty when you all are gone. I really don't mind keeping an eye on him for—"

"It's fine, Hannah." The words come out on a laugh, mostly out of exasperation. I'm not sure why this is so important to her. I know she has been missing her own son, but this is the first time she has been so adamant about it. "I appreciate it, but it's not necessary. We'll all hang out another night, okay?"

Hannah bites her lip and then nods, lifting one hand in surrender. "Sorry. I think I'm a little hungover. I drank too much last night and it has made me crazy. Apparently, I'm a clingy drunk."

"It's fine." I grip her elbow as I pass. "I'm glad you like Theo. It's nice that the two of you are close."

Hannah's mouth pulls into a tight smile and then I head upstairs to get ready for the shoot.

Hannah wasn't wrong, though. Even after a morning of running around upstairs with Viktor, Theo is wild at the shoot. He is blurry in half of the photos and pouting in the other half. Still, it's a good time.

"Come on, bud," Viktor begs. "Give us a happy smile."

Theo pouts and crosses his arms. "I want to play."

I'm about to get stern with Theo, threatening to take toys away if he doesn't smile, when Viktor suddenly tickles Theo under the armpits. Immediately, his face bursts into an open-mouthed grin, and he shrieks.

Distantly, I hear the camera shutter opening and closing, catching every moment, but I'm laughing too hard at Theo's banshee shrieks to think about what we must look like.

Viktor arranged for our pictures to be taken in a photographer's studio downtown. It is a large warehouse-like space with different sets lining the walls. There is one with red barnwood and a broken-down truck filled with hay and another that is half of a carousel with a carnival scene painted on the back. The photographer assures us several times that he will make every scene look entirely real in the final edits.

"You'll have time to do it all in a few hours?" Viktor asked.

The photographer laughed. "With how much you're paying me, I'm motivated enough to do it all in a few minutes."

We change clothes and hair between shots, which is when Theo gets the most upset. It is hard to convince him to get dressed once every day, so costume changes aren't going well. He breaks down between every shoot and has to be tickled into happy tears by Viktor before we continue.

Finally, however, we are done with the family shots and the photographer's assistant takes Theo to a play area in the middle of the room. Of course, they've prepared for the likely possibility that kids will need to be occupied during the photo shoots. While he is busy, Viktor and I are sent into back rooms to change into our final outfits.

The wedding dress Viktor got for me is the same silhouette as the one I wore on our actual (fake) wedding day, but one hundred times more extravagant. Bits of crystal are stitched all across a lacy material, and it hangs from my body like it was made specifically for me. The only difference is that the plunging neckline shows a bit more of my cleavage now that my breasts are larger due to pregnancy hormones. So, when I step out of the room and find Viktor standing in the hallway, his eyes go wide when he sees me.

I can feel his gaze like a physical touch, but I'm too busy devouring the sight of him in his navy-blue suit and crisp white shirt to feel flushed or embarrassed. All I feel is a bottomless kind of warmth deep in my stomach. He looks incredible.

"Beautiful," Viktor whispers, holding out his hand. When I grab it, his fingers whisper over my skin like I'm something precious, and in this moment, I do feel precious. Cherished.

The photographer selects a set with fake flowers dripping from an archway and a pale pink sunset in the background. It feels like the background you'd stand in front of for cruise ship photos, but I am too focused on Viktor to care at all.

There are pictures taken of us holding hands and staring into each other's eyes. Pictures of Viktor standing behind me, his arms wrapped around my body. He presses his palms against my stomach, caressing me and our unborn baby in a way that, no matter what happens, I'll always treasure.

Then, before I can react, Viktor spins me around and dips me backwards. I let out a yelp, but it is lost when his lips press over mine, stealing my breath. My hand holding the bouquet drops back, limp, as my ability to move my own limbs is kissed out of me.

He nibbles my lower lip and tilts his mouth against mine in a way that is intimate and private and sensual ... except, it isn't.

After a while, the photographer clears his throat, and Viktor pulls away from me. I curl my free hand in his hair to keep him close, and he laughs, his breath warm over my mouth. "I think we got carried away."

"Carry me away," I say, giving him permission. "Far away. Right now."

"Family shots," the photographer says, clapping his hands and clearing away the sensual haze that had me almost letting Viktor ravage me in front of a camera. "You two look too good not to have the little guy in there with you.

Theo had on a pair of gray pants and suspenders for the last shot, so they are able to help him shrug on a small jacket and have him ready for these family shots.

"Go stand with your dad," the photographer says.

Viktor opens his mouth to correct him. We've never formally discussed his role in Theo's life, and we've certainly never told Theo Viktor is his dad. But before Viktor can say anything, Theo runs straight towards him, arms outstretched. When Viktor scoops him up, Theo yells, "Dada!"

I see the stunned joy on Viktor's face, and I'm sure my expression is much the same.

Viktor kisses his cheek and then wraps his arm around me.

"This feels real," Viktor says, repeating my words from our argument the other day. Then, he says it again, squeezing me closer to him. "This feels real."

I'm still swimming in the confusing feelings and joy and desire inside of me when there is a loud banging noise from the front of the studio.

The photographer frowns and turns towards the sound. I'm so wrapped up in my little family and the illusion of us standing in front of the fake backgrounds that I don't turn towards the noise until the banging happens again, this time closer.

I look at the double front doors just as they burst open and a group of black-clad men comes pouring through them.

Instinctively, I reach for Theo. He is in Viktor's arms, but Viktor gives him to me immediately, and then moves to stand in front of both of us, his arms outstretched.

"What—?" the photographer asks, backing away slowly. When he notices the men have guns, he turns and full-on sprints across the studio and behind the fake carousel. I don't blame him. I'm tempted to do the same, but I know these men are here for us.

The men rush forward, guns first, and surround us. Each of the ten weapons that I can count is pointed directly at Viktor. At us. I know Viktor has a weapon strapped to his side, but it isn't enough to take on ten or more men. And I'm sure Viktor would have had guards keeping watch outside, but they've apparently been overpowered as well, otherwise there would have been more of a fight out front.

"Who are you?" Viktor growls. We are outnumbered and outmatched, but his deep voice still sends goose bumps down my arms. It sounds like the voice of death himself. "What do you want?"

"Easy, brother."

Viktor stiffens at the voice, and I recognize it immediately.

Fedor.

I peek around Viktor's arm while trying to keep Theo hidden from view. Surely, Fedor knows Theo is here. That is why he is here at all, after all. For Theo. Still, I don't want him to lay a hand or his eyes on my son. On Viktor's son.

"Nobody needs to get hurt," Fedor says. He lifts his hands as though he is the rational one. As though he is trying to keep the situation from escalating, like he didn't just barge into the room with a small army.

"Nobody will get hurt," Viktor says. "Leave. You shouldn't be here."

"Haven't you learned by now, Vik? I can be wherever I want." Fedor folds his hands behind his back and begins pacing back and forth. He looks thinner than the last time I saw him. His cheeks are sunken in and there are dark circles under his eyes. If anything, he looks more dangerous than before. It is obvious his physical health is failing with his mental health, which only makes him more dangerous. He truly has nothing left to lose.

"Or, have you missed all of my little gifts?"

I wonder what he means, but I can tell Viktor understands. His shoulders lift defensively. "You've made your point clear. You are willing to destroy everything Dad and I built. And for what? Vengeance? Does it make you feel good to kill innocent men and ruin my front businesses?"

"It's justice," Fedor snaps, his top lip pulled back in a scowl. Immediately, he seems to regret his loss of control and smooths a hand down his button-down shirt. It is slim but still hangs from his small frame. "You've built yourself a pedestal to stand on. A place where you can feel powerful and in control. I'm simply trying to show you that a big throne makes an easy target."

"What is this about?" Viktor sounds bored, but I can feel the tension behind his words. He is pulled taut, ready to snap at a moment's notice. "Why are you here?"

"I'm here because you've taken something that is mine." Fedor leans to the side, his eyebrows lifted, and catches my eye. He lifts his hand in a wiggling-finger wave. "Where's my little boy?"

A low, primal growl tears out of Viktor's throat. "He isn't yours."

"Then whose is he?" Fedor asks. "He certainly isn't yours. I mean, look at how handsome he is. He clearly got that from me. No offense, Vik, but you are more of the muscled, masculine type. Theo and I are of the pretty handsome variety."

Fedor leans to the other side and grins. "Isn't that right, kiddo?"

I realize too late that Theo has straightened up on my hip and is looking at Fedor over Viktor's shoulder. I twist him down and back, breaking their eye contact. Theo gasps and then buries his face in my neck. I pat his back and whisper quietly in his ear.

"It'll be okay," I whisper, trying to convince myself of the words as well.

"How did you know we'd be here?" Viktor asks. "I kept this location a secret. Only a handful of people knew where we'd be. Who told you?"

Fedor grins and shrugs. "Would you believe that I'm all-knowing?"

"Was it Petr?"

At that, Fedor frowns and it looks genuine. He is confused, and so am

I. Viktor hasn't mentioned any doubts about Petr to me. This is the first I'm hearing about it, and it makes me wonder what else has been going on that I've missed.

"What the fuck does this have to do with Petr?" Fedor asks.

Viktor shakes his head. "Just give it up. I know Petr is working for you. You might as well admit it."

Fedor looks like this is news to him, and I'm tempted to believe his act. "I don't know what you're talking about."

"Phone taps?" Viktor prods. "Or bugs in the apartment? Is that why you sent a goon to the apartment a few weeks back? Not to get Theo, but to leave a mic."

"Damn. Missed opportunity," Fedor says. "That would have been a good idea." He shrugs. "Unfortunately, no. Even if that was true, I still wouldn't tell you. It doesn't matter, anyway."

"It does to me," Viktor says. He reaches back to touch my leg, as if to check I'm still there. I lean into his touch, trying to offer what little reassurance I can.

"Well, it shouldn't. I'm here to end this, brother. Once and for all, and I meant what I said. I don't want anyone to get hurt."

"Tell that to your army," Viktor grumbles.

"Don't put up a fight and they won't shoot." Fedor shrugs like it is that simple. "Believe me, I'd end it quickly if I could. You've more than earned a bullet to the brain by now, but I think it will be easier to bring the rest of your men in line if you are alive. If they see you brought to your knees, they won't respect you anymore. They'll see that I bested you. That I'm the true leader of the Kornilov Bratva."

"Why do you need my men? You've had the Italians sucking your balls for a while now."

Fedor's mouth tenses into a hard line. "They aren't my men. They are helpful to me, but I want my own kin around me. The men I've grown up with, who I trained with. And you are the only one who can help me get them."

Viktor takes one step forward and every gun in the room lifts slightly, ready to take aim should he do something foolish. I reach out and grab the back of his shirt, but it isn't necessary. He is simply leaning forward so Fedor can understand how serious he is about his next few words: "Over my dead body."

I wish he wouldn't say things like that. Fedor's eyes are pitch-black and wild. He is so far gone I'm not sure there is anything human in him left, and he might take Viktor's words as truth. He might believe he can only get what he wants if Viktor is dead and decide to riddle him with bullet holes right now.

"Come on. Be reasonable." Again, Fedor is playing at rationality, but he is incapable of it. "Because it wouldn't be over your dead body, brother. It would be over hers."

I don't need to look up to know he is talking about me, and the meaning is apparently clear enough to Viktor as well, because he growls again.

"Just give them both to me," Fedor says. "I won't hurt them ... much."

"Not a chance in hell." The words are out of Viktor's mouth before Fedor can even finish. "There is no way you are leaving here with them today. None."

Fedor laughs and the sound sends goose bumps down my back. "We'll see about that."

16

VIKTOR

I wish I could turn around and tell Molly it will all be all right. I wish I could squeeze her hand and tell her we'll all get out of this.

Because we will.

She doesn't know it yet, but I planned for this.

Well, not *this*, exactly. But I planned for this possibility.

I knew I had a leak, so I called the men I knew I could trust and posted them in buildings around the photo shoot, ready to strike should anything go wrong. Like, for instance, if Fedor came pouring into the building with ten armed men.

All I need to do is keep him talking, and my men will be here any second. It is easy because Fedor is convinced he is in control right now. He is pacing back and forth slowly, savoring what he believes is his conquest over me.

"Fedor, you don't have to do this," I say, changing my tone. Up until this point, I've been hostile, argumentative. I knew Fedor would want to break me down. He wouldn't want to take me kicking and screaming. He wants me to go out with a whimper, not a bang. So, I whimper. "We used to be a team. A dynamic duo. We can be that again."

Fedor's smile is sad. He is looking at me like I'm an injured animal on the side of the road, and he is trying to decide whether he should put me out of my misery or not.

"Don't beg, brother. It's beneath you."

"Maybe," I admit. "But I don't want things to end badly between us. We are the only family each other has. We shouldn't be enemies. It's not natural."

A flicker of something flashes behind his cold eyes, and I think I catch a glimpse of my real brother. Not the emotionless monster in front of me, but the scared little boy I know is living inside.

Then, Theo whimpers. "Dada."

Whatever guard Fedor may have dropped is hauled back up in an instant, and his eyes are bottomless wells of darkness.

"Do you really believe that?" Fedor asks. "Honestly, Viktor, do you think you would ever forgive me for seducing your now-wife and fathering the child you are trying to claim as your own? Is that something you could look past? That I fucked your woman?"

"Raped," Molly says, stepping out from behind me just far enough to make eye contact with Fedor. "You didn't seduce me, you drugged me. And it wasn't a fuck, it was rape. It was criminal."

Fedor grins, thrilled that he managed to draw her out and into the fight. I want to wrap her in my arms and hold her back, but Molly is unknowingly assisting me in my plan to keep Fedor preoccupied. Because all of his attention is on her now.

"I don't know," Fedor says. "You didn't have any complaints when you took me in your mouth."

Molly flinches, and my vision momentarily goes red. She has told me she doesn't remember that night at all, so there is no way to know whether what Fedor is saying is true, but I have no reason to doubt him. He is a sick fuck, and if I ever get the chance, I'll kill him.

Luckily for Fedor, before I can act on my urges, the door behind him bursts open again. Except, this time, instead of being his men, it is mine.

Twenty men with guns charge in and surround Fedor and his men.

Fedor's eyes go wide, and he turns around to stare at me with betrayal in his eyes. As though I somehow betrayed him rather than the other way around.

"I thought you really wanted to reconcile," he says, his arms flopping at his sides. "Turns out, you were just keeping me talking while your men moved in."

He clicks his tongue in disappointment.

"Leave," I say simply. "My men won't fire if yours don't. If yours do, then we're all dead. No one will make it out of here."

"Mutually assured destruction," Fedor says in a bored voice. "I get it."

I can see him actually thinking it through. Honestly trying to decide whether it is worth it to die here today in order to get revenge on me. And I realize then exactly how far gone Fedor is. Not only is he a homicidal monster, but he is suicidal, too. He has no regard for human life at all, his or anyone else's.

"What happened to you?" I say, almost to myself, though Fedor hears me.

"What do you mean?" Fedor asks with a smile, playing dumb.

"How did you get here? I was there for you. I took care of you our entire childhood. I did my best to support you and care for you. Yet, somehow, you turned into this monster. I don't understand."

Fedor begins to pace again, and I notice my men are keeping their guns trained on him, moving them back and forth to match his pacing. Then, he shrugs.

"You know, I haven't spent much time thinking about it, but when I do, I think it all might have started the night I killed our parents."

My back stiffens. I feel like he just punched me straight in the chest. I'm so startled I can't even manage to inhale. I just stare at him, gaping.

Fedor is enjoying my shock.

"Did you not know that?" he asks, knowing full well I didn't. "I guess it slipped my mind. But yes, I killed them. I set the fire."

I feel Molly's hand resting on my shoulder. She is trying to comfort me, trying to keep me calm, and I lean back slightly into her chest, resting on the reality of her standing behind me.

"You're lying."

"Unfortunately, I'm not." Fedor stops pacing and looks directly in my eyes. "I was just a kid, but I remember the firefighters saying it was an electrical fire. Some bad wiring in the guest room that tore through the wall behind our parents' bed and took them in their sleep. But what the fire chief didn't know is that I was the one who tinkered with the wiring."

I shake my head. "You didn't know what you were doing."

"Maybe not," Fedor shrugs. "But I knew enough to know it was my fault. Curiosity killed the cat. In this case, I had the curiosity, and our parents were the cats. Bad luck for them."

I know he is only telling me this now because his plan failed. Because he is angry and lashing out is what he does best. When he can't get the upper hand, he has always gone for emotional terrorism. He is just trying to rattle me. So, I want to believe it is a lie, but I can see the truth of it in his eyes now.

Fedor was standing there with me when the fire chief told us how the fire started, and I have relived the moment over and over again in the years since. The way Fedor didn't collapse in sobs or fall apart. His face went blank and emotionless, and I assumed he was in shock. Turns out he was, but for an entirely different reason. He was in shock because he started the fire. He is the reason our parents died.

"Why didn't you tell me?"

"It wouldn't have changed anything," Fedor says coldly. "They would always be dead, and it would always be my fault. So, I decided to own it. Let it make me stronger."

If I wasn't so close to being sick, I would laugh. Fedor thinks this is strength. He thinks being murderous and unhinged is power, and it is laughable and pitiable and terrifying.

"If I walk out, will your men shoot me in the back?" Fedor asks.

"Mutually assured destruction," I remind him. "And unlike you, I'm not willing to die for this feud."

He shrugs like that is my personal choice and directs his men to leave.

I don't breathe until they are all gone and my men are standing around us in a circle, guns pointed outwards.

As soon as I'm positive we are all safe, I spin around and wrap my arms around Molly and Theo.

Tears are rolling down Molly's cheeks, and Theo is shaking in her arms, and I wish I could do more to comfort them. All I can do is lead them from the warehouse and into the waiting car.

Once Molly's tears stop, she is shockingly calm. Her face is neutral, eyes blank, and she hugs Theo on her lap and kisses his cheek occasionally, but doesn't say anything else.

Theo manages to fall asleep on the drive home, which only goes to show how adaptable children are, and Molly walks him up to his room and puts him down for a nap while I check the security on the apartment. I triple-check that everything is locked down before I go up and find Molly standing next to the bed.

I walk up behind her and gently wrap my arms around her waist, pressing a kiss to her neck. She doesn't respond at all. Her body stays rigid, and when I look up, I realize why.

There is a suitcase sitting on the edge of the bed.

It is empty, but Molly is standing in front of it, staring down at it like she is waiting for it to begin speaking to her.

"Molly?" I say softly, trying to keep my voice even, free of the fear and rage and confusion clouding my thoughts.

"If this was any other relationship, I'd leave." The words are matter-of-fact and simple. "I'd pack up my things and get out of here ... but I can't."

I feel numb. I'd rather have a gun pointed at my head right now than hear her say these words. I'd rather face down my brother in hand-to-hand combat than listen to Molly wish she could leave me. Because I want her. Only her. Always her.

I've tried my best to stay cold and calculating, to keep my emotions separate from my actions to ensure I make the best decisions for her and Theo and our unborn baby, but it has all been for naught. Because right now, I burn for Molly. I'm not emotionally distant from her. I'm entangled in her. My heart is beating outside of my body, and at any second, Molly could stomp on it and end me.

"And do you want to know the craziest part?" Molly whispers.

No, I think. *I don't.*

Molly turns around and tears are tracking down her cheeks now. She is still in the wedding dress she wore during our photo shoot and mascara is slipping down her face.

"The craziest part is that I'm not sure I *want* to leave."

A sob slips between her lips, and I pull her against my chest. She leans into me, not knowing how much I need this. How much her presence is comforting to me, even if it is wrecking me at the same time.

17

MOLLY

Viktor holds me for a while—how long, I'm not entirely sure—and when he pulls away, his eyes are far away from me.

"I need to—"

"Stay," I say, cutting off whatever he was about to say. "Please. Don't go. Please stay."

Viktor's face softens, and he tucks a strand of hair behind my ear. "You don't need to be afraid. The house is well-guarded."

"I don't feel safe without you." It's true. Not only will I not feel safe, but I'll never be able to relax, wondering where he is and what he is doing. Worried he will go after Fedor for revenge. "Please stay."

After a few seconds of thought, he nods. "Of course. I'll stay."

Viktor undoes his tie and hangs up his suit, and I slip out of my dress and into a pair of jeans and a sweater. Then, we start decorating the house with some of the things Viktor brought from his place. Enough has happened in the last twenty-four hours that I almost forgot about Niamh and Seamus coming over. And honestly, compared to nearly dying, Seamus doubting the truth of our marriage seems like nothing. Certainly not something to risk our lives over.

Still, I'm grateful for the distraction of decorating. I set up some of Viktor's photos in the living room and the office, arranging one on the desk where he brought me to a soul-crushing orgasm only a few days ago. I notice there are no pictures of Fedor in the bunch, and I assume that is on purpose. Probably for my sake, but maybe also for his.

I want to ask how Viktor is taking the news that Fedor is the reason his parents are dead, but I don't want to pry. Besides, I think we both need a distraction from reality right now.

We've just finished with the decorations he brought when the pictures from the photo shoot are delivered in a manila envelope. We planned to print them ourselves, but we were in no state to leave the apartment, so Viktor made a phone call and someone arranged it. It sure is nice being powerful sometimes. I'm surprised the photographer pulled himself together enough to edit them. They aren't perfect, but as long as no one studies them intensely, they won't notice the fake scenes in the background or the slightly inconsistent lighting. For being done on such short notice, they look pretty good.

"What about the toothpaste cap?" Viktor asks from the downstairs bathroom.

"What about it?" I ask, putting down the last frame on a bookshelf and moving to stand in the bathroom.

"Well," he says, pointing to the toothpaste tube I dropped on the back of the sink this morning. "I've noticed you are a barbarian and leave the cap off the toothpaste, but I am civilized and put it back on once I'm done."

A shocked gasp rushes out of me, nearly a laugh. "Excuse me? I'm a barbarian?"

"Unfortunately," he says, pressing his lips into a flat line. "So, should I leave it off to show that we actually live here and are slobs, or should I put the cap on and hide it in the drawer to impress them?"

Despite everything, I have to fight back a laugh. "If those are my only two options, then leave it off."

"Why?" he asks, eyes narrowed.

I lay a hand on his chest and press up onto my tiptoes to give him a soft kiss. "Because I want them to know I always get my way."

I spin out of the bathroom and move up the stairs before Viktor can argue, but I feel him hot on my heels. Just before I get to the bedroom, he wraps an arm around my waist and spins me around, pinning me to the wall.

"Fine, we can put the cap on," I say, holding my hands up in surrender and trying not to dissolve into giggles.

Viktor shakes his head and bends low, his lips less than an inch from mine. "No, we'll leave it off."

"Really?"

He nods. "Yes, but not to show you always get your way. It's to show them you have me wrapped around your finger."

I'm not convinced Seamus and Niamh will use the state of our toothpaste as a direct metaphor for our relationship, but my stomach still flips when he speaks.

This is exactly why it's hard for me to leave. Why I'm torn on what to do.

Because Viktor makes me feel alive. His presence is like a bolt of electricity through me, shocking me back to life. Before him, I muddled through. I had moments of joy playing with Theo, but beyond that, my life was gray. With Viktor, I've experienced every shade of the rainbow. Every emotion and fear and feeling. Some terrible, some amazing. And I'm not sure the terrible outweighs the amazing.

In fact, the more time I spend with Viktor, the more the amazing times start to outweigh everything else. Even the danger.

Viktor loosens his grip on me enough that I twist away and go into the bedroom. There, we have even more to decide.

"I've been sleeping on the right side of the bed, but I prefer the left," Viktor says.

I shake my head. "Tough luck. I'm not sleeping closest to the door."

He frowns. "Why not?"

"Murderers," I say, like it is obvious. That has been my reason for not sleeping close to the door my entire life and it has always sounded absurd. Now, however, it is a real possibility that murderers will pour into our bedroom. But if they do, I'm not sure being two feet further from the door will do much to spare me.

Still, Viktor holds up his hands in defeat. "Fine. I'll sacrifice myself first in the event that someone comes into our room to murder us. You just have to promise that if they do, you'll try to run. I don't want to die for nothing."

"Promise," I say, trying to keep my tone light as I move to the closet. "The other problem is there is no room for your clothes in here."

He comes to stand next to me, his hands on his hips. "How do you have this many clothes?"

"You bought them for me! Don't blame me. You gave me more than I could ever wear."

He sighs and begins riffling through the closet and pulling things out. Quickly, I realize he is pulling out all of my sweaters, T-shirts, and sweatpants and laying them on the bed, leaving behind my dresses, low-cut tops, and jeans.

"What are you doing?"

"Get rid of everything on the bed and keep what's in the closet," he says.

I grab his arm as he threatens to throw my favorite pair of pajama pants over his shoulder. "You're taking all my comfortable clothes and leaving me the skimpy stuff."

He wags his eyebrows mischievously. "Like you said, I bought it all. Shouldn't I be the one to decide what stays and what goes?"

I scoop up the stuff on the bed and begin hanging it back up. "Absolutely not. It all stays. Even these."

I hold up a pair of fuzzy pajama pants with cartoon frogs all over them—the only thing I actually bought myself. Viktor wrinkles his nose. "We can throw away the cap to the toothpaste if you get rid of those."

"Never!" I scream, laughing maniacally.

Viktor walks away, shaking his head, but I see his shoulders shaking with laughter.

Over the next hour, we reorganize some of the furniture to better suit a life together—pushing two armchairs close together, setting out two mugs next to the coffee pot, and putting Viktor's home weights next to my elliptical machine. By the time we are done, it looks like a well-lived in house, and I'm sweaty.

"I need to clean up before they get here. I'm sticky," I say, wiping my arm across my forehead.

When I look over, Viktor is watching me, his eyes more focused than they were just a moment ago. His gaze slips down my body, and I know what he is thinking.

I wasn't thinking it, but I am now.

"Are you going to shower, too?" I ask innocently.

He nods slowly. "I should."

We stare at one another for a long time, and I can feel the unspoken question in the tilt of Viktor's head as he watches me.

Is it too soon? Too soon to want this after what happened today? Are you ready? Are we okay?

Honestly, the right answer might be that it is far too soon. That I'm too raw to make a good decision or think clearly. But right now, I don't care about being right. I'd rather be wrong with Viktor than right without him.

So, in answer, I grab his hand and pull him behind me all the way back upstairs and into the bathroom. I let go only to start the water and let it get warm.

The room quickly starts to fill with steam, and I turn back to him and undo the button of his jeans. Viktor watches my fingers carefully, as though his very life depends upon my next movements. I grab the hem of his shirt, pulling it over his head in one quick motion. He lifts his arms to help, stretching the strong muscles of his abdomen in a way that makes my mouth water. Then, he pushes his jeans down while I start to take my own jeans off.

I only wiggle my hips once to shimmy out of my jeans before Viktor replaces my hands with his own and hooks his fingers in the waistband. He drops to his knees in front of me in nothing more than his boxers and peels the denim down, his eyes taking in the sight of me, inch by inch until I'm free of the pants, and he can sweep his fingers over my skin.

The room is entirely foggy now. The air is thick and warm, but goose bumps still rise over my arms and legs as Viktor grabs the hem of my shirt and pushes it up my body, his palms sliding over my breasts as he lifts it over my head.

As soon as the shirt is gone, his mouth drops to my neck, and I lose track of what happens to my panties and bra, but I don't care. Burn them. I'll never wear undergarments again if the reward is this feeling. This heady, blissed-out warmth that seeps into my head and heart and lungs and makes everything okay.

That is when it hits me that Viktor is a drug.

I've made it a point not to become a statistic. To not be another homeless person on drugs who makes money only to spend it on her next fix. I've always been proud of keeping myself clean.

Yet, here I am, needing Viktor. Despite the lows he has brought into my life, he has also brought the highest highs. Those highs are what I keep chasing.

Having his body close to me, his protection, his loving gaze and warm smile is what keeps me coming back again and again. It is what makes it hard to leave.

Viktor presses my body against his, and I feel his excitement on my hip as he carries me into the shower. He stands with his back to the spray, blocking me from most of the water. When I look up, water is hitting his back and spraying outward, catching the light so it looks like there is a halo around his head.

The image is almost absurd.

My Viktor is as beautiful as an angel, but he is no angel. He should be swathed in shadows and darkness, not light.

My Viktor.

He dips his head, water washing over his shoulders and down his chest, and I follow the path with my fingers, touching each curve of his abdomen and following the slope of the deep indentation that leads from his hip to …

Viktor moans when I wrap my hand around him, and he tips his head back, letting the water hit him directly in the face.

I laugh and stroke him again, but a second later, I'm the one moaning. Viktor's hand slides between my thighs and finds my center easily.

I'm wet and ready for him, and he slides a digit into me and then another, pulsing into me with slow, deliberate movements that make it hard for me to focus on what I set out to do. So, I try to match my hand to the speed of his movements, though they feel clumsy as I start to lose fine motor skills.

I lean forward and rest my cheek against Viktor's strong, damp chest. He kisses my temple, and it feels like the most tender moment I've ever experienced in my life.

We are naked, standing in harsh fluorescent lighting, bringing each other pleasure, and I realize I've never been this close with anyone in my life. Ever. I've never been this vulnerable, this open, this honest.

Tears start to burn in my eyes, and I try to fight them back. I don't want Viktor to get the wrong idea about them. I don't want him to think I don't want this, because I do. More than anything. In fact, I'm tempted to demand we start every day like this. If he is going to live with me, it only makes sense. It will save both water and time.

Viktor slides his fingers from me and grabs my face with his other hand, tilting my chin up so I'm looking into his eyes. Then, he brings his two fingers to his lips and slips them into his mouth, tasting me.

I'm not sure why, but that pushes me over the edge. Tears begin to slip down my cheeks, and I hope maybe he'll think it is just the water from the shower, but Viktor is more observant than that. He grabs my face with both of his hands and begins kissing my face, licking the salty tears away.

"Please," I say softly. It is the only word I can manage, but Viktor knows what I need.

He hooks his hands under my thighs and lifts, and I curve my legs around his waist, hooking my ankles behind his back. Then, he maneuvers my hips, positions himself at my opening, and pushes me onto him like I was built for this very thing. Like our bodies were made for this.

I gasp when he slides into me to the very hilt and grip his body with my legs as hard as I can, desperate to keep him there. I roll my hips against him, and Viktor stumbles forward and presses my back against the tile. It is cold, but I don't care. The heat between our bodies is more than enough to sustain me and keep us both warm.

"You feel so good," he groans, his lips pressed against my neck. I arch my entire body into him, giving myself to him in every way I can. Giving myself to this moment and this sensation and this goodness.

Because there is goodness within him. He is a good man who has done bad things, but who hasn't?

Viktor slides out of me and thrusts back in, and my ability to think about anything other than him dissipates. Soon, we are hands and lips and bodies crashing against one another, aching to be filled by the other in ways both physical and not, and we don't slow until we are both trembling.

My body clenches around him, and Viktor thrusts and holds, releasing everything into me.

He lowers me gently back to the ground and then grabs the soap from the shelf above my head and smooths it down my body.

He washes me with gentle touches, and then I return the favor, soaping him up and rinsing him off, all the while admiring the exquisite shape of his body. The perfect lines and edges and shades of him.

"You're beautiful," I say, not realizing I've said it out loud until Viktor chuckles.

He grabs my chin and presses a kiss to my mouth. "You're perfect."

It might be my post-orgasmic bliss, but the towels feel fluffier, and the air smells sweeter. I definitely have rose-colored glasses on with no intention of taking them off anytime soon.

Then, my phone on the counter vibrates, and I check it to see it is Niamh.

"Oh." I'm embarrassed to admit I nearly forgot about the dinner, despite that being the reason we were both getting ready. I show Viktor who it is and then answer. "Hello?"

"Thank God," she says with a relieved sigh. "Seamus just heard about the attack. Are you all okay?"

Viktor can hear her through the phone, and he frowns and then nods his head at me.

"Fine," I say, following his lead. "We are all okay."

"Good, good," she repeats. "Are you all still up for dinner tonight? We obviously understand if you aren't."

Viktor nods again, and I assure Niamh we're excited, even though Viktor had all but wiped the event from my memory with his shower sex. "We are looking forward to it."

When I hang up with Niamh, I turn to Viktor. "Why are we still doing dinner? Don't we need to be figuring out how Fedor knew where we were and how to attack us? What if he tries it again?"

"We do need to figure all of that out, but we also need to keep up appearances," he says. "Our alliance with Seamus is new, and I don't want him to think I can be so easily shaken. I need him to know I am strong and resilient."

"You are," I assure him. Viktor is all of those things. I only hope I am, too. Right now, I feel shaky.

"So are you," he says, bending down to brush his lips over mine.

Viktor digs clothes out of the dresser—I cleared out a few drawers for the stuff he brought with him from his house—while I dress in a black pair of jeans and a long gray sweater that hugs my waist.

When I turn around, Viktor has his shoes on and is slipping a leather jacket on over his black shirt.

"Are you leaving?"

He nods. "Just for a little bit. There is something I have to do."

I want to ask where he is going, but Viktor told me he would tell me anything that was important.

"You'll be safe?" I ask, pressing my hand to my stomach, which feels suddenly queasy.

"I'll be safe. I'm just going to handle some business." He presses a kiss to my cheek as he leaves.

18

VIKTOR

The sky is a deep orange when I walk into one of Seamus' offices and down the stairs.

There are no windows in the basement, and the air smells damp and coppery. Seamus is saying something to me as he leads me down a long hallway and into a large open space, but his words are lost when he flicks on the fluorescent lights, and I see my consigliere sitting in a metal chair in the middle of the room.

Petr looks smaller chained up. Less powerful. Helpless.

His hands are chained to his ankles and a single chain runs from his ankles to a metal hook in the floor.

There is an angry twisting in my stomach, but I try to ignore it and remain neutral. I asked Seamus to do this, after all. Petr is chained up by my orders. I can't look like I regret it. Especially since I don't. If Petr is guilty, I want him to pay.

He looks up, his eyes squinting against the sudden brightness, and I see there is a rag in his mouth.

"He was screaming," Seamus tells me. "I've soundproofed down here, but there is no such thing as being too cautious."

That is why Seamus will make a good ally. I appreciate cautious. Some people—like Fedor—see it as a weakness, but I recognize it for what it is: smart.

I walk forward just as Petr's eyes adjust to the light. They go wide when he recognizes me. I rip the rag out of his mouth.

"Viktor," he gasps, coughing and taking in huge lungfuls of air. "What the fuck? What happened?"

There is a bruise across his cheek and a cut on his eyebrow, but otherwise he looks unscathed. I'm sure he won't be for long.

"How long have you been working for Fedor?" I ask, cutting straight to the chase.

Petr frowns and his brows knit together. "What are you talking about?"

I rear back and kick the leg of his chair, knocking it sideways and sending him toppling to the floor. He manages to brace himself for impact and avoid hitting his head. The chains pull tight, and he winces as the metal cuffs chafe on his wrists and ankles. He lifts his head, trying to look at me, but since he can't lift himself back to sitting, he has no choice but to lay his cheek on the concrete.

"I'm talking about you selling information to my brother," I snarl, kneeling down in front of him. "What did he pay you? What did he offer to make you turn your back on me so easily?"

Petr is trembling now, but he manages to shake his head. "Viktor. I didn't. I wouldn't."

"I know you lied about your mother." I try to keep my voice level and calm, but rage is curling inside of me like a snake ready to strike. I'm not sure how long I can keep my head. "I visited her, and she isn't sick. She hasn't been sick at all. So, where in the fuck have you been going?"

"Okay, I did lie about my mom," Petr admits, nodding emphatically. "I lied about that, but I'm not working for Fedor. It's not what you think … believe me."

"How can I?" I snap. "I've tracked you going into an Italian stronghold every day for a week. What else am I supposed to think?"

"I know it looks bad, but—"

His words are lost to groans when my foot connects with his stomach.

Despite what many people may think, I don't relish the violence. At least not this violence. But it is necessary. I need Seamus to know that I deal with those who disobey me, and I need Petr to know that our friendship won't mean a damn thing if he is lying to me.

Petr curls in on himself and a sob bursts out of him. "Vik, man. Come on. Listen to me."

"I have been listening to you," I growl. "For years. You've been my number two, and now you are lying to me."

He tries to hold up his hands in surrender, but the chains catch, and his hands end up down by his knees. Still, he shrugs his shoulders and shakes his head. "I am lying. I was, but I'll tell you everything. Right now. You don't have to do this."

I nod for a few of Seamus' men to pick up the chair, and they do. Petr sighs when he is upright, relaxing slightly, and I don't like him thinking he is off the hook.

"You just need to listen—"

My fist smashes against his jaw, and Petr's head snaps to the side.

I shake out my hand and pace away from the chair. "I don't need to just do anything."

Petr spits and blood splatters across the cement floor. "You're right. I'm sorry. Will you, though? Will you let me explain?"

"My family could have died," I roar. My voice echoes around the room, and I remember what Seamus said about the room being soundproofed. Still, I should be cautious. "My wife and son could have been killed at the photo shoot. And Seamus could have died at the dinner, but we still don't know the assassin's entire plan. Would he have gone after me and Molly after Seamus?"

I'm getting angry just thinking about the possibilities. Just thinking about what could have happened to Theo if Molly and I had died or if he had been in the crossfire at the photo shoot. I tighten my fists until my fingernails bite into my palm.

"How did you even know about the photo shoot? I didn't tell you, but we had guards there keeping watch over things. Maybe one of them told you? How many of my men are betraying me? Or maybe it's a phone tap?"

Petr shakes his head. "Please, Vik?"

"Don't call me that!"

"Viktor," he corrects. "Please, Viktor? Let me explain?"

I look over at Seamus, and he nods, letting me know he'll respect whatever decision I make. I don't need his permission, but when I have no one else on my side, it's good to know Seamus is a true ally.

"Fine," I say, spinning around and crossing my arms over my chest. "Say what you need to say. Tell your tale, and I may or may not kill you when it is over."

Petr's eyes go wide, and then he blinks and takes a shuddering breath. Blood is dripping from his mouth, and I can already see a bruise spreading under the skin of his cheek from my fists, but he should feel lucky he is in such good shape. I would never admit it out loud, but if he had been anyone else, I would have had him beaten before questioning.

"You know I've been going into Italian territory, so I'm sure you had me followed to the Italian lieutenant's apartment?" Petr asks.

I press my lips together. He doesn't need to know what I know or how I know it.

When he realizes I'm not going to answer, he continues. "I'm an idiot. We both know that. My entire life, I've made shitty decisions because I'm selfish. But we also both know I've only ever been loyal to you."

"That remains to be seen."

"I've been loyal to you," Petr says again, almost as if trying to convince himself. "I know it looks bad, but the Italian lieutenant was never at the house when I was there. In fact, that was the entire point."

"You broke in?" I ask, eyebrow raised. "Bullshit."

"I was let in," he admits, his eyes on the floor. When he looks up, his eyebrows are pinched together, ashamed. "By his wife."

The room is silent and tense, and I want to make some snarky comment, but I'm riveted. Petr knows it and continues.

"I only went to the house while he was out because ... I'm fucking his wife." Petr groans. "God, I'm so stupid. I know that. I should have told you, but I felt like an asshole. Not only because I was sleeping with another man's wife, but because I was also sleeping with an Italian's wife. It felt like disloyalty in multiple ways, and I didn't want you to think I'd be compromised. Because I wasn't. I never talked to Danielle about you or work at all."

"Danielle?" I sneer. "What did you talk about?"

Petr's cheeks go pink. "How to get her out of her marriage. How I'd protect her ... our future together."

I snort. "So, what? You loved her?"

"Love," Petr corrects. His eyes flick from mine to the floor and back again, nervous. "I love her, which is the reason I acted like an idiot. I mean, tell me you understand."

"How would I understand?"

Petr shrugs. "I mean, Molly ... she is your weakness, and—"

"I don't have a weakness," I say, charging forward, shoving my finger in his face. "And I would never let a woman change my relationship to this Bratva."

Petr smiles, one eyebrow raised. "Viktor, I'm sure you believe that, but you have to know that isn't true. Everything has changed since Molly came into your life. She is your priority now, and no one blames you for that, but ... it's true."

I narrow my eyes, trying to find fault with what he is saying. When I can't, it only makes me more annoyed. I stalk away from him. "Keep your commentary to yourself and finish explaining yourself so I can decide what to do with you. I have to get to dinner with my lady."

"I don't have anything else to say," Petr says. "That was it. I lied to you because I didn't want you to think I was betraying you by sleeping with an Italian's wife, but now you think I betrayed you anyway. So much for that plan. You can think I'm scum if you want, but I can't let you think I'm disloyal. I would never turn my back on you, Viktor. My brothers are dead, and Fedor is crazy. Aside from my mom, you are the closest family I have left."

As much as I want to remain cold, my heart twists.

Petr is the closest thing I have to family, too. He has been like a brother for years, and the thought that he could be betraying me too is physically painful.

"I haven't spoken to Fedor at all outside of our meetings with him. I'm not working for him, and I never would."

Petr's voice is thick with emotion, and it sounds genuine. But what do

I know about genuine emotion? Fedor was lying to me, Petr was keeping secrets from me, and through all of it, I'm still preoccupied with whether or not my fake wife really loves me or not.

Everything in my life is fucked up and twisted in ways that make it hard to see which way is up.

"I wish I could believe you," I say. The words are meant to inspire fear, but they sound weak. More like a plea than a threat.

Frustrated, I turn and storm out of the basement.

∼

George picks up on the second ring. "Well, what did he say?"

He knows I was interrogating Petr and is eager for more information, but so am I.

"I need you to find out if Petr was having an affair with the Italian lieutenant's wife."

"Is that what he is saying?"

"Yes, and I need to know as soon as possible if he can be trusted."

George agrees without any further questions, and when we hang up, I shove my phone in my pocket and lean back against the brick wall. I wish I had a cigarette. I've never been much of a smoker—just now and then when the occasion or the company calls for it—but now I wish I had something to do with my hands.

Usually at this point in an interrogation, I'd be beating the person to a pulp. But I don't want to hurt Petr until I'm certain he deserves it. I'd never forgive myself if I found out he had been telling the truth the entire time.

Though, in regards to the bruises he already has, he deserves those. If he really was lying to me about something as stupid as fucking another man's wife while we are in the middle of a war, then he needs a good beating to teach him what is actually important. I'd rather know he is a home wrecker than think he is disloyal.

The door opens, and I look over as Seamus saunters over to me, hands shoved down in his pockets. "That was entertaining."

"Was it?" I ask, trying to find a friendly smile. "I'm glad. Thanks again for helping me out."

"You saved my life," he says. "I owed you. Besides, I like you."

I raise a brow and look over at him. "Are we going to kiss now?"

He chuckles. "See? You're funny. And Niamh is smitten with Molly. The two of us never had children. It just wasn't in the cards for us, but she has always been a mother at heart. She cares for people, and I can see that she cares about Molly. She wants to protect her."

"I want that, too." More than anyone could possibly know. Molly has been through so much, and she deserves a happy life. I'm just not sure if I'm the kind of person who can give her that.

"I know. Which is why I know you'll do whatever you can to end this war, and that works to my benefit, too."

"How so?"

"Your brother is growing powerful and reckless. He struck one of my laundromats early this morning."

I frown. "I hadn't heard about that."

"You've been busy," he says, tipping his head back towards the building. "But this war is growing larger than just the two of you. Fedor and his men are wild ... savage. They are fanatics following a loose cannon. They'll do whatever he asks of them regardless of the body count. So, I want Fedor taken care of, too, and aligning with you is the best way to ensure that happens."

"Great. Then we are on the same page."

"Are we?" Seamus asks, turning to me.

I frown. "Of course, we are."

"I hope so," he admits. "Because once your brother is gone, his men will be neutralized. Once the figurehead is gone, there will be a power vacuum and his followers will fall into in-fighting. They aren't organized enough to have a Plan B set in place. At that point, they'll be easy to pick off, but we have to get to that point first."

I nod. "I agree."

"Are you prepared to kill your own brother?"

My brother. The man who raped my wife. The man who broke into my properties multiple times to try and kidnap the boy I view as my own son. Of course I want him dead.

But killing him myself?

I've been talking about taking care of Fedor for weeks, but I've avoided the thought of actually killing my brother. Mostly because when I picture it, I see Fedor at five years old. Or eight. I see him with gangly limbs and acne. I see him young and excited and innocent. Or, as innocent as Fedor ever was. I see the sadness in his eyes when he confessed to me that he was the reason our parents died in a fire.

No matter how hard I try, I can't picture myself killing him now.

"Of course I am," I say sharply.

Seamus nods and pats my shoulder. "I sure hope so. Because it has to be you, Viktor. It can't be anyone else."

I know he is right, but I wish he wasn't.

19

MOLLY

Viktor still isn't home when there is a knock at the front door. It has been a long time since I've opened my own front door, but I still stand up and am halfway across the living room when I hear the guard open it.

Old habits die hard.

"I'm here for Molly." I recognize Niamh's voice, and even if I didn't, I would recognize the authority in it. She is a woman comfortable with wielding power over others, even large, muscled men whose job it is to keep her from coming inside.

"Niamh." I step into the hallway, and the guard moves out of sight once he realizes I recognize the woman. "Where's Seamus?"

I wasn't expecting to host them on my own, but I feel more comfortable around Niamh and Seamus than most people. With them, I don't feel like I'm pretending.

"Did Viktor not tell you?" she says with a frown. Then, she waves it away as though it isn't important. "The two of them are off on business. Seamus told me it would be a little bit still, so I figured there was no reason the two of us couldn't talk before they arrive. I'd like some alone time with my designer, anyway."

"Of course." I usher her inside and lead her to the sitting room. I want to ask what the two men are doing, but I don't want to sound like I don't trust Viktor. Or worse, like he doesn't trust me. He promised me he would tell me things that had to do with my safety, so if he didn't tell me, it must mean that it has nothing to do with me.

Though, that doesn't feel right, either.

Anything that has Viktor away from home is my business. Anything that could put him in harm's way concerns me.

"Is Theo here?"

"No, he is with the nanny tonight, but I hope to introduce you all soon."

I was reluctant to part with Theo, especially after what happened this morning, but I didn't want him to be introduced to the leaders of the Irish Mafia just yet. Not until we are absolutely certain they can be trusted. It's nothing personal towards Niamh and Seamus, but I won't take any risks with Theo.

Hannah volunteered to watch him again, but Viktor wouldn't hear of it. So Theo is with the nanny and several guards at Viktor's penthouse, and Hannah has made herself scarce for the evening.

"I'll love him, I'm sure, but I'm anxious to have some adult time with you, anyway." Niamh smiles briefly and then her eyes grow heavy with concern. "How are you doing? I couldn't believe it when we heard about the attack this morning."

"Luckily, it was a near-attack," I say, trying to sound light. "We all left unscathed."

"Thankfully." Niamh presses her lips together and shakes her head. "This life is not for the faint of heart. I would understand if you had needed time to unwind and decompress, but I must admit, I'm impressed that you still had us over for dinner."

"I've been through worse." It's true, but I don't want to elaborate on exactly what that means. Niamh doesn't ask me to.

She nods. "You're built for this life, Molly. You may not feel like it all the time, but believe me, you are."

The words are meant as a compliment, but I'm not sure how to take them. So instead of saying anything, I smile and then launch into talk of her new library design.

"I want a window seat, but I'm not sure how to make that happen without blowing out a wall," Niamh says, pointing to the exterior wall of the library on the floor plan.

I wave her away. "Built-in bookshelves. We can get some made to match the other wall and have them wrap around to this wall. Then, in the middle of the shelves, we'll add in a deep bench seat and cushions. There can even be some shelves below and above the window."

Niamh taps the side of my head lightly and grins. "You're a genius. I'm not sure why I even bothered writing down ideas. Everything you say is so much better."

"It's a collaboration," I assure her. "Your ideas are a great jumping-off point. Plus, you are the one who picked out the wall sconces. I wanted to do a chandelier, but you were totally right; it would have been too bright. The sconces will be the perfect amount of light while still feeling intimate."

Niamh likes all of my ideas for the library, and I really hope she isn't just being nice because for the first time, I feel like an actual designer. Aside from the sconces, everything in the room has been my idea. She is giving me free rein with the color pallet, carpet selection, and décor. The only constraints are nothing rustic and no yellow. Niamh hates the color.

We are just wrapping up the last few items on Niamh's itinerary when the door opens and Viktor and Seamus walk inside. Their voices are low enough that I can't hear what they are saying, but Viktor isn't being as charming as he usually is around other bosses. Based on their somber faces, whatever business they were attending to has followed them to dinner, though they both try to hide it.

Seamus bends and gives his wife a kiss on the cheek, and she squeezes his hand. Viktor sits next to me on the couch and stretches out his long leg next to mine, his warmth seeping into me.

"Is everything okay?" I ask cheerfully, though I turn my head, letting my hair fall down around my face, allowing us a small curtain of privacy. I narrow my eyes.

Viktor nudges me with his hip and smiles. "It will be okay as soon as I eat something. I'm starving."

"Me too," Seamus says. "You two aren't vegetarians, are you?"

"Do vegetarians look like this?" Viktor teases, flexing his bulging bicep. "This body does not run on vegetables alone."

Seamus looks visibly relieved. "Thank God. I'm a carnivore through and through, though I think Niamh could sustain herself on nothing but foraged berries for months. She hardly eats."

"I hardly eat compared to him," she says, hooking a thumb over her shoulder at her husband. "And you'll understand what that means when he eats his way through your entire pantry here in a few minutes."

"He'll have to fight Viktor," I say, wrapping my arm around Viktor's elbow and pulling him to his feet. "Viktor gets what we like to call 'hangry.' If he goes too long without food, he is liable to take down the first warm-blooded thing he sees for sustenance. I have to keep him fed or else things get dangerous."

As we move the party to the dining room, Niamh stops to admire the pictures Viktor and I just hung up earlier in the afternoon.

"You two look so happy," she says, tilting her head to the side and smiling. "I wish we could have been there."

Given what happened only a few minutes after the picture was snapped, she really wouldn't have wanted to be there, but she doesn't know they were only taken this afternoon. She doesn't realize they are all manufactured memories.

"They are such a beautiful couple, aren't they?" Niamh asks, prompting Seamus.

Viktor nudges my arm, grinning down at me, proud of our success. I'm proud, too. I swell slightly at the compliment, thrilled that Viktor and I are viewed as a real couple. Though, there is another part of me that is twisted with worry and shame.

I hope to consider Niamh a true friend, and I'm lying to her. And not about something small like my favorite food or whether I like her haircut. I'm lying to her about being married when I'm really not. I'm pretending to live a life that is entirely different from the one I actually live. And I have to wonder if she would still like me as much if she knew the truth.

"They are definitely a beautiful couple," Seamus agrees. "But do you know what would be even more beautiful? Dinner."

Niamh groans. "You're incorrigible."

Viktor laughs and leads us all to the dining room where the cook has laid out four plates around a crispy and golden roasted chicken. In small trays around the chicken are various vegetables and side dishes.

Niamh tells the story of a time when Seamus ate something unidentified at a business lunch and ended up with swollen lips and a rash because he was allergic to shellfish. Then, Seamus counters with the time Niamh tried out temporary lip injections and looked like a scary movie mask for two weeks.

The two of them are easy with one another, bantering back and forth without any hesitation, and I wonder if Viktor and I will ever have that. I certainly hope so.

Because this is nice. Sitting around a table with friends and talking, it feels normal. This is the kind of life I've always imagined for myself. Or, rather, the life I was too afraid to imagine for myself. Having friends like these and regular dinners like this seemed too good to be true, and I didn't want to be disappointed. Now, it could be a reality.

The trouble is, the life of crime comes right along with it. The two can't be separated, and I have to decide whether one is worth the other.

"We can't thank you enough for having us over," Niamh says at the end of the evening, holding both of my hands in her own. "I want to see you both again soon, but I better be seeing you even sooner, Molly. You have me far too excited about my new library."

"She is telling the truth," Seamus says. "She won't stop talking about it."

"Molly has amazing ideas," Niamh says, smiling up at Viktor. "I may force Seamus into a full remodel of the house if I love the library enough."

Seamus grips his heart like it hurts, but Niamh just rolls her eyes and then pulls me in for a hug. "Take care of yourself, dear."

The men shake hands, and we wave to them from the doorway until they are in the elevator and gone. Then, we slip back inside.

Dinner will be cleaned up by the staff, and I'm eager to get out of my tight dress, so I head upstairs, wash my face, and slip into a loose nightgown. When I get back downstairs, Viktor is still sitting in the same spot on the couch he was when I left, staring straight ahead at the fireplace.

"What are you thinking about?"

He starts at the sound of my voice and then smiles, trying to play it off. "Nothing."

I sit down next to him, my legs curled underneath me. "Is that true? Or do you just not want to tell me?"

Viktor grabs my hand and lays my fingers across his palm. He strokes my knuckles gently with his thumb, looking pensive. "I don't want to worry you."

"Too late."

He frowns, and I realize his beard has been growing in. His stubble has turned to a golden coat across his square jaw, and his hair is longer, too. Unable to resist, I reach out and stroke my fingers through it. Viktor closes his eyes and sighs.

"You and Theo are both safe, but I think I have a traitor in the Bratva."

"You already knew some of your men weren't loyal, though. They left to be with Fedor."

"Not all of them, apparently." He falls back into the couch cushions and pulls me with him, tucking me into his side. "I think someone told Fedor where we would be meeting with the Irish and where the photo shoot would be. I've been trying to keep information limited to only a few people, but it is still getting out."

"That's why you asked about Petr working with Fedor at the photo shoot," I say, remembering his accusations. "You think it is Petr?"

He shrugs, looking more defeated than I've ever seen him. "I don't know. That's what Seamus and I were doing before dinner. George caught Petr going to an Italian lieutenant's house day after day for weeks, but Petr claims he was only there because he is having an affair with the wife."

"Do you believe him?" I ask.

"George texted me during dinner to say that he found compromising pictures of Petr and the woman on Petr's phone, so they are having an affair, but I'm not sure if that is the extent of it."

"It has to be," I say. "I mean, what kind of man would work with his wife's lover? If the Italian lieutenant knew, he'd kill Petr."

"I guess."

"Think about it," I say, draping my leg over Viktor's thigh. "Would you work with a man I was sleeping with?"

His hand tightens on my waist, and he pulls me squarely onto his lap. When he answers, his voice is a growl. "No."

"Then, there you go." I poke my finger into his chest and then drag it down, admiring the patch of golden hair sticking out of the top of his shirt.

"Either way, Petr is locked up until I know for sure," Viktor sighs.

I lay my head on his chest and breathe in the woodsy scent of him. "Then don't worry about it right now."

"I wish I didn't have to." His strong arm wraps around my back, caging me in.

I turn my face and press my lips to his neck. "Let's just live in the afterglow of our successful dinner for a little bit longer. Let's be normal for tonight."

"Normal?" Viktor scoffs. "You couldn't be normal if you tried."

I sit up, frowning, and he immediately smooths the lines in my forehead with the pad of his thumb. "*I mean*, you are far too extraordinary to ever be normal, Molly."

"Yes," I whisper, twisting so I'm straddling his legs. "That is what I'm talking about. Let's forget about traitors and wars and Bratva life for a minute and focus on this."

Viktor must agree with my idea because his lips are on mine in an instant, warm and soft. I melt against him. My arms wrap around his neck, and my fingers tangle in the hair at the base of his neck.

The kiss starts slow but builds quickly. Viktor's hands are strong on my hips, holding me against him, and I arch into his touch, wanting more of him.

This has always been the easy part with Viktor. Touching him and being touched by him is as simple as breathing. I don't need to think about it or plan my next move. It feels like something my body was naturally made to do.

When I feel his hardness between us, I instinctively roll my hips, and Viktor groans. He bucks against me, finding more friction.

His hands slip down my body and then slide up my skin, bunching my nightgown as they go. His fingertips trail fire, and I'm itching by the time his hands encircle my waist. The light brushes of skin aren't enough. They are a drop of water after a week in the desert. They are a crumb of food after I've been starving.

I need more.

"More?" Viktor breathes the word against my skin as he kisses his way up my ribs. I didn't realize I'd said anything out loud.

"More," I sigh, rolling my hips against him again.

Viktor responds by ripping my nightgown over my head. When my breasts bounce free, he presses them together, savoring the view for a second before his mouth circles over my nipple.

His tongue flicks at the sensitive, pebbled skin, and I don't recognize the sounds coming out of my mouth. I never knew such small actions could elicit such strong sensations, but I'm writhing on top of him. I don't want him to stop, but I want his mouth ... everywhere. All at once.

I pull his face away from my breast and kiss him, swirling my tongue in his mouth and biting his lip. Then, I pull away and direct him back to my nipple.

I'm wild and commanding and so out of my mind with lust that I barely notice when Viktor picks me up and lays me back on the couch. Since his tongue never stops flicking against my sensitive skin, I don't care what he does with the rest of me.

"I want you to forget," Viktor says, kissing a line down my stomach to the top of my panties.

"I don't," I gasp, rolling my hips up in search of him. "I want to remember every detail."

"Of this, yes," he says, hooking his fingers under the waistband and tugging down. I feel the cold air against my warm center and shiver. "But I want to be the person who makes you forget everything else. Every bad thought in your head, I want to banish with pleasure."

He cups my calf with gentle hands as he pulls my panties down my legs. He is being so careful, and I don't want careful. I want him hard and fast and, most importantly, now.

"Like a sexy exorcism," I say, trying to make a joke, though my voice is deep and breathy.

"Something like that," Viktor chuckles.

He kneels in front of me on the couch and begins working his way back up my body, pressing kisses to my ankle and the backs of my knees. Every touch of his lips deepens the ache at my center. It is a tease. A hint of what I want, dangled just out of reach. I try to wriggle my hips down closer to his mouth, but Viktor grabs my hips and moves me back into position. I groan, and he smiles, enjoying my torture.

When he finally makes it to my inner thighs, the anticipation feels like a wild animal clawing at the walls of my chest.

I've never sat back and watched someone admire me before. I've never had the view of watching a man enjoy the taste of my skin and the feeling of me underneath him, and there is something sensual and erotic about it.

I can feel my pulse pounding in my throat and my chest, but I feel it most strongly between my legs. I'm ready for him, aching, and I'm not sure his mouth is going to be enough.

I'm about to tell Viktor this when he finally pushes my legs apart and swipes a finger over my opening.

Instantly, I gasp and buck my hips.

He smiles and spreads me with his thumbs, treating me like a delicate flower whose petals he doesn't want to crush.

Then, he buries his face in me, and there is nothing delicate about what his tongue is doing.

Viktor sucks at the sensitive spot at the apex of my thighs and smooths his tongue over the places that are burning for him. Suddenly, I'm worried his mouth is entirely too much.

Then, he adds a finger.

My body arches with his touch, nearly lifting off the couch, and he has to hold me down with a firm hand pressed to my stomach.

He adds a second finger, and I bite down on the heel of my hand to keep quiet.

He pulses his digits in and out of me to the speed of his tongue flicking over my center, and I lose my mind entirely. Heat builds and rages and catches fire inside of me, and I feel like my joints have come undone. I feel as though my entire body is seconds away from blowing apart.

When he curls his fingers inside of me, I fall into darkness.

My eyes are squeezed closed, and I'm not sure where I am or which way is up as I ride the wave of my orgasm.

I come back to myself slowly.

First, I feel his fingers moving slowly inside of me. Then, I feel the soft kisses he presses to my inner thighs. Last, I feel his large, warm hand sliding up my stomach to cover my breast.

I grab his hand with both of mine and cling to him, bringing myself back to Earth.

When I finally open my eyes, Viktor is hovering over me, his elbows on either side of my head. His blue eyes are blown wide with lust, and I slide my hand down his stomach, reaching for what must be the ache between his legs, but he snatches my hand before I can get there and shakes his head. He brings my hand back to his lips and kisses my fingertips, sucking them into his delicious, devastating mouth.

"That was for you. I don't want anything back."

I want to argue, but my arms and legs are jelly. As much as I want to make him black out with lust, I also feel like I might black out myself. So, I wrap my arms around his neck and hug him to my chest, taking deep breaths of his woodsy, lemony scent as I try to stay in this moment forever.

Because for the first time in weeks, I forgot everything except for Viktor.

And it was heaven.

20

MOLLY

When I wake up, I'm in my room upstairs.

I wipe at my eyes and realize I'm naked. I have no memory of coming upstairs, so Viktor must have carried me.

When I roll over, I see him lying in the bed next to me, one strong arm thrown over his head. He is cast in a silhouette against the navy-blue sky visible through the wall of windows behind him. It is late at night or early in the morning—I can't tell which—but either way, I want to tuck myself against his chest and fall back asleep. Because he is my safe place.

The thought hits me like a slap in the face, and I almost gasp from the force of it.

Viktor is my home base. Sometime in the last few weeks, he became the person I feel safest with. Not only that, he became the person I want to keep safe.

Not just physically, but emotionally.

This life is too heavy for any one person to carry alone, and I want to help Viktor carry the weight. I want to talk to him about his day and help him muddle through the decisions that come with leadership. I want to be Viktor's partner, and I want him to be mine.

I'm staring at him, blinking like a crazy person when I finally hear the reason I woke up in the first place. My phone is vibrating on the nightstand.

I grab for my phone, worried it could be an issue with Theo. The few times he has stayed the night away from me, he needs to call and hear my voice in the middle of the night.

Instead of the nanny's name, however, I see Hannah's.

I grab my phone and a throw blanket from the end of the bed and walk into the hallway to answer.

"Hey, what's going on?" The clock on my phone says it is almost three in the morning. If Hannah is calling now, something must be wrong. "Where are you?"

"Outside," she says, sounding breathless. "I'm only a block from your place, and I need to talk to you."

I frown and shake my head, tired and confused. "You said you'd be able to find a place to sleep tonight. If you can't, you can obviously come up and stay in your room. I'll have the guards unlock the door for you."

"That isn't it. I don't need a place to sleep. I'm not tired." She sighs, making me doubt the truth in her statement. "I just need to talk to you."

"Come inside and talk. I'll make some tea. Just come over and—"

"Not while *he* is there," she snaps, venom dripping from her words.

Hannah has been so relaxed since she arrived to stay with me. Even when she found out about Viktor and his penchant for violence, she was worried about me, but calm. So, I'm not sure where this new emotion is coming from. I tell Hannah as much.

"You haven't had an issue with Viktor since you got here. Why now? What happened?"

"I came to my senses, Molly. That's what happened. I hate the way that criminal has lured you in and corrupted you. I've had time to think about it tonight and—and he isn't a good man. I can't stay with you anymore, and you shouldn't either. You need to come talk to me and see sense and let me help you."

"Hannah." I say her name calmly, trying to ease her back from the emotional ledge. "It is late and this is crazy. Just come home, and we'll talk tomorrow."

"That isn't my home!" she screams into the phone.

"Okay, okay." I'm not sure if Hannah has been drinking or doing drugs, but whatever is happening, this isn't her. She isn't acting like herself, and I need to help her. She shouldn't be wandering around the streets late at night like this. I have to go to her. "Stay where you are. I'm coming."

Hannah releases a long sigh that I take to be relief. "Okay. I'm in front of the nail salon."

I know where she is talking about, so I hang up and slip back into my bedroom. Viktor is still sleeping on the bed, and I consider waking him up to tell him where I'm going, but I know he won't approve. He hasn't liked Hannah from the start. If I tell him she thinks I need to leave him, he will insist on coming with me, and then Hannah won't talk to me. She might even run off when she sees him, and I don't want her getting hurt.

So, I silently grab a pair of jeans, a sweater, and a pair of sneakers from my closet and then tiptoe back into the hallway. I change, pull my sex-mussed hair into a ponytail, and walk downstairs as confidently as possible.

The guards stop me at the door.

"Where are you going? No one is supposed to be leaving right now."

The overnight guards are always lower on the totem pole. Young members who are trying to prove themselves. Sometimes, it makes them a little overzealous, but sometimes, it makes them easy to manipulate. I hope these guards are the latter.

"I'm going out to see a friend down the street." If they tell Viktor about it later, I'll already be home and safe, so it won't matter.

One of the guards, a stout man with a bald head, sighs and slides off a stool. "Fine, but give me a second. I need to find my shoes."

"Don't bother. I'll be right back."

He narrows his eyes and frowns. "Someone has to go with you. You aren't supposed to leave alone."

"My husband knows where I am going and told me I could go alone," I snap, pulling my face into a deeply offended scowl. I want this man to feel foolish for questioning me at all. "Do you suddenly outrank your leader?"

The guard's mouth opens and closes several times, and I know I've got him.

"By all means, feel free to go upstairs and question him," I say, leaning back against the wall, arms crossed over my chest like I'm bored. "I'll wait, but I should warn you, he is tired and in a very bad mood."

The man looks towards the stairs as though he is considering it before he reluctantly shakes his head. "Sorry I doubted you."

I raise a brow until he lowers his face in shame. Bratva queens are not to be trifled with.

Only once he is good and shamed do I march through the front door and into the night.

I see the nail salon from a block away, but I don't see Hannah until I'm standing in front of the alley next to the building. She is leaning against the brick wall with her arms wrapped around her middle. She isn't dressed for the cold night, and I can tell she is shivering.

"Hannah?"

She starts and turns around, and that is when I realize she isn't shivering, but sobbing.

Fat tears roll down her cheeks, smearing her mascara, and her entire body is trembling.

"What happened?" I ask, rushing forward to wrap her in a hug. "Whatever is going on, we can fix this, okay?"

I'll let Hannah live with me for years if she needs to. I'll drive her to AA or NA meetings. I'll do whatever I can to help her the way she helped me and Theo all those years ago. She may feel like the debt between us has been paid, but I'm not sure I'll ever feel that way.

"No, you can't," Hannah sobs into my shoulder. Her arms are hanging limply at her sides. "I ruined everything for you, and I'm so sorry."

I step back and rub warmth into her shoulders with my hands. "Nothing is ruined. I'm fine. We can go back to the apartment and talk about this. Everything is fine."

Hannah pulls away from my touch and shakes her head. "I didn't find you with the Find-my-Phone app, Molly. Someone told me where you lived."

I blink, confused. "Someone?"

Hannah's lower lip pouts out, and her chin wobbles. "Fedor."

My heart sinks in my chest and it feels like time has slowed. Like the world has stopped spinning. Everything I thought was true, suddenly isn't.

Hannah knows Fedor. Fedor told her where I lived. She lied to me.

As fear grips my mind, the same thought thumps through me like a heartbeat: *She lied to me. She lied to me. She lied to me.*

"I didn't want to help him, but he threatened me, Molly. He told me I had to or else he'd kill my family."

"What about my family?" I ask weakly, my voice barely audible.

Hannah swipes at her eyes and takes a step towards me, but I wave my hand, keeping her at a distance.

"I know," she sobs. "I told him where you guys were and when you left the house. I felt like shit the whole time, and I tried to get you to leave, but you wouldn't do it. I tried to get you to leave Viktor, but—"

"Am I supposed to thank you?" I spit. "You've been lying to me this entire time. Spying on me."

"I tried to keep Theo safe, too," she says softly. "I wanted him to stay home the day of the photo shoot. I didn't want him to be there for whatever was going to happen."

Hannah was insistent that morning, and I didn't understand why. Now it all makes sense, and my stomach turns. I thought she missed her son and wanted to spend time with Theo. Instead, Hannah knew we were going to be ambushed and attacked. Luckily, what she didn't know is that Viktor had a security team in place.

So many thoughts are running through my head, but one separates from the others and rises to the forefront of my mind. "Why are you telling me this now?"

Hannah doesn't have a chance to answer.

I hear a car door open behind me and turn around just as Fedor steps onto the curb, gun in hand.

"Because I want you to suffer the way I did when you took my son and my brother from me." His eyes are narrowed on me, but the gun is pointed at Hannah. "She's telling you this now because her mission is over."

Hannah sobs and folds over, her body going slack. "Please. No. Please. I did what you asked."

All of my animosity towards Hannah fades the second I realize Fedor is going to kill her.

She doesn't deserve this. Regardless of what she did, she doesn't deserve to die.

A smile spreads across Fedor's face, and for a moment, I'm startled by how much he and Theo look alike. They have the same smiles and the same pointed chins. But where Theo's eyes are warm and brown, Fedor's are electric green. And right now, they are deadly.

I lunge forward before I can second-guess myself and shove Fedor's arm up into the air. "Run, Hannah!"

She takes off running.

Fedor grabs my hair with his free hand and yanks my neck to the side, but I don't let go of his arm until he drops my hair and swings for my stomach. I want to save Hannah if I can, but I won't sacrifice the safety of my baby for her.

I jump back and Fedor aims the gun at me. His smile has been replaced with a sharp frown. His nostrils are flared, and he is breathing heavily. He looks crazed, and I'm convinced he is going to execute me on the spot.

Then, his demeanor changes in a flash. His mouth tilts up in a cocky smirk, and he is all swagger and confidence. "My men will find and kill Hannah later. Right now, I don't care. The slut did her job. She got you here."

The idea of being taken by Fedor is even more terrifying than a sidewalk execution, but just as I spin around to run, more men step out of hiding and move towards me.

I scream, hoping to draw some attention, but before the sound can even leave my throat there is a hand clamped over my mouth. I thrash and flail, but strong arms pin my limbs to my sides and throw me in the back of a waiting van.

∽

The room is small and white and secure.

I walk the small perimeter countless times, desperate to find a secret hatch or a boarded-over window or a key to the door. But even that wouldn't help. The door is locked from the outside and there is no handle on the inside.

I walk along the edges of the small room until hopelessness settles over me like a weight, dragging me to the floor.

Eventually, I lie down and try to rest.

In the van, the men tied my arms and legs, and I prayed they wouldn't notice I'm pregnant. I'm still early enough that it isn't obvious, but if they'd lifted my shirt, they might have noticed the bump. It's popping out a lot sooner than it did when I was pregnant with Theo.

Thankfully, they didn't look at my bare stomach, and I didn't have to endure any additional violence.

Fedor didn't talk to me as we drove across town. I was left to lie in the back of the van, guarded by two of Fedor's men, and he stayed in the front.

Then, when we arrived at our destination, I was blindfolded and carried inside. I could hear gravel crunching under their feet, but that did little to tell me where we were going.

The inside of the building is cold, and even after hours locked inside,

I haven't grown accustomed to it. I slip my arms from the sleeves of my sweater and wrap them around my middle, trying to warm up with my own body heat.

I don't know whether Fedor is keeping the room cold to torture me or whether there is simply no electricity. There are no lights in my room or any lights visible through the small, barred window set into the metal door of my room, so I can't be sure.

Guards walk up and down the hallway every so often, and I don't know if I'm the only prisoner Fedor has or not. I can't hear any other voices, and the silence is starting to make me crazy when suddenly, there is a loud metallic scraping noise.

I yelp and jump to my feet, shoving my arms through the sleeves of my sweater as fast as I can, wanting to be ready for anything. Then, the long, thin rectangular cut into the bottom of the door opens and a tray filled with food is pushed through it.

The tray clatters to the floor, and I'm so unaccustomed to the noise that I shove my hands over my ears.

After almost a minute of silence, I realize whoever left the food is gone, so I crawl forward and pick at it.

It is a microwavable freezer meal. The macaroni is salty mush and the green beans are rubbery. Still, I eat everything. The baby needs nutrients, and even if I don't feel hungry, I can't skip any meals right now.

When I'm done, I shove the tray against the door and lean back against the wall. My hips hurt from sitting on the concrete floor, but I barely feel the pain. I'm far too focused on the burn of betrayal in my chest.

Hannah lied to me. For weeks.

Every laugh we shared, every secret I told her ... she was betraying me. She was spying on me and feeding information to a man who wants to kill me and steal my son.

I drop my face into my hands and cry for the first time since Fedor kidnapped me.

Everything happened so fast: Hannah's admission, Fedor's appearance, and my saving Hannah from being shot. There hasn't been any time to process how I'm feeling, and even now, I'm not sure I want to.

My feelings won't save me right now. Regardless of how I'm feeling, it doesn't change the facts.

I'm away from my family, locked up by my husband's crazy brother, and away from my son.

Viktor doesn't even know what has happened to me. I wonder whether Fedor will try to convince him I ran away.

Surely, Viktor wouldn't believe that.

At least, I hope he wouldn't.

I allow myself another minute of crying before I wipe my face on my sleeve and stand up, shaking off the meltdown.

If I want any chance of getting out of here, I have to stay focused. I have to stay strong. I have to think about Theo and my unborn baby and Viktor.

I have to think about my family.

21

VIKTOR

I wake up to screaming.

Shrieking, rather.

Truly, no one can scream like an upset child. Crying kids seem to reach an entirely new level of sound previously unknown to the human race.

I sit up in bed, searching for the source of the noise.

Then, I see Theo standing next to Molly's side of the bed, his face red and covered in tears.

"What's up, bud?" I reach out for him, and he crawls on the bed and falls against my chest.

"Where's Momma?" I make out his words between sobs and hiccups.

"I'm not sure." I press a kiss to his forehead and then scoop him up as I get out of bed. I'm only in my boxers, but putting him down to find pants would likely result in more screaming, so I don't bother. "She is probably in the shower. Let's go see."

Except, Molly isn't in the shower.

She isn't in any of the rooms upstairs, and when I carry Theo downstairs, I see the nanny sitting in the living room.

Her eyes widen when she sees me in my underwear, and then she glues her eyes on my face. "Sorry. Theo was crying all morning, and I couldn't get ahold of Molly, so I just came over. The guards said she wasn't here, but I thought seeing you might calm him down."

My heart stutters at her words, and I hold out a hand to stop her. "What do you mean Molly isn't here?"

The woman frowns and points towards the front door. "That's what the guards said. She left last night."

The guards on duty now are not the same guards who were watching the house when Molly left. It takes lots of questioning and several phone calls to get the entire story: Molly left the house in the middle of the night, claiming I told her it was okay, and she never came back.

"Why the fuck wasn't I called?" I growl, forgetting Theo is in my arms. I take a deep breath and try to understand what this means.

Did Molly leave us again? She did it before, but only when she thought she was bringing danger to Theo. The incident at the photo shoot yesterday could have scared her, but I doubt she would leave again. Not without Theo.

The guards were afraid to question Molly when she left, and while part of me is proud of her for being able to scare two grown men, a much larger part of me is furious with her for choosing now to step into her role as Bratva queen.

I send men out to patrol the neighborhood for any sign of her, but she isn't around, and just as I'm growing desperate and about to call Seamus for help, my phone rings.

I set Theo down on the couch, pull out my phone, and nearly collapse with relief when I see Molly's name on the screen.

"Where the hell are you?" I ask. I want to sound furious, but the desperation is so thick in my voice. "Why did you leave?"

There is a low laugh on the other end of the phone, and every hair on my body rises.

"Fedor."

"Surprised?" my younger brother asks. "I wish I could see your face."

Theo is looking up at me, eyes wide and brown and just like his mother's, and I can't take this call in front of him. I nod for the nanny to keep an eye on him, and then move into the office at the end of the hallway.

"Where is she?" I growl.

Fedor laughs again, clearly giddy over his success. "You thought she was so safe locked away in that apartment. Were you in bed next to her? Did I steal her right out from under your nose?"

An involuntary growl rises in my throat.

"You hired so many men to watch over her, but you never considered that I was already inside the house."

I spin towards the door, listening for the sounds of Theo and the nanny playing on the other side of it. Theo still has his pouty voice, but I can hear him telling the nanny what he wants for breakfast.

Is Fedor in the house now? Are the guards behind Molly's disappearance?

"Hannah." The single word is an answer to every question in my mind, and I feel like the dumbest man on the planet the moment he says it.

Hannah. Of course.

Of fucking course.

"Who better to lure Molly into complacency than one of her oldest friends?" Fedor says. "It didn't hurt that she wasn't terrible to look at. I thought she might be a distraction for both of you."

The night in the kitchen suddenly comes back to me. "You're the reason Hannah tried to seduce me?"

Fedor laughs. "My hope was to distract you long enough to sneak in and take Molly out of the house. That would have been a sweet victory."

"To what end? Why do you want her?"

"I want Molly for my own reasons," he says. "She and I have unfinished business. Taking her from your house while you fucked her best friend would have simply been fun. Not to mention, I hoped it would finally make you see the consequences of your actions."

"The consequences of *my* actions? You've got to be kidding me."

"See? This is what I'm talking about," Fedor says with a sigh. "You betrayed your own brother, and you don't seem to understand it. You don't realize the depth of the betrayal you've wrought, and I'm not sure how else to show you."

"I'd never betray Molly. That was your mistake."

"Just your own brother, then? Nice, Vik. Real nice." His voice is thick with sarcasm. "Truly, I did underestimate your love for Molly. You're devoted to her, and it is admirable. Though, unfortunately, it won't help you much now."

"Where is she?" I snap. "Tell me what you want. I'm sure you have demands."

"My first demand is that you not rush me," Fedor yells. He sounds unhinged, and I squeeze my eyes closed, trying to imagine where Molly is. Is she nearby? Can she hear this conversation? Is she still alive?

I push that question to the back of my mind. I'm not ready to consider the alternative.

"I've lost too much to you to make my victory quick," Fedor continues. "I'll take my sweet time, and if you try to rush me again, I'll cut off Molly's fingers one by one."

The threat turns my stomach. "How do I know you haven't already?"

"Is there no trust left between us? Do you think I would hurt your wife and not be honest about it?"

"You kidnapped her, so no, I don't exactly trust you. I want to hear her voice. How do I know you even have her?"

"I'm calling you from her phone and she isn't home with you. What more proof do you need?"

I believe Fedor has Molly, but I want to know about her physical well-being. If she is okay enough to talk on the phone, that will reassure me marginally.

"Let me talk to her."

"No." His answer is immediate and sharp. There will be no budging him. "You will talk to her if and only if I allow it."

"Fedor." My voice shakes with emotion. "If you hurt her, so help me—"

"Don't be so dramatic," Fedor says with a laugh. "And don't act like you are above hurting people for your own gain. I'm not the only person you've betrayed."

He is changing the subject, but I'm not sure how to get him back to the topic of Molly without rushing him. And right now, I'm confident he would really cut her fingers off.

"What are you talking about?"

"Did you think the diner was a safe place to meet up with George?"

The question hangs between us, a question and a statement wrapped up in one.

Fedor knows I met with George and where I met him. I try to think about what that means. About how much he may have heard. How much he knows.

"Did you have a spy there, too?"

"A bug," he says. "It was a simple job and very rewarding. It's how I knew you were investigating Petr."

"Was he working for you?" The question is out of my mouth before I can stop it. I just want to know how many people have betrayed us.

"No, but I did little to correct you. It kept you busy and occupied."

It certainly did. I've been such a fool. I fell into all of his traps. Fedor wanted me to be paranoid. He wanted me to isolate myself and trust no one, and I very nearly gave him exactly what he wanted.

Now, though, it doesn't matter. He has what he wants: revenge.

"He has been your second-in-command for years, and you turned on him so quickly. It was sad to watch. But do you know what was worse?" Fedor pauses, waiting for me to answer, but I'm suddenly exhausted. I don't want to play this game anymore. I just want Molly. "Fine. I'll tell you anyway. It was worse to watch you betray Molly."

I stand tall at that, eyebrows knit together. "What are you talking about? I never betrayed Molly."

"Maybe not technically," Fedor says. "Though, you tried. You asked George to hire some men to scare her."

"But I didn't," I say quickly.

"Only because I beat you to it! I took the idea from you, you know?"

My stomach drops. Molly was so terrified that night I came over. Seeing a strange man in her house, holding her son—she was shaken enough to agree to marry me. When I saw how scared she was, I realized how sick with guilt I would have been if I'd caused her to be that afraid. I was grateful I hadn't gone through with it myself.

"Does Molly know?" he asks. "Does she know you were going to terrify her into staying with you? Did you tell her that you were planning to send men in to grab her son? I'm sure not. If you had, she would have left you."

"I didn't tell her because I decided not to do it."

Suddenly, the line goes staticky, and I hear my own voice, garbled through a bad speaker.

"Molly is pregnant, and I need to protect her, but she won't let me. I need to show her how badly she needs my protection."

"What do you have in mind?" George asks.

"I need a few men to break in. They won't hurt her or Theo, but it will scare them."

"Are you sure?"

"It's the only way," I say. "Molly needs to know how bad things can be. She needs to understand what I'm saving her from."

The static fades, and I know Fedor has turned off whatever recording device he was playing back.

"That sounds like a man who is deeply in love with his wife, does it not?" Fedor laughs again, and I want to reach through the phone and strangle him. Before this moment, I hadn't been able to imagine hurting my little brother, but now, I can picture it perfectly. If I ever get my hands on him, I'll squeeze the life out of him. Easily. "Congratulations, by the way. On the baby."

He knows she is pregnant. He has known for weeks. Since he overheard my conversation with George at the diner. I want to beg him not to hurt the baby, but I know it won't matter. In all likelihood, showing any special concern for the child will only make him more excited to hurt it and Molly. So, I pinch my mouth closed and try to keep calm.

"As a gift to the new parents-to-be, I'll let you speak to one another," Fedor says. "Come on, Viktor, don't be shy now. You've been on loudspeaker this entire time."

"Molly?" Part of me hopes he is lying. I don't want Molly to know about the men I nearly hired. I don't want her to know that I was even considering manipulating her into marriage. But a much larger part of me wants to hear her voice. "Are you there?"

I hear what sounds like duct tape being removed, and then screaming.

"Viktor!" In the mess of crying and yelling, I hear my name, and my heart breaks. I drop to my knees in the study and squeeze the phone, desperate to get to her.

"Molly, I—"

"We'll be in touch," Fedor says, cutting me off before I can finish.

Then, the line goes dead.

22

VIKTOR

After I shove my legs into some jeans and pull on a T-shirt, my first thought is to call Petr. A few weeks ago, he would have been the person I took all of this information to. Now, he isn't there. I know he is innocent, so I'll let him out soon, but I need to get my men out in the streets *now*. We need to be looking for Molly every minute until she is found. So, I call my next highest lieutenant.

Alek doesn't answer.

Neither does Moises. Or Lexei.

By the fourth person on the list, I'm cursing under my breath with every ring of the phone. It is midmorning. Everyone should be awake by now. If not, they should have their ringers on so they can be alerted to Bratva business no matter whether they are sleeping or not.

Finally, on the sixth ring, Michail answers.

"Hello."

"Thank fuck," I groan. "No one is answering. I'm trying to get men out on the streets to look for Molly. Fedor has her, and—"

"You want us to look for your girlfriend?"

I frown. "No, my wife."

Michail makes an unconvinced noise. "According to the information we all received this morning, Molly is not your wife, and you lied to us."

Shit. "What information did you receive?"

"Proof that you aren't actually married," Michail says. "Proof that you conducted a sacred swearing-in ceremony under false pretenses since Molly was not your wife."

"Damn it, Michail, I'm sorry, but—"

"I'm not in the city," he said. "Neither are most of the other guys."

"What does that mean? Where are you?" The world feels like it is falling apart around me. I grip the edge of the desk for support. The same desk where Molly and I had sex last week. It feels like a lifetime ago.

"This war is between you and your brother. The rest of us don't want to get killed over your feud."

I slam my fist down on the table. "We're a family. You can't just leave."

"Family doesn't lie," Michail says. With that, he hangs up, leaving me holding onto the useless phone.

I dart out of the room and towards the front door. Theo is eating a bowl of cereal at the table, and he calls my name as I pass, but I'm on a mission.

I peek in on the room just to the right of the front door. There is usually a guard in there, but the stool is empty right now. Then, I tear open the front door and look down on the street below. The space where a guard usually sits is empty.

We are all unprotected.

I drag a hand down my face and squeeze my eyes shut, trying to think. I have to find Molly, but I have to keep Theo safe, too. I can't leave him undefended.

George.

I pull out my phone and call George. He answers on the second ring.

"I need your help," I say, talking faster than my brain can keep up. "Molly is gone, and everything has gone to shit. I can't trust Theo with anyone else but you. Can you do it?"

"I can do it," he says without hesitation. "I'm on my way now."

I silently thank God for one loyal friend and am about to turn inside when I look up and see Sasha walking towards me. He is one of the newest recruits the Bratva has. I barely know him beyond a few short conversations. He is holding a tall coffee in one hand, and he doesn't meet my eyes as he approaches.

"I'm surprised you're still here."

"Me too," he admits with a shrug. Then, he lifts his coffee. "I figure there won't be anyone coming to relieve me anytime soon, so I'll need the caffeine."

The man looks so young, and I'm tempted to tell him to run and hide with the rest of my men. I want to be angry with them, but I've given them no reason to trust me. Time and time again, I chose Molly over them, and while I wouldn't change anything about that, I understand their reluctance to die in this war for me.

Still, I'm so grateful to see Sasha, to know that one other person will be here to look after Theo, that I pat him on the shoulder and walk him back inside the house.

Theo is finishing up breakfast, and he runs to me, wrapping his arms around my legs. "Where is my momma?"

I scoop him up with one arm and nuzzle my face in his small neck. "I'm going to go find her right now."

"Really?" he asks, excited. "Can I come with you?"

"You can't. I'm sorry." He starts to pout, and I pinch his lower lip playfully between my fingers until he smiles. "But I'll be back soon. And George is coming to stay with you for a while."

The nanny meets my eyes over Theo's head and nods, her silent confirmation that she'll stay with Theo as long as it takes.

I kiss Theo on the forehead and send him off to play before I leave to bring his mom home. I hope for both of our sakes I can keep my promise.

∼

Sasha rallies a few Bratva men who are still loyal, and they follow me to Seamus and Niamh's house. Seamus meets me at his front door, eyes wide.

"I should have called," I admit. "But I was afraid you'd say no if I called first."

He studies me for a moment. "I wouldn't have. And if I did, Niamh would kill me. She is beside herself with the news."

"How far has it spread?" I ask.

"Fedor isn't keeping it quiet," Seamus says, ushering me inside. "This is a big victory for him."

"I assume you know Molly and I aren't really married."

He nods, his mouth twisting to the side. "I know, but I don't care. Do you really love her?"

"With all my heart."

He shrugs. "Then that's all I need to know. You did what you did to protect her, and I understand that. I'd do anything to protect Niamh."

I lean back against the wall in their entryway. "You are more understanding than my men. Most of them deserted me because of the swearing-in ceremony. I polluted a Bratva ritual."

Seamus snorts. "Bullshit. Those cowards were looking for an excuse to escape a sinking ship and they found one. Forgive me for being so blunt, but I think you're aware that your Bratva is in a precarious position."

"Too aware," I groan. "But if you help me now, the newly solidified Bratva I form on the other side of this shit storm will be an ally of the Irish for life. No questions asked."

Seamus extends his hand, and we shake. "I'm on your side now and always, friend."

We are barely into the sitting room before Niamh lunges from the couch and throws herself at us, desperate for information. Her eyes are red-rimmed, and her nose is too. It is the least put-together I've ever seen her.

"Do you have any word yet?" she asks, sniffling.

I share an overview of the conversation I had with Fedor. "Beyond that, I have nothing. No idea at all where he could be or where he is holding her."

Niamh worries her bottom lip between her teeth. "Where is Theo? How is he? He can come here if you'd like."

"He's at home with a nanny and a few guards."

"Is the house really safe for him?" Seamus asks. "We have top-of-the-line security here. He is more than welcome to stay here until everything blows over."

I hadn't realized how worried I still was about Theo until that offer presented itself. Immediately, I call George and tell him to bring Theo over.

"George is welcome to stay with Theo while he is here," Niamh says. "Our home is your home for as long as you need it."

She offers her hand, and I grab it, holding it tightly, silently thanking her for her friendship to both me and Molly.

Seamus interrupts us by wrapping his arm around Niamh and pulling her into his side. "Viktor and I have to go to the office and then I'm not sure when I'll be back."

The two of them share a private moment, no doubt planning for the devastation Fedor could wreak if he wins this war, and then they part with a kiss.

When Seamus and I leave, Niamh is wearing a fake smile and pulling out paper and snacks in preparation for Theo's arrival.

~

I haven't eaten anything since dinner the night before, so Seamus buys a drive-thru breakfast sandwich for me on our way to his office. I finish it just as we pull into the lot.

"So, you trust Petr?" he asks as he parks the car.

I nod. "The only thing he seems to be guilty of is sleeping with the enemy, and I can't execute him for that. Honestly, I can't afford to. I'm pretty short on loyal men these days, and Petr is close with the men. If anyone can convince my men to return, it will be Petr."

"Do you think he'll work for you again after you kidnapped him?"

I roll my neck on my shoulders, stretching out my tense muscles. "I guess we'll find out."

Petr was chained to a chair in the basement of the building the last time I saw him, but Seamus had him moved upstairs to a "cell."

I imagined it would be a cement room with a thin mattress and a toilet, but from what I can see through the window in the door, it is actually a smaller version of a hotel room.

There is a twin-sized bed with three pillows, a small table with a half-eaten sandwich on it, and a chair with a shelf of at least twenty books behind it.

Petr is lying across the bed with a book open on his chest. He must have been sleeping because when I knock on the door, he starts, dropping the book on the floor, and jumps to his feet. He smooths down his hair and then stills when he sees me.

"Can I come in?" I have the key to the door and it only opens from the outside, but I still want to ask. I want Petr to know his opinion matters. I want him to know this isn't an interrogation.

He nods, and I walk inside. I leave the door halfway open behind me so he knows he can leave at any time.

"Nice place you got here."

He shoves his hands in his pockets. His face is blotchy with a purple bruise on his cheek and a green-tinged one near his eye, but otherwise, he looks in good health. "It isn't bad. I'm ready to get out, though."

"The door is open."

He looks up at me, eyebrow raised. "You believe me?"

"Your story was verified by some … pictures on your phone."

He grimaces. "I hoped I wouldn't have to show you those."

"I'm sorry, but I didn't have a choice. I had to know for sure."

Petr holds up a hand. "I know. I was a fucking idiot. Lying to you about anything made all of my moves look suspect. I know that, and I'm not mad." He rubs a hand over his sore cheek. "Well, I'm a little mad. My face hurts like hell."

"It looks like hell, too."

His mouth pulls into a half smile, and for the first time in hours, I allow myself to breathe.

Since I opened my eyes this morning, everything has gone to shit. It has been nothing but bad news. Finally, something has gone right. I have my consiglieri back.

Petr shifts into business mode quickly. His smile slips, and he folds his hands behind his back, shoulders back and broad. "I've heard the guards talking about Molly. What's going on?"

I fill him in as quickly as I can, trying to keep my composure. Rehashing the details of Hannah's betrayal and my distraction makes me feel like a bigger idiot each time. I should have noticed something. If I'd been paying closer attention, this never would have happened.

"I should have been there to help you," Petr says, running a hand down his neck. "You wouldn't have been under so much pressure if I'd been there to pick up some of the slack. I'm sorry, Vik. I really am."

I wave his apology away. "We can hash it out another time. Right now, I need to know that we can move forward and work together."

Petr steps forward and holds out a hand. I grasp his, and he pulls me in for a quick hug, patting me once on the back. "We're good. Brothers for life, okay?"

I swallow down an uncharacteristic swell of emotion and nod in agreement. "Brothers for life."

"Then let's get to work." Petr lets go of my hand and bends down to grab the book he dropped on the floor when I knocked. He tucks it into his front pocket and strolls out of the room, tipping his head to the guard as he saunters past.

Til Death Do Us Part

Petr is even more of a miracle worker than I thought. While my connection with the men in the Bratva has been growing more and more tenuous, his has been strengthening. None of them will take my calls, but they answer Petr's calls on the first ring. They don't want to hear talk of coming back to help the Bratva when it is my idea, but as soon as Petr suggests it, they are open to discussing it.

After a painful afternoon of making phone calls and arrangements when I'd rather be making funeral plans for my baby brother, things are finally in motion.

Seamus' promise of Irish assistance holds steady, and his men are at my disposal and willing to take commands from me. Half of the Bratva men who bailed at the news of my betrayal this morning have returned as well. I assure them there are no hard feelings. Mostly because I can't afford to be picky right now. I need every bit of help I can scrounge up if we are going to save Molly.

Though, things aren't quite as desperate as I thought this morning. While a good number of men did bail on me and the Bratva, more than I realized stayed behind. Their loyalty to me and the Bratva remains, and they trust me to end Fedor, regardless of the Bratva rules I broke.

Still, even with the Irish and remaining Russian men looking together, no one is able to find any trace of Molly or the location of Fedor's current hideout.

"We'll find her," Petr says, squeezing my shoulder. "I'm sure of it."

I want to believe him, but more and more, I'm starting to allow myself to consider what will happen if we don't find her. What will life look like if Molly is gone?

I'll take care of Theo no matter what. He is my son, regardless of genetics. But is that what is best for him? I want to be the one who comforts him when he cries and tells him stories about his mom, but maybe Molly was right all along. Maybe he deserves a better man than me.

Niamh and Seamus never had children, but they would be a good, loving home for him. Maybe they would take him.

The thought of him calling someone else 'dad' makes me feel sick, but I'll do whatever is best for Theo. Always. I owe Molly at least that much.

My phone rings, interrupting my thoughts, and I lunge across the table for it.

The number is unknown, and that is more exciting to me than anything else.

Maybe Molly escaped. Maybe she got away from Fedor and is calling me from a random phone somewhere. Maybe I can get in my car and go pick her up and wrap her in my arms.

My heart is hurling itself against my chest by the time I answer.

So, when I hear the female voice on the other end of the line, the disappointment is physically painful.

"Hannah?"

"Don't hang up," she says quickly, her voice desperate.

"Don't tell me what to do, you bitch," I spit at her, standing up and pacing across the small room. Petr is frowning at me, but I'm too livid to explain. My hands are shaking, and I want to throw my phone across the room. "You turned your back on your best friend. You deserve whatever hell comes your way."

"He has my mom," Hannah says, her voice breaking. "He was blackmailing me, and I didn't know what to do. I'm sorry. I'm so ... so sorry."

I hear her crying on the other end of the line, but I have no sympathy for her. She could have chosen not to participate and gone to the police. Or, better yet, she could have come to me. She could have told me what was going on and allowed me to help her, but she didn't. She got Molly kidnapped and maybe killed.

"I should have told you," she says through tears. "I should have told both of you, but I was so scared. I thought if I just did what Fedor wanted that he would give me back my mother, but now I know it was all a lie."

"No shit. I could have told you that. Molly could have, too. We know him better than you, and we could have helped."

"I know, and I'm sorry, but I want to help."

"Why should I listen to you?" I ask. "Better yet, why should I trust you?"

"Because Molly saved me." Her voice is soft, and I hear her sniffle through the phone.

"What do you mean?"

Hannah tells me about the moments leading up to Molly's kidnapping. She tearfully explains that Fedor was going to shoot her and take Molly, but Molly grabbed the gun and told Hannah to run. Even after being lied to and betrayed by her friend for weeks, Molly saved Hannah's life.

"She is a good person," Hannah says. "Probably the best person I know, and I feel like a piece of shit for betraying her. So, I'd like to help."

I want to hang up the phone and forget Hannah exists. Actually, I'd like to hang up the phone, track her down, and make her regret every lie she told—but I know that won't do much to help Molly now.

However, Molly's example shines like a lighthouse in the distance, guiding me home. She saved Hannah as her last act of freedom, and I have to believe it means something. I have to trust her instincts even when my own instincts are screaming at me to disconnect the call.

I drop my face into my hand and shake my head. "How can you help?"

Hannah sighs with relief. "I have an idea."

23

MOLLY

I don't know how long it has been since the phone call with Viktor. It feels like hours since I heard his voice through the speaker, wondering where I was and if I was okay. I could hear the fear in his voice. I could sense how much he loved me. But still, when Fedor revealed that Viktor had hired—or rather, nearly hired—men to break into my house and scare me, it made me doubt everything.

As soon as Fedor hung up, two of his men dragged me back to my cell, and I've been here ever since, trying to understand my own feelings.

I told myself before that feelings didn't matter in here. They wouldn't help me escape. But now, my feelings feel as inescapable as my cell. No matter how hard I try to push them away, they rise back to the surface, demanding to be felt and understood.

Betrayal.

That is the first and strongest emotion.

Viktor was willing to terrify me and invade my privacy and traumatize Theo to get me to marry him.

Whatever Viktor may think his motivation was, it wasn't love. Love does not hurt like that. Love is not vindictive or scheming.

But he chose not to send the men in. He didn't hire anyone to come and scare us—Fedor did. The fact that Fedor got the idea by listening in on Viktor's conversation adds an entirely new and confusing layer to the situation.

I go around in circles, trying to be angry and disgusted with Viktor, but as hard as I try, I still want him here with me. Even while I'm internally screaming at him for being such a bastard, I long to feel his strong arms around me, telling me everything will be okay.

Plus, crazily enough, if I had taken the protection Viktor had offered me and allowed the guards to follow me last night, I probably wouldn't be trapped in this cell right now. But I bypassed those security measures and took my safety into my own hands, and now look where I am.

I run my hands through my oily hair and wonder whether Theo is okay. Will Viktor have told him I was taken? I hope not. I don't want Theo to worry.

Hopefully he is playing right now. Hopefully Viktor is telling him that I'll be home soon.

It might be a lie, but Theo deserves to live in that lie for a little bit longer. He deserves to hear those words of comfort until Viktor is entirely certain they aren't true.

I'm huddled against the back wall of the cell, my knees tucked to my chest, when the door suddenly bursts open.

I scream and jump to my feet. I didn't even hear the key in the lock, so I'm taken off guard, but I come to my senses quickly.

Fedor is standing in the doorway, his green eyes vibrant and wild. My attention snags on the gun in his hand. He is pointing it at me, and I have no reason to believe he isn't going to shoot me dead right now.

His head is tilted oddly to the side, and I realize he is on the phone. He grabs the phone wedged between his chin and shoulder and hits a button so the sound of a ringtone fills the room on speakerphone.

It rings over and over again. So long that I begin to wonder whether this is a new kind of torture I'm unfamiliar with. Given enough time, the sound would certainly drive anyone mad.

"Your fake husband must not have any real feelings for you, after all. He sure is taking a long time to answer," Fedor sneers.

My heart lurches when I realize I might get to hear Viktor again. I'd still be trapped in this tiny cell with his crazy brother as my guard, but hearing his voice would strengthen my resolve to do everything in my power to get out of here.

Fedor opens his mouth to say something else, but before he can, the phone stops ringing. Then, someone answers.

Except, it isn't Viktor.

"Hello?" The voice is female, and I recognize it, though it takes me a second to place. "Fedor, is that you?"

Fedor frowns and looks down at the phone, probably making sure he called the right number. "Who is this?"

"It's Hannah."

Fedor looks at me like maybe I'll understand what is happening, but I'm just as lost as he is. Last time I saw Hannah, she was running down an alley for her life being pursued by some of Fedor's men. How or why she would be answering Viktor's phone is a mystery. One I hope does not involve anything bad happening to Viktor.

"Why are you answering my brother's phone?"

"Because his hands are tied at the moment." I can hear the smile in her voice. The victory. The pride. Whatever is going on, Hannah is thrilled.

"Do you mean that figuratively or …"

"Literally," she says. "He is handcuffed to a chair in the motel bathroom."

I rise up onto my knees as though I can look through the phone and see Viktor, understand what is going on. Fedor points the gun at me and shakes his head, a silent threat. "What do you mean? I thought you were as good as dead."

"Your men couldn't catch me," she says. "I outran them, but I knew I wouldn't be able to run forever. I had to find a way to prove my worth to you. So, I have."

"By handcuffing my brother in a motel bathroom?" Fedor asks, dubious.

"Exactly."

Fedor sucks on his teeth and then barks out an order. "Explain."

"There is nothing Viktor wants more than to get Molly back, so I used his desperation against him," she says. "I called him and told him I knew where she was and how he could get her back. Like a lovesick puppy, he fell for it. He met me at the hotel, and that was that."

Fedor's brow furrows. "How the fuck did you overpower Viktor?"

"You know how he is. He thinks he is stronger and smarter than everyone around him," Hannah sneers. "His guard was down, and I drugged him. Hauling his beefy ass into the bathroom was a real bitch, but I got him in there, and he isn't going anywhere."

I squeeze my eyes closed, wishing I could stop listening to this. Wishing I could shut out Hannah's words and make it not true.

Would Viktor really fall for a trap like that? Would Hannah really do that to him, even after I spared her life?

I should have let Fedor shoot her. After everything she did to me and the danger she put Theo in, I should have let him kill her. I should have let Fedor do it because now, I'll have to kill her myself. This is unforgivable, and I'll gladly put a bullet in her.

"I know you were going to kill me," Hannah says, her voice going soft and seductive. "But that was only because you thought I wasn't useful. Now, I've proven myself to you. I can help you. Plus, I'm just as guilty as you are now. I won't go to the police. When you come pick up your brother, I'll leave town and you'll never see me again. All I want in return is my mom back."

Her mom? I open my eyes and look up at Fedor. The gun is still trained on me, but he is staring straight ahead at the wall. I can almost see the gears in his head turning, trying to decide what to do about Hannah's offer.

"Release my mom, and we'll be even."

"I don't believe you," Fedor says, drawing out the words, his eyes narrowed. "You were sobbing as you betrayed Molly, now you want me to believe you willingly betrayed Viktor?"

"I hate Viktor. I always have." Hannah's words are cold and harsh. I knew she and Viktor didn't get along, but I never imagined she hated him this much. Enough to send him to his death. "He is a criminal and a monster, and he deserves whatever you have planned for him."

"And Molly?" Fedor asks, turning to me, an eyebrow raised in amusement. Whatever Hannah is going to say, he wants me to hear it. This is what Fedor lives for. The emotional torment is as sweet to him as any physical torture.

Hannah sighs and the line goes quiet for a second while she thinks. "Molly brought all of this on herself when she kept your son from you. It is her fault you and your brother are fighting at all. She is my friend, but she is just as guilty as Viktor."

Her words hit like a punch in the stomach, and the pain must register on my face because Fedor grins at me.

"So, do we have a deal?" Hannah asks. "Your brother in exchange for my mom?"

"Of course. Absolutely." Fedor smiles at me and winks. "Now, where the fuck is my brother?"

∽

Fedor is so excited about Hannah's offer that he leaves the room without saying anything else, and I'm relieved. Because the moment he is gone, I bury my face in my hands and cry.

Is everything my fault?

On one hand, I know this is Fedor's doing. He is criminally insane, and if he hadn't raped me four years ago, none of this would be happening. However, Hannah's theory makes a lot of sense, too.

What if I'd told Fedor about Theo? Would he have helped me raise him? Would he have given me money and a place to stay and taken care of us? Maybe Theo and I wouldn't have been homeless.

Though, being homeless might have been preferable to living under Fedor's thumb.

Multiple time lines spin out inside my head, stories where I took Theo and ran far away, leaving this city far behind. Stories where I told Fedor the truth and he took care of us, others where he had me killed before I could even give birth.

I try to stop the noise inside my head, but the words hit me in the chest again and again.

This is all my fault.

For years, I blamed myself for Fedor's actions. I blamed myself for drinking when I was underage, for accepting a drink from a stranger, for wearing a tight dress. I found a thousand different ways that I was at fault, and it took me years to realize that all of the blame landed squarely on Fedor's shoulders.

I can't backtrack now. I can't allow him to break me down and make me feel responsible for his heinous actions.

I swipe at my eyes and stand up.

This is all my fault.

No.

"No," I whisper to the voice in my head. "It's not. This is not your fault."

I repeat the words over and over again until I believe them. Until the voice in my head gets quiet enough for me to think.

Viktor is in trouble. Fedor is headed to him right now, and I'm stuck in this room. Helpless. We are both helpless.

And Theo.

Tears push at the backs of my eyes, and I look up at the ceiling, holding them back. He is helpless, and will be entirely alone in the world if Fedor gets his way.

Or worse, Theo will be under Fedor's care, which would be worse than being alone.

I have to do something.

I go to the door and look through the window. There is a guard visible in the hallway. He is tall and thin with only a few wisps of facial hair on his chin—definitely young.

I back away from the door, double over, and groan. Loudly.

I moan and grasp my stomach and sob, putting on the best performance of my life until I hear a key in the door.

"What's going on in here?" the guard barks.

I glance up just long enough to see that he has a gun in a holster on his hip and the keys to the door still in his hand. Then, I double over again in another bout of fake pain.

"I'm pregnant," I say between gritted teeth. "Something is wrong. It hurts. Help me."

"I'm not a doctor." The words are clipped, but I can hear the uncertainty in them. Fedor is deranged and heartless, but the men who work for him aren't all that way. Some of them are just doing what they can to survive. I pray this man has some humanity left.

"Please," I gasp, stumbling to the side.

Acting on instinct, the man steps forward and grabs my arm to steady me. The moment his hand wraps around my arm, I jerk away from him and drive my elbow into his stomach. He grunts with the blow, bending over the way I just was, and I scramble to grab the gun at his hip.

The holster is open, so the gun slides out easily, but the guard recovers quickly and tries to grab for my wrist. Before he can get a good hold, I kick him straight in the groin. It is painful enough that he drops my hand, and I flip the safety off and aim the gun at him.

"Give me the keys."

The guard looks even younger now, his eyes wide and terrified, sweat dripping across his forehead.

"He'll kill me," he says, voice breaking. "If he finds out I'm the one who let you escape, he'll kill me."

"Interesting," I say with false sincerity. "Because if I stay here, he'll kill me, too. Now, give me the keys."

The man drops his head, sagging forward, and hands me the keys that are still in his other hand. I shove the keys in my pocket and then instruct the guard to put himself in handcuffs. Once he has, I tighten them and then take off his shoes and socks and shove one of the socks in his mouth as a gag. Slipping his belt from his waist, I wedge it into his mouth and tighten it at the back of his head to keep the gag in place.

"Stay quiet or the last thing I do will be to come back to this room and shoot you dead," I warn, pressing the gun against his temple.

He is shaking all over and nods silently.

I check that the hallway is clear before I step out, close the door, and lock it behind me.

Immediately, I realize the building is not silent, after all. My room must have been heavily soundproofed because I can hear voices and laughter coming from all around me. Some of it sounds like it is coming from different floors, but either way, there are plenty of people around here, and I need to move quickly if I want to escape.

I make it to the end of the hallway without incident when I suddenly hear pained moaning.

I consider moving on. If I can escape here and save Viktor and take down Fedor then I will come back for the other prisoners. I'll save them then.

But what if we can't kill Fedor? What if I escape here and die during the effort? What if I can't come back to help anyone and they all die?

I want to stay focused on my own mission, but guilt twists my stomach, and I stop at the last door in the hallway and look through the window.

The room is dim, but I can make out two shapes lying on the ground. It takes my eyes a second to adjust, but as they do, I realize I recognize the men. One is older with a round middle and the other is a younger version of the other. Clearly related.

They are the Italian dons. The same men who promised Viktor they would help him keep an eye on Fedor only to betray Viktor and take Fedor's side. Clearly, they are regretting that decision now.

The younger don, Rio, looks up at the window, squinting to make out who is looking at him. When he sees me, his eyes go wide. "You're Viktor's woman, right? What are you doing here? Is Viktor here?"

Mario Mazzeo stirs next to his son, but it is obvious he is in rough shape. His eyes are sunken in and bruised, and he has a hard time moving. "Who is here?"

Rio jumps up and moves to the door, his hands bound behind his back. "Get us out of here. Fedor locked us up, and we'll die if you don't help."

His voice is soft through the thick door, but I can still make it out.

"I thought someone innocent might be in here," I say, my voice surprisingly cold. "I'm not going to waste my time on you."

I turn to leave, but Rio's muffled voice stops me. "You'll never make it out alive. This place is too heavily guarded."

I freeze, wishing I could keep walking. But I realize all at once that I don't know my way out of this building. I have no idea where to go or how many men are here.

I spin around. "What do you know about this building?"

"Everything. We've walked it many times. We can help you out of here, but you have to help us escape."

I look down at the keys in my hand, and Rio follows my eyes. When he sees the keys, he becomes more desperate. "Please. Please help us. We'll pledge our allegiance to Viktor. Or you. Whatever you want. Help us."

He sounds nothing like the cocky don I remember from before, and it becomes apparent how efficiently Fedor has beaten the man down.

"I'll kill you if you betray me," I growl, grabbing the key and shoving it in the door. "If you do anything at all that makes me doubt your loyalty, I'll shoot you in the head. Do you understand?"

He nods vigorously. "Understood. Just let us out."

I turn the key and it works. The door opens and Rio spins around to help his elderly father to his feet. Mario nods in thanks as they walk out of the room, hands still tied behind their backs.

"Wait." I grab Mario Mazzeo's shoulder and turn him around. Ropes are wound around his liver-spotted hands. Too thick to cut through with a key. "We need to untie you."

"There's a utility closet just there." Rio points to a door two down from their cell. "I've seen guards go in and out for supplies.

I ready my gun to take out anyone who may be inside and then throw the door open. The room is empty, so I step in and flip the light switch, and then say a silent prayer of thanks.

The room is not just a utility closet. It is a weapons room. Guns and bullets and knives line the shelves. I grab another gun, check to see it is loaded, and shove it in the waistband of my jeans. Then, I stash one knife in my back pocket and grab a second before walking into the hallway to free the two men. Then, I point them towards the room.

"There are weapons in there. Arm yourselves and then we move."

Mario and Rio are both comfortable with weapons, and they come out armed with handguns, semiautomatic rifles, and plenty of magazines. Mario looks like he is bowing under the weight, but I don't have time to worry about him. I freed him from the cell and gave him a weapon; that is my good deed for the day.

"I can't believe they'd leave all of these in an unlocked room," Rio says, admiring the gun around his chest.

"I can," I say, rolling my eyes. "Fedor is a cocky son of a bitch. He would never imagine we could escape."

I'm hoping Fedor's cockiness will continue to play to my advantage. He never imagined I would fight back. He never imagined I would be able to overpower one of his guards and free his other prisoners. So, I plan to continue bucking his expectations. I will surprise him until Viktor is safe, and together, we bring Fedor to his knees.

"Help me escape, and your betrayal will be forgiven," I say, leading the two men down the hallway towards a stairwell.

"By whose authority?" Rio asks. "Are you sure Viktor feels the same way?"

I stop him at the doorway, one arm blocking their path forward. Before we move any further, I need them to understand who they are protecting. "It doesn't matter how Viktor feels. I'm his wife, and I am promising you immunity if you get me out of here alive. Don't worry about Viktor, worry about me."

Rio's eyes narrow for a moment, and then he and his father both nod in understanding.

"Good." I lower my arm and let them pass in front of me. "Now, get me out of here so I can save my husband."

24

VIKTOR

Hannah is pacing by the door, waiting for Fedor to arrive, and it takes everything in me not to scream at her.

She helped me set a trap for Fedor just like she said she would, but it doesn't change the fact that she betrayed Molly and put her in danger in the first place. Her mother was kidnapped and held by Fedor, and I understand how bad that must have been for her, but it is no excuse to turn on an innocent person. Especially when that innocent person is as sweet and gentle as Molly.

I hate Hannah, but right now, she is helping us, and I have to shove aside my hate until Molly is safe.

"I think he is here," Hannah says, looking through the peephole of the motel door. "Three cars just pulled into the parking lot."

I push her aside and look through the hole. Three black cars are idling at the far end of the lot closest to the check-in desk.

"Call him," I say. "Tell him you see him and give him the room number."

Hannah does as I ask and calls Fedor. His voice is faint and indecipherable through the phone, but Hannah says exactly what I told her to and then hangs up.

"He's coming." She takes a deep breath, and I can practically see her heart pounding through her shirt.

I nod for her to go hide, and she goes into the bathroom and climbs into the tub. I adjust my bulletproof vest and prepare myself.

This is it. I'm going to kill my brother.

The thought still fills me with mixed emotions, but I focus on the fact that Fedor is here to kill me right now. That is his sole purpose in being here. He wouldn't hesitate to end my life, so I can't hesitate to end his. I can't. It is either him or Molly, and there is no competition. I'll choose Molly every time.

Seamus and his men are in the rooms surrounding the one I'm in, ready to jump out and fight off Fedor and his men as soon as I give the signal.

I wanted Hannah to be the one to answer the door. I wanted her to lure Fedor into the room so I could kill him more easily, but at the end of the day, I can't trust her. She stuck to her end of the bargain in getting Fedor here, but she is clearly a survivor. Her main goal is to get out of this alive, and I can't trust that she won't flip sides on me again. So, it is safer to just do it myself, even if it might be messier.

When three knocks sound on the door, I grip my gun against my chest and take a deep breath.

This is it.

I grab the doorknob and start to open the door, but just as I do, I realize I never gave the signal. I was so nervous about facing Fedor that I never knocked on the door adjoining the two motel rooms. Seamus and his men don't know Fedor is here yet.

I freeze, the door partway open, unsure what to do.

"Hello?" Fedor asks, sounding suspicious. "Hannah?"

I could open the door and shoot at Fedor, but his guards would gun me down moments later. I have to alert Seamus, but I'm not sure how to do that without letting Fedor know this is a trap and giving him the upper hand.

"What the fuck is going on?" Fedor asks.

I'm out of time and options, so I do the only thing I can think of. I cup a hand around my mouth and yell, "He's here!"

"Shit." Fedor curses on the other side of the door. I hear him and his men scrambling to get away, but I also hear the doors around me open. I follow suit and step into the breezeway.

Irish members move into the breezeway and the parking lot, backing Fedor and his men into the corner, but they aren't going quietly. Bullets are flying and by the time I step outside ,there are already two men on the ground, blood pooling around them.

"I'm sorry," I yell to Seamus as I advance on my brother. "I fucked it up."

He waves me away and points to Fedor, directing me to focus, and I'm trying. I really am.

I've never been this frazzled before. Perhaps it is because I know this is it. I know this is the last battle I'm going to have with Fedor. Only one of us is going to walk away from this. Either I'll kill him, or I'll die trying.

I take a sobering breath and begin firing.

My men and Seamus' men are shooting at Fedor's guards, but I aim for their cars. I can't let them escape this.

One by one, I blow out the tires on their vehicles and shatter the windshields. Then and only then do I turn on his men.

I step out from behind the pillar I was using for cover, and immediately, I feel a burning sensation in the center of my chest. I don't need to look down to know someone hit me in my bulletproof vest. I'm alive, but it still hurts like a motherfucker.

When I look up, I see Fedor lowering his gun and ducking behind one of their wasted cars.

He hit me in the chest without a second thought.

Suddenly, the doubt I've been experiencing fades away. I can no longer remember why I was hesitating.

I don't want to be the one to kill my younger brother, but my baby brother has been dead for a long time. And I didn't kill him. Fedor did.

This new version of Fedor strangled the innocent, kind version of my brother I've been holding onto. The little boy I loved and protected is gone, and now, I'm left to deal with the cold murderer in his stead.

I shake off the pain in my chest and charge forward, taking out two of Fedor's men in the blink of an eye.

Fedor sees me approaching through a shattered window in the car and has the good sense to look terrified.

He grabs one of his guards and makes a run for the front lobby of the motel, ducking inside the shabby building.

Instead of following him, I duck into a maintenance hallway that splits the motel into two separate buildings with an overhang between and run to the back of the building. The grass is slick with dew, and I slide around the turn but manage to keep my footing as I head towards the back door.

That is where Fedor is going. I know it.

His men are out front fighting on his behalf and dying, but he doesn't care. He is like a rat searching for dry ground in a flood. He will leave them all to die if it means he will live. He is going to run away.

A gunshot slices through the air, closer than the ones happening at the front of the building, and I spin around searching for Fedor, assuming he shot me. Then, I see a middle-aged man poking around the corner of the hallway I just ran through. He is chasing after me, still trying to protect his "fearless" leader, even as his leader is making a run for it.

I lift my arm to shoot him and a sharp pain burns through my muscle. My arm seizes up, and I nearly drop the gun. He shot me in the arm. In almost the exact same place where I was sliced in the arm a week ago. Molly was worried the slice would leave a scar and now there is no doubt about it. I'll definitely have a scar.

I switch hands and fire at the corner, hitting the man's exposed knee. He screams in pain and falls to the ground, cradling his leg, and I take him out.

Usually, I reserve kill shots for necessity only, but there is more than just my life on the line. I have Theo and Molly and our unborn baby to think about. I'll singlehandedly slaughter every person on the motel's property if it means keeping them safe. I have no regrets.

I spin around just as the back door of the motel bursts open and Fedor comes sprinting out of it. He doesn't even look around to see if the coast is clear. He keeps his arms close to his sides, head down, and sprints for the tree line in the distance that borders the drainage ditch.

If he makes it through the trees, he could very well escape, and I can't let that happen.

I aim for him and fire, shooting once, twice.

Grass and dirt explode just behind him, and Fedor jumps and then picks up his pace. I adjust my aim a bit higher, and I see the blood spurt from his thigh. A direct hit.

He stumbles, rolling over his shoulder in the grass before getting his good leg under him again. If I wasn't the one chasing him, I'd be impressed with the show of agility. As it is, I'm annoyed he won't just stay down.

Fedor glares at me, and I barely recognize him. His pupils have eaten up the usual electric green of his eyes, and he looks like a man possessed. He lifts his gun just as I lift mine, and we shoot at the same time like it is an old-timey duel.

I feel the shot hit me in the vest just above my heart, and I drop to my knees with the force of it. Fedor, too, drops to the ground, but whereas I'm unscathed, I see a red stain spreading across his gray T-shirt just over his stomach. He presses his hand to the spot and then looks at me, his eyes wide enough that even from a distance, I can see the whites around his irises.

He fires at me again, and I hear the shot shatter a window on the back of the motel. I fall down in the grass, but when he pulls the trigger again, it is just a useless click.

He's empty.

I crawl forward on my knees and elbows, eventually making it back to my feet, and run for him. My arm is burning, but it isn't life-threatening. Not like Fedor's wound. My brother tries to run for the trees again, but he only makes it a few steps before he stumbles over his own feet and rolls in the grass. This time, rather than deftly maneuvering to his feet, he staggers on his hands and knees. He looks like a wounded animal, and it is pathetic.

"Enough," I call after him, my boots squishing into the soft earth. "Face me and let's end this."

"Easy for you to say; you have a weapon," he says, rolling onto his back. "It isn't exactly a fair fight."

"Was it a fair fight when you kidnapped Molly? Did you give her time to arm herself and give her a fighting chance?"

He doesn't answer and scoots away from me on the ground. His face is paler than I've ever seen it and the blood is spreading across his shirt so quickly that it's hard to tell what color the fabric was originally.

I can still hear shots coming from the front of the building, but they are happening less often than before. Whatever is happening up there, it is about to wrap up. I hope Seamus and his men come out victorious.

If not, at least I'll have this victory before Fedor's men kill me.

"That's what I thought," I say, standing over him. "That's kind of your thing, isn't it, Fedor? Overpowering those who are weaker than you? Beating people who can't fight back?"

Fedor's mouth turns up in a smirk, but the expression doesn't reach his eyes. His eyes are those of a cornered animal, searching desperately for escape. He keeps checking the building to see if any of his men are coming to save him. "Is this about me kidnapping Molly or when I impregnated her?"

"*Raped her*," I correct. "You drugged her and raped her, and I should have known the moment she told me what you did that you were unredeemable, but I thought maybe I could help you."

"Help me?" He snorts. "Is that what you call keeping my son from me? Is that what you call lying to me and sleeping with the mother of my child? Were you helping me? Well, excuse me for being confused."

"I was helping them," I say. "I was keeping them safe from you and hoping that you would turn it around and become a human again. But no matter how hard I tried, you became more and more of a monster, and now, you are irredeemable. There's nothing else to be done."

His breathing is growing heavy, and I know that even without a final shot, Fedor will bleed out back here. He will lie in the grass and spill his blood until there is nothing left. It may take a while, but he'll die.

"Giving up on me so easily?" he gasps. "I thought you would always protect me, Vik."

His voice is a mix between a sneer and a plea, and I know it is his way of begging for his life. He is trying to appeal to my big-brother heart. He is trying to make me feel something for him, but he is too late.

"I am protecting you," I say, kneeling down in front of him, looking into his eyes. "I'm protecting you from yourself."

He opens his mouth to say something else, but before he can, I press my gun to his temple and pull the trigger.

25

MOLLY

We are backed into a dead end and Mario Mazzeo does not look well.

"Come on, Dad. We have to keep going," Rio says, trying to rouse his father. But I can tell by the look in his eyes that he is wondering whether to go down with this ship or try to save himself.

Regardless of what he decides, I'm going to try to save myself. I'm not dying here like this.

We made it out of the hallway with the prison cells all right, but the moment we walked out of the stairwell on the first floor, all hell broke loose. Fedor has even more men fighting for him than I thought, and they were all congregated in the large entrance hall. They started fighting the moment we opened the door and haven't stopped since.

The Italian dons put up a good fight, especially considering they were fighting a lot of their own men who went to Fedor's side when they realized their leaders were locked in a prison cell upstairs. Mario is a hell of a shot, and Rio gave his dad as much cover as he could. I did my best to clear a path from the stairwell to a more covered location. It helped that many of the men weren't armed. Apparently, they hadn't been expecting three of their captives to burst into the room armed to the teeth.

But now, we are trapped in a back room with the door barricaded while Fedor's men arm themselves and prepare to kill us all.

I circle the room several times in search of a window or a back door, but there is nothing. Unlike the room upstairs, this closet is not filled with weapons, but produce. It is some kind of pantry, and unless the Mazzeos know how to turn protein bars into weapons of mass destruction, I don't see how we are going to get out of here alive.

Suddenly, there is a piercing alarm that fills the air and the sound of voices on the other side of the door fades to stunned silence.

Then, the alarm goes quiet, and I hear it. The sound I've been dying to hear for hours … days … weeks.

Viktor's voice.

"Fedor is dead."

Mario gasps and moves towards the door, pressing his ear against it to hear better.

"Fedor is dead," Viktor repeats, talking through some kind of megaphone. "Put down your weapons and live or be shot on sight."

"Holy shit," Mario says, a smile spreading across his face. "Holy shit, we're going to live."

I run to the door and push him aside. I don't know what is happening on the other side of that door, but I need to see Viktor. Now.

I ready my gun, take a calming breath, and open the door.

Fedor's soldiers are standing around the room, looking confused, and when I walk out, they all return to high alert. Too many guns to count are pointed at me.

Then, the front door of the building bursts open and Viktor comes storming in.

"Put down your weapons," he shouts, his voice echoing off the walls.

No one moves, and Viktor lifts his gun and shoots the first man he encounters. The bullet tears through his hand, forcing him to drop the weapon, and Viktor raises an eyebrow at everyone else. "Drop. Your. Weapons."

Immediately, the sound of guns clattering to the floor echoes around the room, and I meet his eyes.

His face is blood splattered and muddy, and his clothes are full of holes, but he is whole and breathing and staring at me like I'm a ghost. Like he can't believe what he is seeing.

Men surge forward around him, beginning the arduous process of getting Fedor's men under control, but I ignore all of it and rush towards Viktor. I just need to feel him in my arms. I need to know he is okay.

I'm only a few steps away from him when he stumbles. Then, just as I reach him, he drops to one knee and then the other.

"Viktor?" I try to catch him, but he is too heavy, and we both fall to the floor. His head lands in my lap, and I smooth his hair back from his forehead as his eyes flutter closed.

There is blood on his arm, two holes in the front of his shirt where bullets hit his vest, and then I see the bloodstain on his leg. He is hurt, and even though I'm desperate for him to scoop me up and carry me out of here, I have to be the one who is strong.

Right now, I have to save him.

"Pick him up," I bark at two of the men standing closest. "Careful with his wounds. Get him in a car. Now."

The men hesitate for only a second before they follow my

commands. I stand up and smooth down my dirty clothes. I know I don't look the part of a Bratva queen, but it is more important than ever that I play it. If Viktor was telling the truth and Fedor really is dead, these men are all looking for someone to follow.

And right now, they are going to follow me.

～

I'm sitting in an uncomfortable chair with a scratchy blanket wrapped around my legs when I hear my favorite sound in the entire world: Theo's laughter.

"She's in there," Niamh says, appearing in the doorway, ushering in my dark-haired angel.

I fall out of the chair and onto the tile floor. I open my arms wide as Theo runs into them, burying his face in my neck. I plaster him with kisses as he tries to tell me all of the fun things he and Niamh did together.

Once I got Viktor admitted to the hospital and stabilized, Seamus called and told me Theo was asleep at his house with Niamh, and she would bring him in the morning. He also asked me what I wanted done with the Italian dons.

"They are saying you promised them immunity?"

I was so confident back at the warehouse, making promises I wasn't sure I'd be able to keep. Part of me wanted to bend to Seamus' will and tell him to do what he wanted with them, but another part of me wasn't ready to get rid of the power I claimed while I was locked up. I came out of that warehouse a stronger, more confident woman, and I don't want all of that pain and trauma to be for nothing.

"I did offer them immunity. They fought for me, and they are loyal to me now. To us."

Without hesitation, Seamus agreed. "Okay. Now, what can my men do to help?"

It felt crazy to have the boss of a crime family asking me for orders, but I gave them like it was the most natural thing in the world. "Have them chase down Fedor's men. Get them out of the city or kill them. Either way, I don't care, but we don't want them here anymore."

"Done," Seamus says. "I'll put an Irish guard on you guys at the hospital and the Italian dons. You just worry about getting your husband healthy, okay?"

So, that is what I did.

All night, I've held Viktor's hand and waited for him to regain consciousness.

"Is Daddy okay?" Theo asks, running to Viktor's bedside, staring at the tubes coming out of his arms.

"He is getting better," I assure him. "He is resting right now so he can get strong."

"He's already strong," Theo frowns. "The strongest."

I smile, tears welling in my eyes as I meet Niamh's gaze over Viktor's hospital bed. "He is the strongest, babe. You're right."

∼

Theo is with Seamus and Niamh when Viktor finally wakes up two days later.

"Molly?" His voice is harsh and dry, and I look up from the magazine I've been flipping through, and blink at him.

For the last two days, I've had nothing but time to think about what I learned while I was held captive. About Viktor nearly hiring men to pretend to kidnap Theo.

I'm angry with him. So fucking angry.

But I was even more angry that he wouldn't wake up so I could tell him how angry I was. I was more upset that he was unconscious and injured and sick than anything else, and therein lies the answer to my unspoken question.

"Molly?" Viktor asks again, squinting at me. "Are you okay? Are you hurt? Where's Theo?"

The heart monitors next to his bed start beeping faster, and I jump out of my chair and kneel next to his bed. "We're all fine. You're the one who is hurt. You lost a lot of blood."

He tries to sit up in his bed, and I press him back down and then work the lever on the railing to lift the back of the mattress forward until he is sitting half up.

"I should call for a nurse," I say, laying my hand over his. Immediately, though, Viktor closes my hand with both of his and shakes his head.

"Not yet. Please."

"But—"

"I'm sorry," he says, cutting off my protests. "I'm so sorry, Molly. About everything. I should have never even considered hiring men to scare you, and I shouldn't have tried to manipulate you into marrying me. And I should have been paying better attention and known that Hannah was up to something. I messed up, and I'm so fucking sorry. You have no idea. If I could go back and change things then I would."

"I wouldn't," I say quickly, realizing all at once that I truly mean the words. Viktor looks up at me like I'm crazy, his eyebrows pulled together in the center, and I smile at him. His hair is mussed from days of lying down, and his face is creased from his pillow. He looks so much younger like this, and I reach out and stroke my hand across his cheek. "I wouldn't change anything because ... we're here. We're alive. We are all okay."

He blinks and then lays his hand over mine, pinning my palm to his cheek. "We are?"

I nod. "We are, but you do have to promise me something."

"Anything," he says without pause.

"You can't ever lie to me again. About anything." I shake my head. "If we are going to do this, there has to be honesty between us. Always."

Viktor's lips are dry when they pull up into a smile. "If we are going to do what thing?"

The hope in his voice cracks the ice around my heart, and I can't keep back my smile. "Life. Marriage."

His grin splits his face, and he looks happier than I've ever seen him. Despite his horrible breath and his sweaty forehead and the tubes and wires and monitors, I lean down and brush my lips across his, leaning into the comfort of his kiss.

"So, you're staying?" he asks when I pull away.

I shrug. "If you can promise me that—"

"Done," he says before I can finish. "Done. Definitely. Whatever you want, it's yours."

I laugh. "You might come to regret that."

He runs his thumb over my knuckles, staring down at my hand like it is the most precious thing he has ever seen. When he looks into my eyes, I want to melt. "Regret isn't possible where you're concerned, Molly. I could never regret you. I love you."

The tears I've been holding back for days finally spill over my cheeks, and I swipe at them with my free hand, laughing at myself. Viktor pulls me towards him, curling his strong arm around my back, and I bury my face in his newly grown-in whiskers. "I love you, too."

"Daddy?" Theo's small voice breaks through our moment, and Viktor tenses under me.

"Theo?" His voice breaks when he sees Theo crawling over the bed to get to him, and I uncurl myself from his chest and let the two of them hug. Theo is the only person I'd allow Viktor to choose over me.

Theo is talking too fast to keep up with, telling us about all the things we've missed while we've been away, and while he talks, Viktor reaches out and grabs my hand, pulling me to the edge of the bed. We sit there, holding hands, listening to Theo regale us with stories of life as a four-year-old, and it is the most perfect beginning to our new life together I could ever imagine.

For the first time in years, I think that everything just might be all right.

EPILOGUE

MOLLY

One Month Later

"You're late!"

I slip out of my heels and tuck them in the closet by the front door. It used to be where my full-time security team set up shop, but now it hardly gets any use, so we use it more as a coat closet.

"I know, I'm so sorry. I got to talking with Hannah and Niamh about Niamh's upstairs bathroom remodel, and we lost track of time."

"Bathroom?" Viktor asks. "I thought you were doing the library."

"We are, but we're almost finished with that. Now, Niamh wants the bathroom done, too."

"Seamus loves that, I'm sure," Viktor says, sarcasm thick in his voice.

I pad barefoot into the kitchen, expecting to see Viktor, but he isn't in there. I grab a glass from the cabinet and fill it with water, leaning back against the counter to drink it.

"Seamus doesn't have much of a say."

Viktor laughs and then hesitates. Even from a room away, I can feel his tension. "And things with Hannah are okay?"

Viktor still hates Hannah. He doesn't trust her or forgive her, and I understand his anger, but I don't feel the same way. She made a mistake under serious duress and then did her best to fix it. She kept her distance for weeks after everything happened, but just last week she called me to talk. We spent two hours on the phone that night and again the next night. Eventually, we went for coffee and then lunch. Now, she has been helping me with Niamh's remodel projects. Niamh hasn't come out and said it directly, but I know she has a soft spot for Hannah. Niamh has a soft spot for anything that needs a little work, interior design related or otherwise. She likes to fix things up, and Hannah is the perfect project.

"They are great," I say. "She has been a big help with the library, and she and Niamh are really hitting it off."

"Great." Again, his sarcasm is obvious, but I ignore him. Either he'll come to stand Hannah or he won't. But either way, he'll have to deal with her presence in my life.

I set my glass in the sink and walk into the living room. "What did you and Theo do for dinner?"

I expect him to be lounging on the couch, but he isn't there.

"Where are you?" I ask, spinning in a circle. Just as I'm finishing the full three-sixty, I see him standing in the doorway to the balcony wearing a pair of dress pants and the blue cashmere sweater I tell him brings out the color of his eyes. He has a red rose in his hands.

I blink at him, stunned by how handsome he is, and shake my head. "What are you doing?"

He smiles, effectively stopping my heart, and nods for me to come closer. "I think you already have a good idea."

My heart is hammering against my ribs as I cross the room to stand in front of him. He bends down and brushes a soft kiss against my lips before stepping to the side and revealing the candlelit dinner on the balcony. There is sparkling grape juice—since my pregnancy doesn't allow for champagne—and two covered plates of food. But the thing that catches my eye is the little velvet box on the edge of the table. Viktor reaches for it and turns back to me, his throat bobbing as he swallows down his nerves.

"Viktor," I say, tears already welling in my eyes.

He holds up a hand and shakes his head. "Hold yourself together or else I'll lose it, too." He pulls a folded-up piece of paper from his pocket and waves it in front of me. "I wrote it down so I wouldn't forget."

Silent tears are rolling down my cheeks as he unfolds the paper and begins to read.

"Molly," he starts, looking at me with soft blue eyes. "I've given a version of this speech twice before. I laid out the practical reasons why you should marry me for the safety of yourself and our children. I made good arguments that I stand behind, but the thing I failed to mention in both proposals is the depth of my love for you. So, here's hoping the third time is the charm."

I choke back a sob, and Viktor reaches out and grabs my hand, smoothing his thumb over my knuckles.

"From the first moment I saw you and Theo, I wanted nothing more than to take care of you. For a long time, I thought it was because I wanted to make right the crimes of the past, but now, I recognize my motivations for what they truly were: love. I loved you from the moment I saw you, and I love you still. Our love story has not been easy or simple. It has been star-crossed in a thousand different ways, yet every single time, regardless of the obstacle, we come back together."

I'm full-on weeping now, barely able to stand, and Viktor wraps an arm around my waist and hugs me against his chest as he finishes his speech.

"I want you to know right now that even if you refuse this proposal flat out and turn me down, I'll still choose you, Molly. I'll choose to respect your wishes. I'll choose to co-parent our baby and Theo, because he is as much mine now as he is yours. I will choose to do whatever is best for your mental, physical, and emotional well-being, even if it means breaking my own heart."

His voice cracks, and I wrap my arms around him and bury my face in his chest, listening to the sound of his heart beating.

"But if you accept me." He sighs with the very thought. "If you accept me, then I will make you the happiest woman on earth. I will protect you, cherish you, and respect you until my dying breath."

Viktor unwraps me from his body and drops down to one knee, wincing from the wound in his leg, and opens the velvet box. The ring inside is huge and shining, but nothing can compare to the hope shimmering in his bright blue eyes.

"Molly Reyes, make me the happiest man in the world and marry me. Please."

The sight of him on his knees in front of me is the most magnificent thing I've ever seen, and it feels like my brain explodes. I grab the box from his hands, place it on the table, and throw myself at him.

Viktor laughs as I kiss his face and his neck. As my hands skim down the soft cashmere of his sweater and begin undoing his belt.

"Is that a yes?" he chuckles, lifting his arms to let me pull his sweater over his head.

"Hell yes," I growl, smoothing my hands down his flat, strong stomach. "Absolutely."

He lies back on the balcony, letting me straddle his hips, and grips my waist in his big hands. "Usually, consummating the marriage comes after the wedding."

I yank my dress over my head in one motion and rock my hips against his growing hardness, drawing a moan from him.

"We've never been very traditional, so why start now?"

Viktor's eyes rake over my body, and he finds the clasp of my bra and flicks it open, slipping the lacy material from my body. "Great question," he growls.

The sex is fast and wild. He keeps his pants on and just pushes my panties to the side, and we find pleasure in each other's bodies as the cool night air bites against our skin and the sounds of the city drift up to us.

Viktor throws a hand over my mouth as I come, screaming out his name, and he bites down on my shoulder when release finds him, rocking his hips up and into my body, spilling inside of me.

By the time we clean up and get dressed, the food is cold, but neither of us cares. Viktor scoops me up, careful of his wounds, and takes me upstairs for round two. On the way, we stop outside of Theo's door. Viktor put him to bed before I arrived home, and he is breathing deeply in his room, clutching a teddy bear Viktor bought for him.

Viktor sets me down on the ground and wraps an arm around my waist, pulling me against his warmth. I smile up at him, unable to believe this is going to be my life.

Then, he kisses me, and the fire in my belly reignites.

I close Theo's door and push Viktor towards the bedroom we share. When he falls back on the bed, I close the door with no intention of opening it again before dawn.

Tonight, he is mine.

Thanks for reading, but don't stop now! Get the exclusive Extended Epilogue to TIL DEATH DO US PART.

Click here to keep reading Viktor and Molly's happily ever after.

SNEAK PREVIEW (BROKEN VOWS)

Keep reading for a sneak preview of my bestselling mafia romance novel, BROKEN VOWS!

She's my fake wife, my property… and my last chance at redemption.

She's beautiful. An angel.

I'm dangerous. A killer.

She's my fake bride for a single reason – so I can crush her father's resistance.

But marrying Eve brings me far more than I bargained for.

She's fiery. Feisty. Won't take no for an answer.

She makes me believe that I might be worth redemption.

Until I discover a past she's been hiding from me.

One that threatens everything.

Now, I know that our wedding vows are not enough.

I need to make sure she's mine for good.

A baby in her belly is the only way to seal the deal.

In the end, the Bratva always gets what it wants.

∼

Luka

Their fear tingles against my skin like a whisper. As my leather-soled shoes tap against the concrete floor, I can sense it in the way their eyes dart towards and away from me. In the way they scurry around the production floor like mice, meek and unseen in the shadows. I enjoy it.

Even before I rose through the ranks of my family, I could inspire fear. Being a large man made that simple. But now, with brawn and power behind me, people cower. These people—the employees at the soda factory—don't even know why they fear me. Other than me being the owner's son, they have no real reason to be afraid of me, and yet, like prey in the grasslands, they sense the lion is near. I observe each of them as I weave my way around conveyors filled with plastic bottles and aluminum cans, carbonated soda being pumped into them, filling the room with a syrupy sweet smell.

I recognize their faces, though not their names. The people upstairs don't concern me. Or, at least, they shouldn't. The soda factory is a cover for the real operation downstairs, which must be protected at all costs. It's why I'm here on a Friday evening sniffing around for rats. For anyone who looks unfamiliar or out of place.

The floor manager—a Hispanic woman with a severe braid running down her back—calls out orders to the employees on the floor below in both English and Spanish, directing attention where necessary. She doesn't look at me once.

Noise permeates the metal shell of the building. The whirr of conveyor belts and grinding of gears makes the concrete floors feel like they are vibrating from the sheer power of the sound waves. A lot of people find the sights and smells overwhelming, but I've never minded. You don't become a mob underboss by shrinking in the face of chaos.

A group of employees in blue polos gather around a conveyor belt, smoothing out some kink in the production line. They pull a few aluminum cans from the line and drop them in a recycling bin, jockeying the rest of the cans back into a smooth line. The larger of the three men—a bald man with a doughy face and no obvious chin—flips a red switch. An alarm sounds and the cans begin moving again. He gives the floor manager a thumbs up and then turns to me, his hand flattening into a small wave. I raise an eyebrow in response. His face reddens, and he turns back to his work.

I don't recognize him, but he can't be in law enforcement. Undercover cops are more fit than he could ever dream to be. Plus, he wouldn't have drawn attention to himself. Likely, he is just a new hire, unaware of my position in the company. I resolve to go over new hires with the site manager and find out the man's name.

When I make it to the back of the production floor, the lights are dimmed—the back half of the factory not being utilized overnight—and I fumble with my keys for a moment before finding the right one to unlock the basement door. The stairway down is dark, and as soon as the metal door slams shut behind me, I'm left in blackness, my other senses heightening. The sounds of the production floor are but a whisper behind me, but the most pressing difference is the smell. Rather than the syrupy sweetness of the factory, there is an ether, chemical-like smell that makes my nose itch.

"That you, Luka?" Simon Oakley, the main chemist, doesn't wait for me to answer. "I've got a line here for you. We've perfected the chemistry. Best coke you'll ever try."

I pull back a thick curtain at the base of the stairs and step into the bright white light of the real production floor. I blink as my eyes adjust, and see Simon alone at the first metal table, three other men working in the back of the room. Like the employees upstairs, they don't look up as I enter. Simon, however, smiles and points to the line.

"I don't need to try it," I say flatly. "I'll know whether it's good or not when I see how much our profits increase."

"Well," Simon balks. "It can take time for word to spread. We may not see a rise in income until—"

"I'm not here to chat." I walk around the end of the table and stand next to Simon. He is an entire head shorter than me, his skin pale from spending so much time in the basement. "There have been nasty rumors going around among my men."

His bushy brows furrow in concern. "Rumors about what? You know we basement dwellers are often the last to hear just about everything." He tries to chuckle, but it dies as soon as he sees that I'm not here to fuck around.

"Disloyalty." I purse my lips and run my tongue over my top teeth. "The rumbling is that someone has turned their back on the family."

Fear dilates his pupils, and his fingers drum against the metal tabletop. "See? That is what I'm saying. I haven't heard a single thing about any of that."

"You haven't?" I hum in thought, taking a step closer. I can tell Simon wants to back away, but he stays put. I commend him for his bravery even as I loath him for it. "That is interesting."

His Adam's apple bobs in his throat. "Why is that interesting?"

Before he can even finish the sentence, my hand is around his neck. I strike like a snake, squeezing his windpipe in my hand and walking him back towards the stone wall. I hear the men in the back of the room jump and murmur, but they make no move to help their boss. Because I outrank Simon by a mile.

"It's interesting, Simon, because I have reliable information that says you met with members of the Furino mafia." I slam his head against the wall once, twice. "Is it true?"

His face is turning red, eyeballs beginning to bulge out, and he claws at my hand for air. I don't give him any.

"Why would you go behind my back and meet with another family? Have I not welcomed you into our fold? Have I not made your life here comfortable?"

Simon's eyes are rolling back in his head, his fingers becoming limp noodles on my wrist, weak and ineffective. Just before his body can sag into unconsciousness, I release him. He drops to the floor, falling onto his hands and knees and gasping for air. I let him get two breaths before I kick him in the ribs.

"I didn't meet with them," he rasps. When he looks up at me, I can already see the beginnings of bruises wrapping around his neck.

I kick him again. The force knocks the air out of him, and he collapses on his face, forehead pressed to the cement floor.

"Okay," he says, voice muffled. "I talked with them. Once."

I pressed the sole of my shoe into his ribs, rolling him onto his back. "Speak up."

"I met with them once," he admits, tears streaming down his face from the pain. "They reached out to me."

"Yet you did not tell me?"

"I didn't know what they wanted," he says, sitting up and leaning against the wall.

"All the more reason you should have told me." I reach down and grab his shirt, hauling him to his feet and pinning him against the wall. "Men who are loyal to me do not meet with my enemies."

"They offered me money," he says, wincing in preparation for the next blow. "They offered me a larger cut of the profits. I shouldn't have gone, but I have a family, and—"

I was raised to be an observer of people. To spot their weaknesses and know when I am being deceived. So, I know immediately Simon is not telling me the entire story. The Furinos would not reach out to our chemist and offer him more money unless there had been communication between them prior, unless they had some connection Simon is not telling me about. He thinks I am a fool. He thinks I will forgive him because of his wife and child, but he does not know the depths of my apathy. Simon thinks he can appeal to my humanity, but he does not realize I do not have any.

I press my hand into the bruises around his neck. Simon grabs my wrist, trying to pull me away, but I squeeze again, enjoying the feeling of his life in my hands. I like knowing that with one blow to the neck, I could break his trachea and watch him suffocate on the floor. I am in complete control.

"And your family will be dead before dawn unless you tell me why you met with the Furinos," I spit. I want nothing more than to kill Simon for being disloyal. I can figure out the truth without him. But it is not why I was sent here. Killing indiscriminately does not create the kind of controlled fear we need to keep our family standing. It only creates anarchy. So, reluctantly, I let Simon go. Once again, he falls to the floor, gasping, and I step away so I won't be tempted to beat him.

"I'll tell you," he says, his voice high-pitched, like the words are being released slowly from a balloon. "I'll tell you anything, just don't hurt my family."

I nod for him to continue. This is his only chance to come clean. If he lies to me again, I'll kill him.

Simon opens his mouth, but before he can say anything, I hear a loud bang upstairs and a scream. Just as I turn around, the door at the top of the stairs opens, and I know immediately something is wrong. Forgetting all about Simon, I grab the nearest table and tip it over, not worrying about the potential lost profits. Footsteps pound down the stairs and no sooner have I crouched down, the room erupts in bullets.

I see one of the men in the back of the room drop, clutching his stomach. The other two follow my lead and dive behind tables. Simon crawls over to lay on the floor next to me, his lips purple.

The room is filled with the pounding of footsteps, the ring of bullets, and the moans of the fallen man. It is chaos, but I am steady. My heart rate is even as I grab my phone, turn on the front facing camera, and lift it over the table. There are eight shoulders spread out around the room, guns at the ready. Two of them are at the base of the stairs, the other six are spread out in three-foot increments, forming a barrier in front of the stairs. No one here is supposed to get out alive.

But they do not know who is hiding behind the table. If they did, they'd be running.

I look over at one of the chemists. They are not our family's soldiers, but they are trained like anyone else. He has his gun at the ready, waiting for my order. I nod my head once, twice, and on three, we both turn and fire.

One man falls immediately, my bullet striking him in the neck, blood spraying against the wall like splattered paint. It is a kind of artwork, shooting a man. Years of training, placing the bullet just so. Art is meant to incite a reaction and a bullet certainly does that. The man drops his weapon, his hand flying to his neck. Before he can experience too much pain, I place another bullet in his forehead. He drops to his knees, but before he falls flat on his face, I shoot his friend.

The men expected this ambush to be simple, so they are still in shock, still scrambling to collect themselves. It makes it easy for my men to knock them off. Another two men drop as I chase my second target around the room, firing shot after shot at him. He ducks behind a table, and I wait, gun aimed. It is a deadly game of Whack-a-mole, and it requires patience. His gun pops up first, followed shortly by his head, which I blow off with one shot. His scream dies on his lips as he bleeds out, red seeping out from under the table and spreading across the floor.

There are three men left, and I'm out of bullets. I stash my gun in my pocket and pull out my KA-BAR knife. The blade feels like an old friend in my hand. I crawl past a shivering Simon, wishing I'd killed him just so I wouldn't have to see him looking so pathetic, and out from behind the table. I slide my feet under me, moving into a crouch. The remaining men are wounded, and they are focused on the back corner where shots are still coming from my men. They do not see me approaching from the side.

I lunge at the first man—a young kid with golden brown hair and a tattoo on his neck. It is half-hidden under the collar of his shirt, so I cannot make it out. When my knife cuts into his side, he spins to fight me off, but I knock his gun from his hand with my left arm and then drive the knife in under his ribs and upward. He freezes for a moment before blood leaks from his mouth.

The man next to him falls from multiple bullets in the chest and stomach. I kick his gun away from him as he falls to the floor, and advance on the last attacker. He is hiding behind a metal table, palm pressing into a wound on his shoulder. He scrambles to lift his gun as I approach, but I drop to my knees and slide next to him, knife pressed to his neck. His eyes go wide, and then they squeeze shut as he drops his weapon.

The blade of my knife is biting into his skin, and I see the same tattoo creeping up from beneath his collar. I slide the blade down, pushing his shirt aside, and I recognize it at once.

"You are with the Furinos?" I ask.

The man answers by squeezing his eyes shut even tighter.

"You should know who is in a room before you attack," I hiss. "I am Luka Volkov, and I could slit your throat right now."

His entire body is trembling, blood from his shoulder wound leaking through his clothes and onto the floor. Every ounce of me wants this kill. I feel like a dog who has not been fed, desperate for a hunk of flesh, but warfare is not endless bloodshed. It is tactical.

"But I will not," I say, pulling the blade back. The man blinks, unbelieving. "Get out of here and tell your boss what happened. Tell him this attack is a declaration of war, and the Volkov family will live up to our merciless reputation."

He hesitates, and I slash the blade across his cheek, drawing a thin line of blood from the corner of his mouth to his ear. "Go!" I roar.

The man scrambles to his feet and towards the stairs, blood dripping in his wake. As soon as he is gone, I clean my knife with the hem of my shirt and slide it back into place on my hip.

This will not end well.

Eve

I hold up a bag of raisins and a bag of prunes a few inches from the cook's face.

"Do you see the difference?" I ask. The question is rhetorical. Anyone with eyes could see the difference. And a cook—a properly trained cook—should be able to smell, feel, and sense the difference, as well.

Still, Felix wrinkles his forehead and studies the bags like it is a pop quiz.

"Raisins are small, Felix!" My shouting makes him jump, but I'm far too stressed out to care. "Prunes are huge. As big as a baby's fist. Raisins are tiny. They taste very different because they start out as different fruits. Do you see the problem?"

He stares at me blankly, and I wonder if being sous chef gives me the authority to fire someone. Because this man has got to go.

"You've ruined an entire roast duck, Felix." I drop the bags on the counter and run a hand down my sweaty face. I grab the towel from my back pocket and towel off. "Throw it out and start again, but use *prunes* this time."

He smiles and nods, and I wonder how many times he must have hit his head to be so slow. I motion for another cook to come talk to me. He moves quickly, hands folded behind his back, waiting for my order.

"Chop up the duck and make a confit salad. We can toss it with more raisins, fennel—that kind of thing—and make it work."

He nods and shuffles away, and I mop my forehead again.

At the start of my shift, I strode into the kitchen like I owned the place. I was finally sous chef to Cal Higgs, genius chef in charge at The Floating Crown. After graduating culinary school, I didn't know where I'd get a job or where I'd be on the totem pole, and I certainly never imagined I'd be a sous chef so soon, but here I am. And now that I'm here, I can't help but wonder if it wasn't some sort of trick. Did Cal give into my father's wishes easily and give me this job because he needed a break from the insanity?

I've been assured by several members of staff that the dishwasher, whose name I can't remember, has been working at the kitchen for over a year, but he seems to be stuck on slow motion tonight. He is washing and drying plates seconds before the cooks are plating them up and sending them back out to the dining room. And two of the cooks, who were apparently dating, decided that the middle of dinner rush would be the perfect time to discuss their relationship, and they broke up. Dylan stormed out without a word, and Sarah, who should be okay since she was the dumper, not the dumpee, is hiding in the bathroom bawling her eyes out. I've knocked on the door once every ten minutes for an hour, but she refuses to let me in. Cal has a key, but he has been shut away in his office all night, and I don't want to go explain what a shitshow the kitchen is, so we are making do. Barely.

"Sarah?" I knock on the door. "If you don't come out in five minutes, you're fired."

For the first time, there is a break in the crying. "You can't do that."

"Yes, I can," I lie. "You'll leave here tonight without your apron. Single and jobless. Just imagine that shame."

I feel bad rubbing salt in her wound, threatening her, but I'm out of options. I tried comforting her and offering her some of the dark chocolate from the dessert pantry, but she refused to budge. Threats are my last recourse.

There is a long pause, and I wonder if I'm going to have to admit that I actually can't fire her—I don't think—and tell the staff to start using the bathrooms on the customer side, when finally, Sarah emerges. Mascara is smeared down her cheeks, and her eyes are red and puffy from crying, but she is out of the bathroom. As soon as she steps through the doorway, one of the waitresses darts in after her and slams the door shut.

"I'm sorry, Eve," she blubbers, covering her face with her hands.

I grab her wrists and pry her palms from her eyes. When she looks up, her eyes are still closed, tears leaking from the corners.

"Go to the sinks and help with the dishes," I say firmly. "You're in no state to cook right now. Just focus on cleaning plates, okay?"

Sarah nods, her lower lip wobbling.

"Everything is fine," I say, speaking to her like she is a wild animal who might attack. "You won't lose your job. Cal never needs to know, okay? Just go wash dishes. Now."

She turns away from me in a daze and heads back to help the dishwasher whose name I can't for the life of me remember, and I take a deep breath. I've finally put out all the fires, and I lean against the counter and watch the kitchen move around me. It is like a living, breathing machine. Each person has to play their part or everything falls apart. And tonight, I'm barely holding them together.

When the kitchen door swings open, I hope it is Makayla. She has been a waitress at The Floating Crown for five years, and while she has no formal culinary training, she knows this kitchen better than anyone. I've asked her for help tonight more times than I'm comfortable with, but at this point, just seeing one, capable, smiling face would be enough to keep me from crying. But when I turn and instead see a man in a suit, the tie loose and askew around his neck, and his eyes glassy, I almost sag to the floor.

"You can't be back here, sir," I say, moving forward to block his access to the rest of the kitchen. "We have hot stoves and fire and sharp knives, and you are already unstable on your feet."

Makayla told me a businessman at the bar had been demanding macaroni and cheese all night between shots. Apparently, he would not take 'no' for an answer.

"Macaroni and cheese," he mutters, falling against my palms, his feet sliding out from underneath him. "I need macaroni and cheese to soak up the alcohol."

I turn to the nearest person for help, but Felix is still looking at the bags of raisins and prunes like he might seriously still be confused which is which, and I don't want to distract him lest he ruin another duck. I could call out for help from someone else or call the police, but I don't want to cause a scene. Cal is just in the next room. He may have hired me because my father is Don of the Furino family, but even my father can't be angry if Cal fires me for sheer incompetence. I have to prove that I'm capable.

"Sir, we don't have macaroni and cheese, but may I recommend our scoglio?"

"What is that?" he asks, top lip curled back.

"A delicious seafood pasta. Mussels, clams, shrimp, and scallops in a tomato sauce with herbs and spices. Truly delicious. One of my favorite meals on the menu."

"No cheese?"

I sigh. "No. No cheese."

He shakes his head and pushes past me, running his hands along the counters like he might stumble upon a prepared bowl of cheesy pasta.

"Sir, you can't be back here."

"I can be wherever I like," he shouts. "This is America, isn't it?"

"It is, but this is a private restaurant and our insurance does not cover diners being back in the kitchen, so I have to ask you—"

"Oh, say can you see by the dawn's early light!"

"Is that 'The Star-Spangled Banner'?" I ask, looking around to see whether anyone else can see this man or whether I'm having some sort of exhausted fever dream.

"What so proudly we hailed at the twilight's last gleaming?"

This is absurd. Truly absurd. Beyond calling the police, the easiest thing to do seems to be to give in to his demands, so I lay a hand on his shoulder and lead him to the corner of the kitchen. I pat the counter, and he jumps up like he is a child.

I listen to the National Anthem six times before I hand the man a bowl of whole grain linguini with a sharp cheddar cheese sauce on top. "Can you please take this back to the bar and leave me alone?"

He grabs the bowl from my hands, takes a bite, and then breaks into yet another rousing rendition of "The Star-Spangled Banner." This time in falsetto with accompanying dance moves.

I sigh and push him towards the door. "Come on, man."

The dining room is loud enough that no one pays the man too much attention. Plus, he has been drunk out here for an hour before ambushing the kitchen. A few guests shake their heads at the man and then smile at me, giving me the understanding and recognition I sought from the kitchen staff. I lead the man back to the bar, tell the bartender to get rid of him as soon as the pasta is gone, and then make my way back through the dining room.

"She isn't the chef," says a deep voice at normal volume. "Chefs don't look like *that*."

I don't turn towards the table because I don't want to give them the satisfaction of knowing I heard them, of knowing they had any kind of power over me.

"Whatever she makes, it can't taste half as good as her muffin," another man says to raucous laughter.

I roll my eyes and speed up. I'm used to the comments and the cat calls. I've been dealing with it since I sprouted boobs. Even my father's men would whisper things about me. It is part of the reason I chose a path outside the scope of the family business. I couldn't imagine working with the kind of men my father employed. They were crass and mean and treated women like possessions. Unfortunately, the more I learn of the world beyond the Bratva, the more I realize men everywhere are like that. It is the reason I'll never get married. I won't belong to anyone.

I hear the men's deep voices as I walk back towards the kitchen, but I don't listen. I let the words roll off of me like water on a windowpane and step back into the safe chaos of the kitchen.

The kitchen seems to calm down as dinner service goes on, and I'm able to take a step back from micro-managing everything to work on an order of chicken tikka masala. While letting the tomato puree and spices simmer, I realize my stomach is growling. I was too nervous before shift to eat anything, and now that things have finally settled into an easy rhythm, my body is about to absorb itself. So, I casually walk over to where two giant stock pots are simmering with the starter soups for the day and scoop myself out a hearty ladle of lobster and bacon soup. Cal doesn't like for anyone to eat while on service, but he has been in his office all evening, and based on the smell slipping out from under his door, he will be far too stoned to notice or care.

The soup is warm and filling, and I close my eyes as I eat, enjoying the blissful moment of peace before more chaos ensues.

The kitchen door opens, and this time it really is Makayla. I wave her over, eager to see how everyone is enjoying the food and whether the drunk patriot finally left the restaurant, but she doesn't see me and walks with purpose through the kitchen and straight to Cal's office door. She opens it and steps inside, and I wonder what she needed Cal for and why she couldn't come to me. Lord knows I've handled every other situation that arose all night.

I'm just finished the last bite of my soup when Cal's office door slams open, bouncing off the wall, and he stomps his way across the kitchen.

"Eve!"

I shove the bowl to the back of the counter, throwing a dish towel over top to hide the evidence, and then wipe my mouth quickly.

"Yes, chef?"

"Front and center," he barks like we are in the military rather than a kitchen.

Despite the offense I take with his tone—especially after everything I've done to keep the place running all night—I move quickly to follow his order. Because that is what a good sous chef does. I follow the chef's orders, no matter how demeaning.

Cal Higgs is a large man in every sense of the word. He is tall, round, and thick. His head sits on top of his shoulders with no neck in sight, and just walking across the room looks like a chore. I imagine being in his body would be like wearing a winter coat and scarf all the time.

"What is the problem, Chef?"

He hitches a thumb over his shoulder, and Makayla gives me an apologetic wince. "Someone complained about the food, and they want to see the chef."

I wrinkled my forehead. I'd personally tasted every dish that went out. Unless Felix managed to slide another dish past me with raisins in it instead of prunes, I'm not sure what the complaint could be.

"Was there something wrong with the dish or did they simply not like it?"

"Does it matter?" he snaps. His eyes are bloodshot and glassy, yet his temper is as sharp as ever. "I don't like unhappy customers, and you need to fix it."

"But you're the chef," I say, realizing too late I should have stayed quiet.

Cal steps forward, and I swear I can feel the floor quake under his weight. "But you made the food. Should I go out there and apologize on your behalf? No, this is your mess, and you will take care of it."

"Of course," I say, looking down at the ground. "You're right. I'll go out there and make this right."

Before Cal can find another reason to yell at me, I retie my apron around my waist, straighten my white jacket, and march through the swinging kitchen doors.

The dining room is quieter than before. The drunk man is no longer singing the National Anthem at the bar and several of the tables are empty, the bussers clearing away empty plates. Happy plates, I might add. Clearly, they didn't have an issue with the food.

I didn't ask Makayla who complained about the food, but as soon as I walk into the main dining area, it is obvious. There is a small gathering at the corner booth, and a salt and pepper-haired man in his late fifties or early sixties raising a hand in the air and waves me over without looking directly at me. I haven't even spoken to the man yet, and I already hate him.

I'm standing at their table, staring at the man, but he doesn't speak to me until I announce my presence.

"I heard someone wanted to speak with the chef," I say.

He turns to me, one eyebrow raised. "You are the chef?"

I recognize a Russian accent when I hear one, and this man is Russian without a doubt. I wonder if I know him. Or if my father does. Would he be complaining to me if he knew my father was head of the Furino family? I would never throw my family name around in order to scare people, but for just a second, I have the inclination.

"Sous chef," I say with as much confidence as I can muster. "I ran the kitchen tonight, so I'll be hearing the complaints."

His eyes move down my body slowly like he is inspecting a cut of meat in a butcher shop. I cross my arms over my chest and spread my feet hip-width apart. "So, was there an issue with the food? I'd love to correct any problems."

"Soup was cold." He nudges his empty bowl to the center of the table with three fingers. "The portions were too small, and I ordered my steak medium-rare, not raw."

Every plate on the table is empty. Not a single crumb in sight. Apparently, the issues were not bad enough he couldn't finish his meal.

"Do you have any of the steak left?" I ask, making a show of looking around the table. "If one of my cooks undercooked the meat, I'd like to be able to inform them."

"If? I just told you the meet was undercooked. Are you doubting me?"

"Of course not," I say. *Yes, absolutely I am.* "It is just that if the meat was undercooked, I do not understand why you waited until you'd eaten everything to inform me of the problem?"

The man looks around the table at his companions. They are all smiling, and I can practically see them sharpening their teeth, preparing to rip me to shreds. When he turns back to me, his smile is acidic, deadly. "How did you get this position—sous chef? Surely not by skill. You are pretty, which I'm sure did you a favor. Did you sleep with the chef? Maybe—" he moves his hand in an obscene gesture—"'service' the boss to earn your place in the kitchen?

Surely your 'talent' didn't get you the job, seeing as how you have none."

I physically bite my tongue and then take a deep breath. "If you'd like me to remake anything for you or bring out a complimentary dessert, I'm happy to do that. If not, I apologize for the issues and hope you will not hold it against us. We'd love to have you again."

Lies. Lies. Lies. I'm smiling and being friendly the way I was taught in culinary school. I actually took a class on dealing with customers, and this man is being even more outrageous than the overexaggerated angry customer played by my professor.

"Why would I want more food from you if the things you already sent out were terrible?" He snorts and shakes his head. "I see you do not have a ring on. That is no surprise. Men like a woman who can cook. Men don't care if you know your way around a professional kitchen if you don't know your way around a dinner plate."

The older gentleman is speaking, but I hear my father's words in my head. *You do not need to go to culinary school to find a husband, Eve. Your aunties can teach you to cook good food for your man.*

My entire life has been preparation for finding a husband. The validity of every hobby is judged by whether it will fetch me a suitor or not. My father wants me to be happy, but he mostly wants me to be married. Single, I'm a disappointment. Married, I'm a vessel for future Furino mafia members.

Years of anger and resentment begin to bubble and hiss inside of me until I'm boiling. My hands are shaking, and I can feel adrenaline pulsing through me, lighting every inch of me on fire. This time, I don't bite my tongue.

"I'd rather die alone than spent another minute near a man like you," I spit, stepping forward and laying my palms flat on the table. "The fact that you ate all of the food you apparently hated shows you are a pig in more ways than one."

In the back of my mind, I recognize that my voice is echoing around the restaurant and the chatter in the rest of the room has gone quiet, but blood is whirring in my ears, and I can't stop. I've stayed quiet and docile for too long. Now, it is my turn to speak my mind.

"You and your friends may be wealthy and respected, but I see you for what you are—spineless, cowardly assholes who are so insecure they have to take their rage out on everybody else."

I want to spin on my heel and storm away, making a grand exit, but in classic Eve fashion, my heel catches on the tablecloth, and I nearly trip. I fall sideways and throw an arm out to catch myself, knocking a nearly full bottle of wine on the table over. The glass shatters and red wine splashes across the tablecloth and onto the guests in the booth like a river of blood.

I pause long enough to note the old Russian man's shirt is splattered like he has been shot before I continue my exit and head straight for the doors.

I suck in the night air. The evening is warm and humid, summer strangling the city in its hold, and I want to rip off my clothes for some relief. I feel like I'm being strangled. Like there is a hand around my neck, squeezing the life out of me.

Breathing in and out slowly helps, but as the physical panic begins to ebb away, emotional panic flows in.

What have I done? Cal Higgs is going to find out about the altercation any minute, and then what? Will he fire me? And if he does, will I ever be able to get another chef position? I was only offered this position because of my father, and I doubt he will help me earn another kitchen position, especially since I'm no closer to finding a boyfriend (or husband) since I left for culinary school.

Despite it all, I want to call my dad. He has always made it clear he will move heaven and earth to take care of me, to make sure no one is mean to me, and I want his support right now. But the support he offered me when a girl tripped me during soccer practice and made me miss the net won't apply here. He will tell me to come home. To put down my apron and knife and focus on more meaningful pursuits. And that is the last thing I want to hear right now.

I pull out my phone and scroll through my contacts list, hoping to see a spark of hope amidst the names, but there is nothing. I've lost touch with everyone since I started culinary school. There hasn't been time for friends.

This is probably the kind of situation where most girls would turn to their moms, but she hasn't been in the picture since I was six years old. Even if I had her number, I wouldn't call her. Dad hasn't always been perfect, but at least he was there. At least he cared enough to stay.

I untie my apron and pull it over my head, leaning back against the brick side of the restaurant.

"Take it off, baby!"

I look up and see a man on a motorcycle with his hair in a bun parked along the curb. He is waggling his eyebrows at me like I'm supposed to fall in love with him for harassing me on the street, and the fire that filled my veins inside hasn't died out yet. The embers are still there, burning under the skin, and I step towards him, lips pulled back in a smile.

He looks surprised, and I'm sure he is. That move has probably never worked for him before. He smiles back at me, his tongue darting out to lick his lower lip.

"Is that your bike?" I purr.

He nods. "Want a ride?"

My voice is still sticky sweet as I respond, "So sweet of you to offer. I'd rather choke and die on that grease ball you call a man bun, but thanks anyway, hon."

It takes him a second to realize my words don't match the tone. When it hits him, he snarls, "Bitch."

"Asshole." I flip him the bird over my shoulder and start the long walk home.

∼

__Click here__ to keep reading BROKEN VOWS.

MAILING LIST

Sign up to my mailing list!
New subscribers receive a FREE steamy bad boy romance novel.

Click the link below to join.
http://bit.ly/NicoleFoxNewsletter

ALSO BY NICOLE FOX

De Maggio Mafia Duet

Devil in a Suit (Book 1)

Devil at the Altar (Book 2)

Kornilov Bratva Duet

Married to the Don (Book 1)

Til Death Do Us Part (Book 2)

Volkov Bratva

Broken Vows (Book 1)

Broken Hope (Book 2)

Broken Sins *(standalone)*

Heirs to the Bratva Empire

*Can be read in any order

Kostya

Maksim

Andrei

Tsezar Bratva

Nightfall (Book 1)

Daybreak (Book 2)

Russian Crime Brotherhood

*Can be read in any order

Owned by the Mob Boss

Unprotected with the Mob Boss

Knocked Up by the Mob Boss

Sold to the Mob Boss

Stolen by the Mob Boss

Trapped with the Mob Boss

Other Standalones

Vin: A Mafia Romance

Box Sets

Bratva Mob Bosses (Russian Crime Brotherhood Books 1-6)

Tsezar Bratva (Tsezar Bratva Duet Books 1-2)

Printed in Great Britain
by Amazon